THE
CONCIERGE

THE
CONCIERGE

ABBY CORSON

ultimo
press

Published in 2024 by Ultimo Press,
an imprint of Hardie Grant Publishing

Ultimo Press
Gadigal Country
7, 45 Jones Street
Ultimo, NSW 2007
ultimopress.com.au

   ultimopress

 A catalogue record for this
book is available from the
National Library of Australia

The Concierge
ISBN 978 1 76115 296 2 (paperback)

Cover design Amy Daoud
Text design Simon Paterson and Samantha Collins, Bookhouse
Typesetting Bookhouse, Sydney | 11.6/17.5 pt Baskerville MT Pro
Copyeditor Ali Lavau
Proofreader Rebecca Hamilton

10 9 8 7 6 5 4 3 2 1

Printed in Australia by Opus Group Pty Ltd, an Accredited ISO AS/NZS 14001 Environmental
Management System printer.

 The paper this book is printed on is certified against the
Forest Stewardship Council® Standards.
Griffin Press – a member of the Opus Group – holds
chain of custody certification SCS-COC-001185. FSC®
promotes environmentally responsible, socially beneficial
and economically viable management of the world's forests.

Ultimo Press acknowledges the Traditional Owners of the Country on which we work,
the Gadigal People of the Eora Nation and the Wurundjeri People of the Kulin Nation,
and recognises their continuing connection to the land, waters and culture. We pay our
respects to their Elders past and present.

For Philip

CHAPTER 1

Tap one. Tap two. Tap three.

Sorry about that. I have to tap my head three times when I have a bad or intrusive thought. That time I was thinking about how much worse everything would have been if my father was still alive.

You can delete that bit from the transcript, Helen. Actually, leave it in. I guess it adds to the authenticity of the tale.

I suppose it would be fitting to explain that I am talking into a dictaphone and the lovely Helen will be typing out my story for you to read. She will have a certain amount of creative control—sorting out moments when I get a bit tongue-tied or slightly muddled—but I have told her to leave in as much as possible, so as not to miss any of the important bits. This is my account of the Cavengreen Hotel murder, best we get that bit in early on.

Tap one. Tap two. Tap three.

That was me remembering the moment I found the body.

Note to Helen: remind me to remind you to ask me if I still want all my head taps to be left in before publishing. I know we spoke before about how my OCD is important to the story, but let's have another chat about it when you're writing this up.

You are probably wondering why I can't write my own book and need the assistance of Helen. I am a seventy-three-year-old man, you see. And before you say it, I know a lot of seventy-year-olds who can use computers too; I just don't happen to be one of them. Prefer the classic pen and paper. When Helen and I first spoke about writing my story, she took one look at my handwriting and suggested I use the dictaphone. Apparently it is easier to decipher my Yorkshire accent than my scribbles. I am not offended, though. Aside from the odd lines and circles on maps to highlight local walks and pubs for the hotel guests, it isn't often I use a pen and paper for anything other than my own reminders. To buy milk and the like.

And about the head tapping, that's something I've always done. A way of coping after my dad started whacking me when I was eight. I don't normally recite the taps out loud. But I will do that for Helen, so she can decide if she wants to put them in the book or not. It is always three taps. Everything is done in threes. Flicking light switches on and off three times before leaving a room. Three tight squeezes of the steering wheel before setting off in the car. Three taps on a glass before a first sip. Three twists of the knob to find the right temperature. (That only works on my sinks at home, not the fancy new automatic ones in the hotel.) And when I found the body, I remember blinking three times before running for help. The pause while I did it was one of the things that made them suspect it was me. Supposedly, it was long enough to kill someone. We will get to that bit later.

Right, so, this might embarrass her a bit, but I want to start by thanking Helen for turning my ramblings into a book. She's a good 'un, is Helen. I've known her for donkey's years. She and my younger sister went to school together. Helen organised the funeral when she died. Everything down to the purple tulips and little photograph of my dearest Josie on the order of service.

This book was Helen's idea. She relocated down to London years back to work in some swish publishing house, and we lost touch for a while. But, just like everyone else, she moved back up north for the fresh country air once she retired, and we've rekindled our friendship. She says she'll do anything for a good book. I suppose that's why she's offered to give me a helping hand. Misses the work. And it's just as well; I wouldn't get very far doing this by myself.

Helen has given me a list of what to talk about and in what order, since she knows how a book should go. It starts with a bit of this and that about my background, then my job at the hotel, and then I move on to the murder and how I ended up here. You're probably wondering where 'here' is. For a bit of fun, I'm not going to tell you just yet. I could be in a prison cell, or my little cottage in the Dales, or some beach on the Costa del Sol. (I'll give you a hint: I'm not in Spain.)

Last thing for this chapter. My name is Hector. Hector Harrow.

CHAPTER

2

Helen popped her head round the door just now to tell me I don't need to introduce the chapter by giving an overview of what will be contained within it. I suppose I have just let the cat out of the bag about my location. Helen doesn't mosey in and out of prison cells willy-nilly. So, I confess—I am at home. In my lounge room to be exact. In a big, reddish brown Chesterfield armchair holding a cup of English breakfast, no milk, and looking out at my little garden, complete with a stone wall at the end and a few pairs of socks and undies on a washing line. Must remember to fetch those in before the rain comes.

Hopefully that admission didn't spoil anything for you. There are plenty more surprises along the way, don't you worry about that.

❧

I have never been one to talk about myself. I've always assumed no one cared what I had to say. Occasionally some guests—usually Americans—would be curious about what life was like growing up in the Yorkshire Dales, but I would answer in as few words as possible, and it was never the truth. What was I going to say? 'Well, my father used to beat the living daylights out of me for no reason, but my mother made a fantastic apple pie, and the country views were a delight.' That would just make them uncomfortable. And I'm sure management would have had something to say about my bothering the guests. Not that I ever would have. Always the professional, that's me. Except that one time they interrogated me for over four hours. Wouldn't even let me have a glass of water. And I was parched after the shock of seeing all that blood.

Tap one. Tap two. Tap three.

That was the first time in my life I ever lost my temper. It felt like I was possessed by my father. I will talk a bit about him now.

My father—Rodney was his name. He'd be down there in hell. There is no doubt about that. He was an alcoholic from the day I was born to the day he dropped dead. There is always an alcoholic parent in troubled tales like this.

Helen made me laugh when we first talked about this part of the book. She said that I make the perfect protagonist because of—she used a good word that I have forgotten now.

Helen, make a note to type that word here please.

The juxtaposition *[editor's note]* of my awful upbringing with the quite nice life I went on to lead, working in one of England's finest countryside hotels.

School was always a bit of an escape for me. Not that I was any good at it. Just the local comprehensive—I wasn't clever enough for grammar school, let alone university. And anyway, I knew I'd be having to get a job straight off. It's a funny story, how I got my start at Cavengreen Hotel. I was only sixteen. My father needed a refill of some tablets that would hopefully *not* prolong the life of his liver, so I cycled to the local pharmacy to pick them up. On the way, I saw a man with a posh car pulled over on the side of the road. He had a wispy grey moustache and an olive-green three-piece suit. Back then, I had never seen someone look so smart—not in real life, that is. The man looked stressed, and as I got closer I saw his tyre was as flat as a squashed cigarette butt.

'Young lad!' he called out to me. 'Come here!'

I braked to a stop and rested my bike against the wobbly stone wall that ran alongside the road. It was a sunny day and I remember shuffling from foot to foot to try and find the exact position in which the man's head would block the sun from my eyes.

'I'll give you two pounds if you help me change this tyre,' the man offered. 'Three if you do it in under ten minutes.'

I had seen my dad change the odd tyre, and two, possibly three pounds was a lot of money back then, so I got stuck into it.

The man didn't say anything as I worked, but I noticed him tapping his foot impatiently and he checked his pocket watch several times. When I was done, I stood up, dusted some of the black off my hands and asked the man how long it had taken me.

'Ten minutes, three seconds,' he announced. 'Here's your two pounds.'

He handed me two notes.

I mustn't have looked best pleased because he asked if there was something wrong. I knew better than to offend a toff, so I thanked him for the opportunity and said I hoped I could use the experience to find a job.

He smiled at me. It was a crooked smile, but it was kind. He invited me to come to a place called Cavengreen Hotel at six the next morning to do some odd jobs for him. Shoeshining, polishing floors, cleaning bird poo off the walls and the like, he said. And that is how it all started. I was the happiest birdshit cleaner the world ever did see.

CHAPTER

3

Bloomin' Paula McDavidson from the *Yorkshire Sun* newspaper has been knocking again. She never listens. That's another reason I want to do this book sharpish: so none of the others that were there at the hotel can tell my story first. There are three main characters in this: one is me, one is dead, and the other is the murderer. Fat chance either of the others are going to try and publish a book, so it is down to me to get the truth out there before the twins or American Dave flood the world with a pack of lies. I told Paula that she will find out all she needs to know in due course. That won't stop her, though. She'll be hammering on the door again in a couple of days, mark my words.

Helen gave me some feedback on what I recorded yesterday. She told me she liked it, so that has given me a little confidence boost. She said that, despite my thick accent, I speak very clearly, which is probably thanks to my many years at Cavengreen. When I started out as a young lad, I'd say things like 'eh up' for 'hello', and ''ow do?' for 'how are you?', but the out-of-town guests hadn't the foggiest what I was on about. Helen's only criticism was that I probably didn't need to list what was on my washing line, but she said she would trim that bit down when she writes this up. Today, Helen wants me to chat a bit about the hotel. Setting the scene is what she called it.

The man that I mentioned, the one I changed the tyre for, his name was Mr Thomas. He was the hotel manager at the time. It wasn't until his funeral twenty years after I met him that I found out his first name was Basil. He was the nicest man I have ever known. He gave a young lad a chance when he didn't have to, and I will always remember him fondly. Every day at 6 am, seven days a week, I would cycle the thirty minutes to the hotel. Wind, rain, shine, the storm of '72, I never missed a day. One time I turned up with chickenpox because I didn't want to let the team down. They sent me home right away, but Mr Thomas still gave me my wages, even when I was off sick. I learnt everything I know about hard work from that man.

As you will probably have gathered from the title of this book, I eventually climbed the ladder up to hotel concierge, but along the way I worked as a porter, then valet. I did a few months in the kitchen, but that wasn't for me, so they moved me to the butler position, and after that I became the concierge. It was my job to make sure that the guests' every want and need was taken care of. Whether it was a taxi at 3 am for a lady they'd met at the hotel bar to travel home in, a plate of French fries with all the crunchy bits removed, or a marriage proposal staged on the lawn, I handled it all. Helen has suggested I talk about the strangest request I ever had. That would probably be the time I set up a screening of the Disney movie *One Hundred and One Dalmatians* in one of the suites, complete with treats and cosy bedding on the floor. The audience was the guest's two beloved poodles. There were plenty of other strange requests over the years, most of which involve very famous people from Hollywood, but I would never breach confidentiality.

You are probably getting the picture by now that Cavengreen was and is not your average hotel. No, no. The hotel proudly displays five stars on the front of the archway that sits at the end of a four-hundred-yard-long gravel driveway. Chauffeurs escort their guests around a large turning circle with a fountain in the middle that lights up at night and has speakers built into the sides that play Vivaldi and the like. Three full-time horticulturists look after the gardens, which include a hedge maze, a rose garden, and a small pond dotted with lily pads. I never get sick of walking through them. Loads of people bring along those fancy cameras with the big lenses or look at everything through their phones, but I prefer to enjoy the smells and colours without distraction.

If you were to see it from above, the hotel is shaped like a T. The top of the T is the part that guests see when they first arrive. The whole building is made from limestone and the entire front is lined with columns. Couples like to take their wedding photographs there. The climbing ivy makes for quite the backdrop.

The west wing houses the hotel's Michelin-starred restaurant, Lavender Plates. As you would imagine, all the chinaware is lavender-coloured with golden rims. The custom-designed wallpaper is hand-painted with watercolour sketches of lavender over the top of a white silk background. The ceilings in Lavender Plates are double the height of anywhere else in the hotel and a huge sparkly chandelier was imported from the United Arab Emirates to add some glitz to the place. Towering floor-to-ceiling glass double doors lead out onto a terrace overlooking the hotel's driveway. In summer, we would open the doors and allow a light breeze to flow through. The guests loved it.

All the seats are upholstered with cream velvet and the white marble tables have ornate gold legs. The waiters and waitresses set the tables in a very particular way; every spoon, fork and knife has its place and must be a certain distance from the plates and glassware. You would be hard pressed to find fault with Lavender Plates. It is very smart. Serves a seasonal tasting menu of seven tiny dishes. I much prefer one big meal, but the few times I have eaten there it has been very good indeed. The kitchen is completely open so everyone in the restaurant can see what is going on. From memory, the last time I dined there I had some type of fish with a burnt honey glaze and a white chocolate dessert with roasted cherries. If you like that sort of thing, fancy stuff, you'd like Lavender Plates. It was all a bit wasted on me. I am a pie-and-mash kind of man. But no one would deny it is good food. And at two hundred quid a pop, you would expect so. I dined for free, of course. Staff were always recruited to taste the new dishes.

Then there is Hugo's cocktail bar, modelled on a moody whisky lounge in Tokyo. The hotel brought in a light-up onyx countertop from Japan, as well as golden light fixtures and a particular type of tumbler that keeps the ice separate from the alcohol, so as not to water down the flavour. It is all in the details at Cavengreen, that is what I am trying to get across.

In the east wing of the hotel there are some offices for the manager, reservations and marketing. There is also a library, where we would hold wine tastings and serve pre-dinner canapés every evening. There is a fireplace and lots of old books that are dusted every fortnight. Think squeaky leather sofas, a royal blue carpet, lots of dark wood, and you are probably on the right track. Some of the books in there would be worth a bob or two. I reckon there are some valuable originals. I am partial to a good murder mystery myself and would often borrow a novel for a weekend of reading at home.

Between the east and west wings was my domain: the lobby. The first point of contact for guests visiting the hotel. This was the place where first and last impressions were formed, so everyone was always on their best behaviour. The lovely ladies on reception (plus Kyle on Saturdays and Sundays) were always smiling and ever so kind to me. They used to say I was 'cute' and that they wished I was their grandpa. A little patronising, but nice nonetheless. At the time of the murder, there was Monique, Chloe and Shamila working on the front desk. Fiona was their boss, and she'd been managing the reception team for the past fifteen years. She's still there, in fact. She's a very dear friend of mine. Lost her husband to cancer two years ago. Lovely fella. It is a shame, really.

My desk was on the other side of the staircase to reception. I had a telephone, lots of maps and information booklets about the local area, a directory of contacts that I used to source whatever the guests needed, and a little fridge with bottled water and a few soft drinks should anyone want a refreshment. I used to burn candles all around the lobby, so subtle notes of vanilla, pepper and grapefruit filled the air. Many years ago, we worked with a perfumery to bottle the perfect Cavengreen scent. Candles and diffusers were available for the guests to purchase, should they so choose.

Now, to the bottom part of the T, the trunk. That is the south wing. This is where you'll find all the rooms—two floors of them, to be precise. In the last refurbishment, they painted all the walls white and rolled out a soft pale-pink carpet. Each suite has the black outline of a flower painted onto a white door. There are all sorts: tulips, roses, poppies, lilies and so on. Every room at Cavengreen Hotel is a suite. That means they've all got a separate sitting area and powder room, as well as either a balcony or terrace and a large master bathroom with a roll-top bath. We got lots of requests for romantic baths, and I always made sure I had plenty of rose petals, bath bombs, candles and massage oils in stock so I could put together a little pack for those guests who requested it.

On the top level of the south wing there are a few luxury suites, as we called them. These have their own bar stocked with alcohol and snacks—all free to the guests. Except it is actually included in the room price. I probably shouldn't have said that, but surely it is assumed. I suppose my loose lips don't matter so much now. All the luxury suites have a jacuzzi spa on the balcony and a fireplace that separates the lounge from the bedroom. The rooms are classic with traditional details like sconces, cornices, and ceiling roses, but they have also been fitted with all the mod cons that people don't seem to be able to live without nowadays. I would rather sit in silence than watch that drivel on television. But that is just me. Wi-Fi is available too, of course. It is near impossible to get phone signal out here so the Wi-Fi is the only way to stay connected.

There is even a special bridal suite which is spread over two levels. As well as the above, it has a dressing room with hair and make-up stations. Each suite is attended to by the hotel's twenty-four-hour butler service; there are twelve of them on staff. Plus there are chefs, maids, security guards, wedding planners, maintenance men, waitstaff and so many more people. You will be introduced to some of them as I tell this story.

That bloomin' busybody Paula McDavidson is opening my gate again. What the devil could she possibly want? I tell you what, I am going to take the dictaphone to the door with me, then Helen can transcribe exactly what her raspy, chain-smoking gob says.

Helen, you might have to change Paula's name and the name of the newspaper.

> Hector: Paula, I've already told you I'm not going to give you any information.
>
> Paula: I need a comment from you for my story.
>
> Hector: No comment. I told you that this morning. I'm closing the door now.
>
> Paula: Wait—this is for a different article. The twins have decided to tell their story.
>
> Hector: Those twins know nothing. They were hiding in their room, drinking champagne the whole time the hotel was on lockdown.
>
> Paula: And why is that?
>
> Hector: Because they knew I'd be after them once I found out what they said I'd done.
>
> Paula: And what exactly did you do, Hector?
>
> Hector: None of your damn business! Goodbye!

That woman could make enemies in the depths of hell. Calls herself a journalist. She is just a nosy so-and-so on a salary. Gets everyone to write her stories for her and then scribbles her name on the top line. And I have gone and walked right into her trap, like the classic fool that I am. The twins will twist my words in their own way to make it sound like I am some nutter who got away with murder. They knew it wasn't me, but that didn't stop them lying to the police, did it?

Tap one. Tap two. Tap three.

I am just going to pause a moment to take some deep breaths. And now my brew has gone cold! This could not get much worse.

Right, Helen, I think I'm going to have to call it a day. Paula has rattled me. A good night's sleep is what I need. Tomorrow I will pick up from where I left off and we'll talk about the guests that checked in that week. The murder week . . .

CHAPTER

It was an odd kind of week, the murder week. Mr Potts called an all-in staff meeting for eight o'clock Monday morning. Mr Potts was the hotel's manager at the time. I have seen plenty of managers come and go through the years, some good, some not so good. Mr Potts would sit somewhere in the middle, I would say. He is a tall, lanky fellow, probably in his late forties, early fifties. If he is reading this, I hope that doesn't offend him. But then again, it doesn't matter so much now if it does. Let us say mid-forties, just to be polite. Whatever his age, he has done well not to get any grey hairs yet. I went grey in my mid-thirties. My hairline has stayed pretty set in place, luckily. But Mr Potts has a great head of raven-black hair. He obviously gets his eyebrows done and probably has his nails manicured too. Nothing wrong with that.

Mr Potts has an interesting temperament. Some days he would be on the warpath, and you would want to steer clear. Other days, he would stop and share a joke with the staff, but he would always catch himself after a minute or so and return to his staunch, very formal demeanour. Sometimes people in positions of power are just like that. Think they have to be stand-offish to command respect.

All the staff gathered in the library, which was closed to guests until 4 pm. Some of the young ones slumped on the leather sofas, a couple fiddled with the lid of the globe bar that hid a few bottles of nice Scotch. I would never let myself fully relax at work. That is not professional, in my opinion. There was always an at-work Hector and an at-home Hector. At-work Hector stood up straight, shoulders back, and maintained a soft, approachable smile. At-home Hector likes to eat fish and chips on the settee while doing newspaper puzzles. I am just saying, different environment, different Hector. Anyhow, Mr Potts stood by the unlit fireplace with the head of marketing, Sandra, on one side, and the head of finance, Rosanne, on the other. Serious faces all round.

'The Cavengreen family have made the decision to sell the hotel,' Mr Potts said, after he had shushed the room several times. He was very matter-of-fact about it. Naturally, people shared worried glances. In the whole time I had worked at the hotel, it had never changed hands. I still haven't ever met the Cavengreens. They never interfered, but as far as I know they were nice people who wanted to employ locals and keep them employed. None of this 'redundancies every few months' malarky like you get at the big chains. A change of owners would almost certainly mean a staff shake-up. And the likes of me, being seventy-three and not as shiny as the young 'uns, I was sure I would be first to get the boot.

There was not much more left to be said. Little groups of employees gossiped in the hallways after the meeting, exchanging baseless opinions on what they thought might happen. It is always dangerous to speculate, so I just got back to work behind my desk. That is not to say it wasn't on my mind.

After lunch, Fiona came over and let me know that she had overheard Mr Potts telling Rosanne that the new owners—Americans by the sound of it—were planning on replacing the concierge service with some fancy iPad system that would be available in each suite. I would be out of a job. What's more, the new owners were due to arrive at the hotel that evening, to survey their purchase.

To them, we were just another drop in their property portfolio. To us, the people working at the hotel, this was our livelihood. The police would call this 'motive' when they tried to pin the murder on me. And believe you me when I say it was hard to wriggle my way out of that narrative.

Back to the guests. The hotel was at seventy-five per cent capacity that week, due to be one hundred per cent by the weekend. But by the time the weekend came, the hotel was on lockdown and no guests were allowed to check in—or check out, for that matter. Seventy-five per cent capacity was par for the course, given it was mid spring and we were coming off the back of a busy and unusually humid Easter. Check-in days are Mondays, Wednesdays and Fridays, and guests are required to pay and stay for a minimum of two nights. If they want to stay longer, they can, but they must stay an even number of nights so as not to mess up the system. But at over one thousand quid a night, most people only stay for two.

The murder happened on a Thursday, so if you're following, you'll have realised that we might have had some leftover guests from the Monday check-in (and we did have a few), but mostly they would have been Wednesday arrivals. I am not going to reel off the names of everyone present in the hotel, but I will describe the main players, those who are essential to the story. And that includes the victim, of course.

Monday evening, as rumoured, the Americans arrived: four of them. They were already complaining loudly about the wet weather when they filed through the door at quarter past seven. They thought May would have been a little sunnier for them. Mr Potts had gathered a sample of his favourite employees, the ones who presented the best, myself included, to greet them in a line at the entrance like they were the royal family. Fiona handed out champagne but two of them didn't drink alcohol. It was a rocky start.

You might remember me mentioning American Dave earlier; he was one of this lot. From the moment I met him, I knew he was a loud-mouthed good-for-nothing, with his obnoxiously sized cowboy hat and blue Ralph Lauren jumper draped over his shoulders. Who wears a cowboy hat in the Yorkshire Dales? One big gust of wind and it would be up and over the hills. Some of the girls on reception swooned when they first saw him. The word 'hunk' was thrown around. Apparently they liked his suntan and sandy blond hair. 'Dreamy,' they said. I know he is already in talks to release his own book about the goings-on at Cavengreen, but hopefully mine will hit the shelves first. His will be full of exaggerations and blurred memories from his late-night whisky-drinking. Not to mention, I have my reputation to protect; I doubt he'd have many nice things to say about me.

Tanya—another of the Americans—was American Dave's shadow. She wore a wedding ring but was inappropriately touchy-feely with American Dave whenever the two Yanky paper pushers weren't around. You see these things as a concierge.

Riley and Jackson were the names of the other two, I think. Very American names. Not my cup of tea. Don't expect them to feature much in this story. God knows where they were during all this. Those two lingered in the background, clearly there for show rather than their opinions. One was in charge of social media or some nonsense, and the other was an accountant. I forget which one was which.

The group took up four of the rooms, a suite each. The only other Monday check-ins who were still at the hotel on the murder day were Sue and Martin Bainbridge, and Olive—Sue's daughter, Martin's stepdaughter. Olive was due to have her wedding at the hotel Wednesday afternoon. The bride-to-be spent the first two days of her stay bossing the staff around and making her wedding planner cry. That is it for Monday check-ins.

Olive's husband-to-be, Patrick, checked in on Wednesday morning. He looked bleary-eyed, as his mates Ray and Jamil had organised a stag-do at a pub not too far from Cavengreen. Ray and Jamil shared a suite, and that was where Patrick stayed before joining his new wife in the bridal suite after the wedding celebrations. Aside from being hungover on his wedding day, Patrick seemed like a decent man. He was mostly polite and softly spoken.

His groomsmen, on the other hand, were abrasive and out of place. Public school education, that much was obvious, but still too young to appreciate the elegance of Cavengreen. Money, yes, it was clear that they had plenty, but they would have been more at home on a booze cruise around Ibiza. Nevertheless, I treat all guests equally. That is what a good concierge must do. And really, who am I to look down on anyone? I am just a concierge, at the end of the day.

The twins, Ruby and Oksana, also checked in on the Wednesday. They were the kind of girls who were born with a silver spoon and no manners. Used to getting whatever they wanted and unable to show appreciation. They arrived with a Mercedes-Benz boot full of suitcases that they demanded be taken up to their suite *immediately*.

A nervous-looking make-up artist and hair stylist carrying bags of kit trailed behind them as the twins were shown their room, which apparently was not up to their expected standard. That is what the porter, Joe, told me. He said they had yelled this at him.

Ruby and Oksana were Olive's bridesmaids. They were identical, but after a few glances it was easy to tell them apart. Ruby was the louder and ruder of the two; Oksana was the sheep. Oksana had a slightly rounded face, while Ruby's was pointed. They were both nasty. Blessed with good looks but horrid personalities, they made quite the impact when they entered a room. If I had to hazard a guess, I'd say they were of either Serbian or Croatian descent. Both girls had long, straight, light brown hair, blue eyes and puffy lips that did not look natural. At one point during their stay, I heard them giggling about how they were sure they would upstage the bride. On her wedding day of all days!

They would strut through the lobby and fling their handbags on my desk before making their demands. As if I'd have any interest in your bloomin' handbag—it could be from the charity shop for all I care. Fiona let me know that the bags were Chanel. Very expensive, so I hear. Well, I saw a lot of expensive bags during my time as the concierge. On the first day, the twins demanded a specific type of tonic water that, after an hour of telephone calls, I finally tracked down at a boutique gin shop in Manchester. Do you know how long that drive is? I had to send one of the porters. Anyway, they got the tonic water, but of course there were hissy fits all round when it didn't arrive on time. They also wanted silk pillowcases, a dehumidifier for their room, and cornflakes with skim milk and raspberries. These were easier to attain.

I will continue to reveal the horrors of the twins as this story goes on, but next I want to introduce a gentleman from Scotland named Alec Maclean who arrived at around 11.30 am on Wednesday. He asked me if I could arrange to have the bangers and mash from the local pub delivered, which I was happy to do for him. Nigel at the Ferret Inn is a long-time acquaintance of mine, so he delivered the meal himself, piping hot.

Alec told me he had come to the hotel to work on his novel as he was suffering from writer's block and needed a change of scenery. Writer's block is something I have yet to encounter, perhaps because I am telling a true story. Maybe I will get talker's block at some point. If that happens, I am sure Helen will have some tips for me after her decades in the book business. Alec had a deep, booming voice, and a messy, wiry beard that he seemed to have neglected due to his writing ailment. He carried a pen everywhere he went, and he chewed on it when he had nothing else to do with his hands. I believe his book will be published posthumously. Read into that what you will.

Lastly, a gentleman named Bruno Tatterson checked in. It was odd because he didn't have a suitcase, claiming that he only intended to go from his room to the spa and back, for which he would wear the robe provided, and then to dinner in the clothes he arrived in. The hotel supplied all the additional amenities a man could need. He rolled his eyes when I reminded him that a wedding would be taking place in the gardens the next day and suggested he avoid that area between four and six. Whenever there was a wedding, I would always inform guests who weren't attending in advance and offer them a complimentary spa treatment or cocktails at Hugo's as a way of keeping them occupied in an area of the hotel where they could avoid any disruptions. No one wants to be around a wedding they are not invited to. But weddings are the hotel's bread and butter, so the show had to go on.

Bruno happily accepted a complimentary massage. He briefly mentioned that he was recovering from a recent heartbreak, so he was enjoying a bit of R & R in the countryside. Naturally, I didn't pry, but I was prepared to listen should he wish to discuss his personal life further. In my many years as a concierge, I would often play the part of a therapist, among other things.

That is a bit of an overview of everyone you need to know about, guest wise. Two of the people I mentioned in this chapter will die at the hotel, though only one will be murdered.

It is no wonder you encouraged me to write this book, Helen. It is quite the story.

Helen was over yesterday, helping me consolidate my thoughts. I think I jinxed myself the other day by saying I'd not yet encountered writer's—or talker's—block.

Whenever Helen comes over, she always does the same three things before she sits down for a brew.

I hope you don't mind me sharing this, Helen.

First, she opens all the windows to let in some fresh air. She says it is stuffy in here, but that is not something I notice. Next, she washes her hands and dries them on the tea towel that hangs on the oven handle. I have to use all my strength not to refold it into a perfect three-fold after she has unravelled it. This normally involves me leaving the kitchen and going into the lounge. Helen follows and, third, starts fussing over me, making sure I am comfortable and well fed.

Sorry, Helen. I am not saying I don't appreciate your kindness; you are a very good friend. But, as you know, I have kept myself alive these last seventy-three years, so there is no need to fuss too much.

She says she worries because I live alone, although I believe she does too, not that she shares much.

Helen, I feel like you know everything under the bloomin' sun there is to know about me, but I don't even know if you're currently romantically involved with anyone. Before she died, Josie mentioned that you were hoping for a proposal from some mystery man whose name you didn't share. I don't know what happened with that, but I don't recall spotting a ring. What a terrible friend I am—although, in my defence, you've always been very private. But things are too *me, me, me* right now, and we've still got lots to catch up on about your time away in London. Over a hot brew, next time I see you.

As I was saying, living alone is not something that has ever really bothered me. It would have been nice to have a wife and kids, but it just didn't happen like that for me. I had my heart broken three times, and after that I decided to stop looking for love. So, I live alone. And that suits me and my little habits quite well. Everything is just as I like it, except for the occasional tea towel out of place. But I fix that as soon as Helen leaves.

Sorry again, Helen.

This cottage is the same one I have lived in my whole life. My father left it to me and my sister in his will. It was the least he could do. And my sister left me her half when she passed away, bless her. It has been paid off for a while now, but it guzzles gas and electricity like a sports car, so that's where a lot of my pension goes each month. The limestone wall out the front has had to be fixed a few times. I used to do it myself, but I can't be doing things like that until I get my hip done. I can barely lift the shopping, let alone slabs of stone. The wall props up a slightly wonky wrought-iron gate and then a small path leads to my white front door. It's not much, but it's a nice home for one.

Three bedrooms, though all very small. One lavatory upstairs and one downstairs. I repainted the entire house cream once Dad dropped dead. Redid the carpets too. I didn't want even the tiniest skin cell from him remaining. I sold most of the furniture at a car boot, but I kept all my mum's cake trays and the like. My father never bothered with the kitchen, so I didn't have to do much in there. Just a few appliance upgrades. I keep the door to their old bedroom closed and never go in. That means my room is not the biggest, but it will do, considering it is only me. It is just about big enough for a double bed, and that is big enough for someone who lives alone.

Yesterday, Helen got me to sit in front of a mirror and describe myself. She said that you readers would like to have a clear picture of me, which is fair enough since we are going to be spending a fair amount of time together. Helen will insert a transcript of that audio here.

You know, Helen, I can't say I have ever sat in front of a mirror and studied myself like this before. Right: from top to bottom, you say? Well, I have a shortish mop of grey hair on my head. Or should I say silver? Does that make me sound more dashing? Let's go with silver. My eyebrows are grey—or silver—too. I have to comb them with a little brush in the mornings as they're normally this way, that way and every which way when I wake up. I have blue-grey eyes and pale skin. Even if I go on holiday I'll always burn and never tan. Not that I sit in the sun much.

I've never been a big drinker, so I don't have any of them spider veins that you see on those down the pub. My father had them all over his big, bulbous nose. He never made it to my age, but even by the time he died he looked older than I do now. Not to toot my own horn, but my skin is pretty smooth, all things considered. A few new wrinkles popped up on the forehead after all this murder malarky, though.

I wouldn't say I'm tall, but I'm not short. Five foot ten and a half. Don't forget the half. And I am slim but not skinny. You might say I've got a slight frame. I walk with a bit of a hobble now that the old hip has carked it. I've been on the waitlist for a replacement since last year.

Clothes. When I'm at home, I normally like to wear comfortable trousers and a shirt. I have different shirts for different occasions. Once I find something I like, I normally buy it in a few colours. And when I was working at Cavengreen, my uniform was a smart navy suit with the hotel's logo on the breast pocket, a crisp white shirt, a blue tie that I attached my gold name pin to, and my always-shined black shoes. The top hat wasn't mandatory, but I thought it was a nice touch. I kept the name pin when I left. It is on the mantelpiece as a reminder to always stay true to who I am, no matter the circumstance.

I must say, now that I have done it, I am glad Helen suggested that mirror exercise. Otherwise, I would be struggling to find many more adjectives for myself other than old and grey.

Helen also told me to run through a regular day with you, but I am not sure how helpful that would be in pushing this story along, considering a regular day now looks very different to a regular day back then. Instead, I will recap the day before the murder. That way you will get an idea of what a normal day looked like at Cavengreen, but with some bits relevant to this book in there too.

That morning, like every morning, I woke at 5 am and took three deep breaths before getting out of bed on the left side. The tap in my shower has always been a bit dodgy, but it is close to three twists to find the perfect temperature. Three small pumps of body wash and then three laps around my mouth with my toothbrush. Three, or possibly six, squares of lavatory roll for my business and then I got dressed and headed out to the car. I upgraded from a bicycle to a car about ten years ago, when the hip first started playing silly buggers. Before I set off, I tapped the steering wheel three times.

At Cavengreen, I parked in the same spot as I did every other day. The hotel made a RESERVED plaque for me because I would get flustered if a new staff member or one of the young folk would park where I normally did. I was there by ten to six, which left just enough time to make sure that everything on my desk was neatly back in place after the night cleaners had been. That meant my pen and paper were perfectly aligned, the labels on the water bottles in the fridge were all facing forward, and my maps and guides were stacked in three perfect rows. Fiona always picked up coffees for me and herself on her way in, and mine was in my hand by 6 am. That morning, she'd written a little message on the side of the paper cup: 'have a good day'. Then the workday began with a briefing from Fiona on all the important goings on.

Once the clock ticked over to 9 am, I started telephoning anyone who had recently made a booking. It was part of our personal concierge service to make them feel special from the moment they booked to the moment they arrived back home. I asked them things like their dietary requirements, if they were staying at the hotel for a particular occasion, what kind of pillow they liked, if they would like me to book the hotel restaurant for them one evening, and if they had any special requests. It was normally just a five- or ten-minute conversation, and I would get one of the girls on reception to pop the notes on their file so that we had everything ready for them when they checked in. We would always try to greet our guests with a personal touch, like,

'Happy fourth anniversary,' or, 'Welcome to the Yorkshire Dales,' if they had never been here before. Just to make them feel a bit special.

On this particular day, the day before the murder, the bride, Olive, came down for breakfast just after 9 am. Her hair was all bunched up in those rollers that make women look like Medusa. She seemed stressed. Her mother was scuttling after her, also in a bit of a frenzy. On their way through the lobby, I heard the bride asking her mother to just give her some space. The bride was only at breakfast for fifteen minutes before returning to her suite in tears. The twins, Ruby and Oksana, trailed along, telling her everything would be okay, but smirking behind her back. Like I said, it was not my business to pry, but those were the sort of things I noticed. To the guests, it was almost like I was a piece of furniture rather than a human with eyes and ears. You would be surprised how openly they displayed their emotions in front of me. Sometimes I felt like one of those oil paintings whose eyes seem to follow you wherever you go.

Check-in at the hotel was from eleven. The groom and his two groomsmen arrived first. They had a lot of suit bags, so I helped the porters take everything up to their suite, making sure to check the coast was clear to avoid a premature run-in with an emotional bride. Luckily, Fiona had carefully planned this arrival and the boys' room was downstairs, while the entrance to the bridal suite was at the far end of the top-floor corridor. There was whisky and ice already waiting for the trio, something they had requested during our pre-arrival telephone call. They also wanted burgers, presumedly to cure their hangovers. I quietly offered to send up some rehydration sachets and painkillers. We needed that groom looking and feeling his best by the afternoon. In my day, I have seen many an angry bride lose their cool over a too-drunk or too-hungover husband at the altar. The groom accepted my offer and, as far as I know, it worked.

By the time I returned to my desk, Alec Maclean, the Scottish writer, was checking in and, as you know, I arranged for his bangers and mash to be delivered. About half an hour after that, Bruno Tatterson arrived, bagless. I noticed Fiona giggling shyly and fluttering her eyelashes as he checked in, which she does when a guest is a bit of a looker, which I suppose he was, but in a more mature, rugged way than American Dave. About ten years younger than me, I'd say. Bruno looked familiar—perhaps from the telly or maybe movies. The hotel is often frequented by celebrities and royalty. Half of them I don't have the foggiest idea who they are, but Bruno rang some sort of bell for me. The most famous person we've had at the hotel is *[name removed for legal reasons]*. I mean, the whole world knows who he is, even an old fart like me. He arrived at the hotel with one younger lady on the Monday, pretended to check out with her on the Wednesday, and then arrived back at the hotel an hour later with another young lady. It was funny watching him pretend to ooh and aah at things he had already seen earlier that day. But the staff were under strict instructions to play along. Discretion is factored into the price tag at a place like Cavengreen.

Mr Potts would circle the hotel like a hawk from about 11.30 am. He checked every surface for dust and then twisted the vases this way and that until he found the angle that best showcased the flowers. This was quite grating for me, as I normally gave the vase on my desk three swift twists to set its position. I would find myself twitching a little when Mr Potts came over and twisted it two or four times. When he had finished his loop of the lobby, I would normally give the vase three more turns, just to resettle my angsty hands.

If anything was not as it should be in the lobby, the blame normally fell on Fiona. It was—and still is, I suppose—her job to make sure everything was spick and span at all times. Mr Potts was particularly hard on her. She never crumbled though, and always took his comments on the chin. She is a strong woman, even stronger after she lost her husband. But some days after work we would head to the pub for a glass of wine, and she would let it all out. It is best not to keep things bottled up for too long and I am always willing to lend an ear to a friend.

As was the norm when we had a wedding at the hotel, there was an influx of suppliers the morning of. Florists, musicians, the cake supplier, the marquee hire company, it all happened in those last few hours. The hotel has its own dedicated commercial kitchen down back, where the chefs make all the food for weddings and events. It is more profitable than bringing in an external caterer, I believe. The couple getting married would usually come in for a tasting about two months before the wedding and sample all the options before deciding what dishes they wanted on their menu. From memory, I think they chose the smoked salmon and vegetable tart for the entrees, and then the pork belly, gnocchi and kingfish for the mains. The wedding cake would be served for dessert and they requested mini beef sliders to come out around 10 pm as a little late-night snack to fuel the dancefloor.

I know the florist, Laurina, quite well. She is the preferred supplier here at Cavengreen, and on the morning of the wedding she turned up with the most beautiful peonies neatly tied into bridal bouquets. All the flowers were white, which I always think looks very elegant. Around 1 pm I went and had a little peek at the wedding set-up, and it looked simply spectacular. But that is what you get when you marry at Cavengreen. It is not a venue for those who are short of a bob or two.

Everything that day proceeded as normal. That was until 2 pm rolled around and Mr Potts and the Americans entered the lobby. The tall fellow, American Dave, had the loudest voice. He sounded like a cowboy, and his brash tone was like nails on a chalkboard in our refined hotel. Or *his* refined hotel, I should say. Mr Potts pointed out various features to the Americans, the two ducklings at the back taking notes. Then they came my way.

'Hector? That's your name, isn't it?' American Dave asked. He placed his giant hands on my counter, leaving smudges when he eventually peeled them off.

I politely confirmed my identity and wondered where this could be going. I would be lying if I said that I wasn't a little concerned after what Fiona had told me about them replacing the concierge system with some new technology.

'A word, Hector?' Mr Potts gestured towards the library, and I followed him and the Americans into the room.

'Hector,' American Dave boomed. 'Pottsy here tells me you've worked at the hotel for over fifty years.' He didn't pause for me to agree or disagree. 'That's a mighty long time. You must have seen some things in your day?'

I nodded but he wasn't looking for a response.

'That may be the case,' he went on, 'but we think the concierge service at Cavengreen could do with a little refresh.'

'A refresh?' I said.

'A refresh. That's right. We want to take Cavengreen into the future and we're going to need your help.' I felt like I was being recruited into the army. 'Do you know what an iPad is?' One of the other Yanks handed him a device.

'Of course.' I withheld my offence as I replied. I might be seventy-three and not able to use a computer, but I am not a bloody imbecile.

'Great!' American Dave thumped his hand down on the mahogany coffee table and I tried not to grimace. Mr Potts gasped a little for both of us. 'Our team back in Dallas has been working hard to develop brand-new software especially for this hotel. Our digital concierge service will now be available in every suite at Cavengreen, allowing guests to make their requests without having to deal directly with you. It will save you time and you won't have to make small talk.'

'I quite like chatting to the guests,' I protested. 'It's no bother.'

But American Dave wasn't interested. 'This is the future, Hector. Nobody wants to speak to a human anymore. The world is all about convenience and this is just part of it.'

'With all due respect, Dave,' Mr Potts began, noticing the horror on my face, 'Hector has worked at the hotel for many years and our regular guests look forward to seeing him. He is part of the experience.'

'And he still will be, Pottsy—he'll just be inside one of these iPads, that's all.' American Dave waved the device in his hand. 'Let me show you the software: you're gonna love it.'

American Dave made us sit either side of him on the sofa as he poked at the screen. The software in question allowed people to request a new pillow from a menu, order room service directly from the kitchen, book dinner at Lavender Plates and make other special requests that would be sent through to the appropriate staff member who could fulfil them. I would have an iPad on my desk through which I would be able to see any guest requests that were relevant to me, he explained. As far as I could see, my new role was that of a donkey. Instead of talking to guests, I was reduced to merely a fetcher and carrier. Most of the requests that I would normally have handled would now go straight to an iPad set up in the porter's quarters. I am no fool, so I asked them straight.

'This is all very well and good for the future and technology, but what does it mean for my job?'

'Hector, relax.' American Dave held up his palms to soothe me, as if I were acting like some lunatic. 'This is merely a trial period to see if it improves guest satisfaction. If they don't like it, we'll take it away.'

'And if they do like it?' Mr Potts asked nervously.

'Then we've done our job right!' American Dave clapped his hands together and his minions all nodded along like those dog figurines that builders have on their dashboards.

After the meeting concluded, Mr Potts pulled me to one side and told me he was going to protect my job at all costs. But we both knew that American Dave and his iPads were likely going to mean the end of my career at Cavengreen. And I will admit it: I was angry.

CHAPTER

6

Normally, I start recording at 7 am, after the morning paper has arrived and I have had one of my two cups of English breakfast. But today, that did not happen, and let me tell you why. That good-for-nothing Paula McDavidson! The newspaper boy flung today's black-and-white at my front door and it landed with a particularly loud thud. I put the kettle on, then stepped outside to pick it up. My heart stopped when I saw my ugly mug on the front page. I haven't read it yet. I just got off the telephone with Helen and she said I should read it to you lot so you can have my real, as-it-happens reaction.

The headline says: CONCIERGE OR CONMAN? Well, I never! Concierge or conman? I haven't devoted the last fifty-odd years of my life to Cavengreen just to be labelled a conman by the local newspaper. Of course, Paula McDavidson is responsible for this. There is a little photo of her next to the word 'journalist'. If she is a journalist, then I am the bloody sultan of Taiwan. A fiction writer is what she is. A make-believe storyteller. On the plus side, the photo she has used isn't the worst I have seen of me. It is from Cavengreen's website. The Americans mustn't have had the chance to update it yet. It was taken about ten years ago now and shows me looking rather smart in my uniform outside the front of the hotel.

Next to the picture of me is a photograph of the twins, Ruby and Oksana. I am not sure what being in a bikini on the beach in Dubai has to do with the murder investigation. The caption underneath the photo says that they are the daughters of a millionaire property investor, and they live in a five-million-pound house in Chelsea, London. They have even put in how much my cottage is worth! It hasn't been sold in over eighty years, so I am not sure where Paula McDavidson has plucked that number from. Why does the newspaper have to mention that? The lower the home value, the more likely the owner is to murder someone? Are people supposed to make judgements on a person's character based on the price of their house? I am already getting riled up and I haven't even started reading the bloomin' thing yet. I am sure this will be a pack of lies, but here goes:

> Cavengreen Hotel may be one of the most luxurious places to stay in the United Kingdom, but recently it was embroiled in a scandal fit for the movies. In an exclusive for the *Yorkshire Sun*, two of the guests staying at the hotel at the time of the notorious Cavengreen murder have decided to come forward. This is their story . . .

Spare me the dramatics! There is no point in me telling my story if the others keep coming out of the woodwork with their made-up nonsense. But then again, I must remember: exposing the truth is why I am doing this.

> Twins Ruby and Osksana Farrinucha are daughters of million-aire property investor Roman Farrinucha and currently reside in

Chelsea, London. In April of this year, the girls were invited to Cavengreen Hotel in the Yorkshire Dales to act as bridesmaids at the wedding of their friend Olive Nixon. During their stay they witnessed the brutal murder of—

WITNESSED? Witnessed, my arse. Not a single person in that hotel witnessed anything. The only people who saw the dead body were me, the police and the murderer. They may have seen the body bag as it was wheeled out of the hotel, but I doubt it; I think I was the only one awake for that. I can't read any more of this nonsense without talking to Helen.

I turned the dictaphone off for a bit. I just needed to gather my thoughts. Helen had to talk me into continuing with this book. Sometimes I think she is the only one on my side. When we first discussed writing this, I told her that if I was going to do it, it had to be the full truth. No fluff or lies. And I stand by that. But it is going to be hard to convince people that this is the true version when there are half-a-dozen other versions out there. Just you wait until American Dave has his chat with the media. We finally got confirmation of that today. Instead of a book, he is planning on releasing a documentary with some American production company and now I feel like it is a race between me and him.

I told Helen I was tempted to just pack it in and let the truth stay hidden forever. But she persuaded me that not only would I be letting myself down by not telling my story, I would be letting her down, after all the effort she's already put into this. She is really enjoying getting stuck into a book project again. It has been a welcome distraction from her recent break-up, so she tells me. Plus, she added, withholding the truth would be letting the victim down.

A good telling-off was all I needed. I'm going to pull myself together and finish what I started. Not today, though; today I need to rest. And as for this pathetic excuse for journalism, this can be tomorrow's fish-and-chip wrapping.

And yes, Helen, that sound was me flinging the newspaper across the room.

Yesterday was a bit rocky but I am in a much finer mood today. Onwards and upwards. It is time to get back to my story. Today we are returning to the hotel and picking up where we left off on the day before the murder. You might remember that I had just been given a lesson in technology from American Dave. It was nice to know that Mr Potts supported me. Whether the Americans would listen to him or not would be another matter.

American Dave left an iPad on my desk so I put on my glasses and tried to have a click around with it. Fiona didn't half chuckle when she saw me. As someone who still has one of those old types of mobile telephones, made just for calls, I am sure I was quite the sight trying to navigate an iPad. Fiona showed me the ropes, and after a few goes I understood the basics. A little pop-up message appeared on the screen reading: TEST TEST TEST. DAVE. TEST TEST TEST. He was just as loud over iPad as in real life. The new devices were to be placed in the guests' rooms during the day's scheduled housekeeping rounds. I was apprehensive to see just how many people preferred to use them.

In the meantime, Alec Maclean, the Scottish writer, called my desk requesting fresh glasses and a bowl of mixed nuts. When I knocked on his door, his voice boomed at me to enter. The curtains in his suite were drawn and just a sliver of bright light spilt through onto his face. There was a humming noise and it took me a few seconds to realise it was coming from Alec. He was sitting at a desk with his laptop open, his hair all in disarray. When he turned around, it was immediately apparent from his grey complexion, drooping eyelids and red eyes that he had spent the few hours since checking in getting very well acquainted with the hotel's complimentary whisky.

'It helps me write,' he mumbled, and then coughed.

'I've heard that Lewis Carroll took hallucinogens when writing *Alice in Wonderland*,' I said, in an attempt to reassure him.

'I don't suppose you have any of those behind that desk of yours,' Alec joked.

'I'm afraid we're all out. Is there anything else I can get you?'

'Opening the curtains might make things a little less depressing in here.'

That seemed like a marvellous idea. A button on the wall next to the fireplace controlled the curtains and with one quick press they whirred open like the beginning of a theatre production.

'How's that writer's block going?' I asked, trying to sound upbeat.

'I thought a little lubrication might help.' He tipped his whisky glass from side to side and watched the liquid sway. 'But I was wrong. Any tips?'

'I could barely read or write when I was at school. It still takes me a while to get through a good murder mystery novel, but perseverance is key in challenging moments. I'd love to be able to write a story one day.

Don't they say everyone's got one good book in them?' I said to him. Irony, that's what that is.

'You could write about life here at the hotel,' Alec suggested.

'And who would want to read about that?'

'You'd have to make it interesting. Every good book needs an event, a twist and a resolution. Get those three, add a few messed-up characters, and there's no reason why you can't write a good book. In fact, I've been writing about some of the people here in the hotel myself. I often do that. I write about conversations or moments I witness, just in case I want to use them later. Not that I know shite about writing a good book. I'm stuck on the twist.' He sighed.

'Well, what have you so far?' I asked.

You might find it odd that I lingered in Alec's room given that, as I told you, I was always the professional, and as such I wasn't in the habit of getting too close to the guests. But this was a funny kind of day, having learnt that my human interaction was about to be replaced with a machine, and since Alec seemed like he wanted to chat, I saw no harm in a little conversation. Plus, the topic was of interest.

Alec ran me through the plot of his book. I don't want to say too much because, like I said before, it is to be published posthumously—by Helen's old firm, as it happens. The story is about a Scottish fisherman who lives on a remote island where strange things keep happening. It's one of those dark and mysterious tales and he uses a lot of adjectives like 'crashing' waves and 'howling' wind to set the scene. He only read part of it to me, but I could tell how cold and miserable it would be in the place the fisherman lived. I guess that is what a good writer does.

In the end we brainstormed three potential twists that could take place to explain the strange occurrences on the island. We quickly ruled out Alec's suggestion of aliens, followed by my recommendation that the fisherman had a long-lost twin brother who had been put up for adoption by their parents and was now back to seek revenge on the family that disowned him. Alec described that as too far-fetched, which I thought was a little rich coming from the drunk who wanted to blame everything on extraterrestrials. But I was pleased with where we landed and happy to have helped Alec overcome his writer's block. When I left him, he was busy tap-tapping on his computer and opening another bottle of whisky. I will say now, with the benefit of hindsight, there is something very dangerous about a man with an empty bottle of whisky—even more so when there is a full one waiting next to it.

I left Alec's room, closing the door behind me quietly, not wanting to disturb his flow of words. A few doors down, someone else was doing some sneaking around too. I saw American Dave zip up his trousers with a satisfied smile on his face as he closed the door to his colleague Tanya's suite. It was my job to turn a blind eye to such dalliances, but I am sure Mrs American Dave won't be best pleased if she ever reads my book. A man like that could convince the Pope that Jesus doesn't exist, though, so I am sure he'll wheedle his way out of it somehow.

'Ready to try out those iPads, my man?' he bellowed as he caught sight of me.

I gave him a thumbs-up, because that seemed the appropriate form of communication with such a man in such a moment. He returned the gesture, seeming completely unfazed by my having caught him in the midst of a tryst. But that goes back to what I was saying before about people feeling like they can be their true selves around me, because it is only the concierge watching—no one important.

Around 3.30 pm, the wedding guests began to arrive in coachloads. The hotel isn't large enough to accommodate hordes of rowdy guests, so we usually suggest that the bride and groom's immediate family stay

in the suites, and that other guests book their own accommodation at one of the neighbouring hotels or bed and breakfasts. I stood by the door with Fiona and the girls from reception, trying to catch a glimpse of the attendees. This lot looked like a very well-to-do bunch as they stepped off the coaches. They were directed around the side of the hotel rather than through the lobby, so as not to bother the regular guests. A rainbow of colourfully dressed women was broken up by the dark tones of designer three-piece suits on well-groomed men who spoke like royalty. One woman seemed determined to outdo the bride in a flowing cream gown made of what appeared to be feathers.

Fiona coordinated some pre-wedding drinks for the groom and his groomsmen in the library. Patrick was complaining that his parents couldn't make it, having been caught up on business in the Middle East. Some people have all the money in the world, but don't put their family first, so what is the point? I would rather have had wonderful parents growing up than millions of pounds. As it turns out, I had neither. That is unfair to my mother, but she was not around that long.

My mother died when I was thirteen. Heart attack. My father found her dead in her favourite chair with a full glass of sherry and an uneaten slice of apple pie next to her. She didn't even get to enjoy her last meal. My mum was a lovely woman. Anna-Elise was her name. She used to paint watercolours of the landscape and sell them at the local pub to tourists passing through. My sister tried to track down some of her work a few years ago. She came close to getting one back for us once, but the greedy seller wanted more than three months' wages for it. Maybe if I sell enough of these books, I could buy it.

Our father's drinking got worse after our mother died. It was a good thing for me, though, because he spent more time down the pub than at home. Then he would pass out almost as soon as he came through the front door, and I would sneak out before he woke the next morning. We were like ships in the night. Sometimes I would get to school three hours early just to avoid him. On the weekends, I would walk up the hill behind our cottage and sit in the grass until I saw him leave for the day.

Anyhoo, after they'd had their drinks, Fiona escorted the groom and his men out to greet the guests. I caught a glimpse of Patrick's face as he passed through reception. Why is it that some grooms look like they are walking to their execution when they are on their way to marry the supposed love of their life?

When Fiona returned, she told me that the groom was having second thoughts. That he wasn't sure if Olive was going to make him happy forever. He said she was selfish, constantly dissatisfied, and always expecting too much. Fiona said she made a joke about divorce that went down like a lead balloon. Fiona has never had the tact for those sorts of situations. I have always found her very funny, though. Nevertheless, it seemed a bit late in the day for the groom to be having cold feet. I have seen a few instances of pre-wedding jitters in my time but I can't recall one single occasion where the wedding hasn't gone ahead. No doubt there are a fair few divorced couples out there now, but a wedding at Cavengreen costs an arm and a leg and no one wants the embarrassment of explaining to a group of snooty guests that a fancy do has been cancelled. I bet Fiona ten pounds that the wedding would still go ahead and later that day she paid up. I tried to refuse—a gentleman never accepts money off a lady from a lost bet—but she tucked the banknote in my breast pocket and told me I could buy her a glass of wine on Friday. That sounded like a good plan to me. Not that we made it to the pub in the end.

Olive's parents were bickering when they came down to the lobby. Something about him not saying her hair looked okay when prompted. Sue's snappishness probably stemmed from mother-of-the-bride nerves rather than a lack of compliments from her husband. Martin was sighing and looked like he would rather be elsewhere. I don't know the ins and outs of the Bainbridge family dynamics, and the whereabouts of Olive's biological father is still unknown to me, so don't expect him to suddenly appear to murder someone. You can cross him off your list of potential suspects.

The bickering stopped when the twins came stumbling along the corridor—a few champagnes in, it seemed. They were laughing loudly and taking pictures every couple of steps. They wore slinky peach dresses with no backs, and had matching half-up, half-down hairstyles. The wedding photographer got some photos of them, and then some more, as they demanded to be shot from every angle. Poor Olive waited in the wings for several minutes before she was called forward for her big reveal. And what a reveal it was. Her mother and stepfather cried happy tears as their little darling emerged in a huge white meringue with a veil that stretched a good way down the hallway. They all posed for pictures on the hotel stairs. Those stairs have been the backdrop for many a beautiful photograph in their day. From newlyweds to celebrities and royals, they have seen it all. You do have to watch out for the odd interruption of a passing guest, mind you. In this case, an inebriated Alec came bounding down, squeezing between Ruby and the bride. Ruby called him a host of offensive names, but Alec ignored her, making a beeline for my desk. It was essential that I join him in his suite immediately to help with the final part of his story, he insisted.

'Are you not going to do something about him?' Ruby shouted in my direction. 'He nearly knocked the bride down the stairs!'

This was a tricky situation for me. I wasn't employed as hotel security and Alec had every right to use the main staircase regardless of their photo shoot. Unfortunately he went about it like a bull in a china shop.

'I am ever so sorry,' I said. 'Fiona will arrange for some more champagne before you make your entrance.'

My words appeased the bride, but the twins weren't satisfied, making it clear that not only was I a silly old man who was beneath them, but noting that it was no surprise to them that I didn't wear a wedding ring given that I had amounted to nothing more than a hotel concierge.

Fiona gave me an apologetic look as she shepherded the bridal party into the library for some champagne and more photographs.

When I look back, it is very clear that the twins were gunning for me from the start. To them, I was an easy target. But I had no time to process the insults because a flushed-looking Alec was practically dragging me up the stairs towards his suite. When I suggested that it might be a better idea if we conversed the following day, when we were both fresher, he shouted something incoherent and spit-laden, then thumped back upstairs alone, tripping once or twice on his way.

The lobby felt like a hurricane had just blown through it and I took three deep breaths to reset myself. Fiona returned to reception, rolling her eyes about the 'twin twits', as she called them. Mind you, this isn't even the half of my experience with the Farrinucha girls. There is more to come, but maybe you're starting to see why I was less than pleased to learn they were telling their story to the *Yorkshire Sun*. Those two girls are menaces.

CHAPTER

8

Paula McDavidson has been round again. This time she wants a quote in response to her interview with the twins. Fat chance of that. I slammed the door in her face and told her not to come back ever again. As if that will stop her. Helen is here today. Something is wrong, I can tell, but she keeps repeating that she is 'fine'. She is sitting in the corner acting all shy because she doesn't want her voice on today's recording. Even when I said pretty please, she folded her arms and looked away. I won't be too pushy. Perhaps when I turn off the dictaphone she will open up.

Helen has come to gauge where I am up to in the story and to give me some helpful tips to make sure I don't forget anything important. She has brought along some vanilla tarts from Maude's Bakery, so excuse me while I munch on one of these and tell you about Bruno Tatterson. I told you I recognised him from somewhere; I wasn't the only one. Fiona said that she knew him from somewhere too. An older movie, she reckoned. Fiona loves her British crime films, and she swore that she'd seen Bruno in one of them. She winced when I cheekily suggested she subtly ask him if he was an actor. At Cavengreen we pride ourselves on our discretion. It is a place where the most famous person in the world can get some privacy.

Bruno spent most of the day in the spa, eventually emerging to head back to his suite around 5 pm. That is what Fiona told me. I wasn't there to see him as Alec had requested a new pillow as a way of luring me to his suite to help again with his writer's block. As it happened, the reason he wanted my assistance so desperately is that he was using me as inspiration for his main character. I already knew he had used little snippets of me in his book, but Helen has since told me I feature quite heavily in his manuscript. The main character looks just like me, she said, and even has many of my mannerisms. He is me but with a Scottish accent. Funnily enough, I do quite a good impression of a Scotsman. Not that you will be able to hear it if I do it for the dictaphone. I did it for Helen earlier and she will not admit it, but I know she was impressed. I even saw a glimmer of a smile as she lost herself for just a moment recalling a Scottish man she dated before her recent on–off relationship ended. In typical Helen style, she caught herself before revealing much more than that.

You've always been a mysterious one. For years we didn't hear from you while you were making books down in London. There are quite a few blanks to fill in, Helen—if that is indeed your real name.

She knows I'm joking. I even heard a little giggle from behind the vanilla tart that is making its way up to her mouth.

Alec wanted me to tell him about a memorable time in my life, so I recited the story of how I changed Mr Thomas's tyre that one time. He smiled and typed as I spoke. He then asked me to tell him about my relationship with my parents, which made me tap my head three times. He noticed and asked what that was all about. I was hesitant at first but then I spoke about my father, about the beatings. I did it without thinking, opening up in a way I wouldn't normally. Not before writing this book, anyway. I told him the head tapping was not the first thing. Just before that, I developed a stammer. That is all gone now. Though when I am very, very stressed, a slight one can creep back in. It used to drive my father up the wall. I suspect that, deep down, he knew he had done that to me. He stopped forcing me to apologise for things because of how long it would take to get the s out when I said 'sorry'. But the beatings didn't stop. It was always three heavy lashes across my lower back.

Realising I had shared too much, I decided it was time to make my excuses and leave. Alec got up hurriedly from the desk. He staggered, then lurched forward to grab me, begging me to stay for five more minutes, to tell him just a few things more. Unfortunately, he tugged too hard and ripped my suit at the shoulder seam. He was apologetic, but not overly so. He knew he had to let me go, though, and I slid out the door, reassuring him that no harm was done. It is an interesting dynamic, that of guest and concierge. Outside the hotel, a man would never imagine he could simply get away with ripping another man's suit. It would only happen during a heated fight of sorts. But because I was the concierge, and he was a paying guest, somehow that made it okay.

Usually, I liked to check in with all the guests at least once a day, whether that meant catching them when they returned from a walk, or when they were on their way to dinner. After what happened with Alec, I was hardly in the mood to make small talk, but I wanted to catch Bruno before I went home. I knew he had a 7 pm booking at Lavender Plates, so around 7.15, right before I was to head home for the evening, I popped my head into the restaurant to say a quick hello. I placed my torn suit jacket, neatly folded, on Fiona's desk on my way past. Excellent seamstress, she is; she said she would have it looking spanking new by morning.

Bruno was engrossed in his mobile telephone and had a bottle of fine Italian wine opened on his table. It was not my intention to startle him, but that's indeed what happened when I coughed to alert him to my presence. The conversation was short and uncomfortable. I got the impression I had interrupted something important on his mobile telephone, so I kept it brief. I advised that I hoped he'd had a pleasant day and to let the nightstaff know if there was anything he needed. I would be back at 6 am, I advised, and then I left. He didn't acknowledge my exit, but I never took such things personally.

Back at my concierge desk, I grabbed my car keys and said goodnight to Fiona, who was leaving herself. No sooner had she walked out the door than Bruno entered the lobby. He apologised for having been so rude, though this was unnecessary, as I had already moved on from our interaction. When you work in hospitality, the sooner you realise that you shouldn't expect an apology for abrupt guest behaviour, the better. Bruno's timing was rather annoying, as I was looking forward to getting home. I told him it was no bother and nothing to worry about, but he appeared angst-ridden, waving his arms in the air erratically as he described how much pressure he had been under recently and expressing regret that he had taken it out on me.

It was at that moment, with Bruno mid-flail, that the twins made their way through reception. They both raised their eyebrows at me as if to say, *Causing trouble again?* Ruby sucked in her cheeks to contain her smirk, while Oksana whispered something in her sister's ear. Those girls may as well have wooden spoons for arms, the amount of trouble they like to cause. Of course, they were gone by the time I had diffused the situation. Had they gawked at us a little longer, they would have seen us shake hands and wish each other a pleasant evening.

And that's it. That was the day before the murder. Yes, I have highlighted some moments of mild disturbance, but these things happened from time to time at Cavengreen. Certainly nothing occurred that would lead me to suspect what was to come the very next day. But before I get to that, this seems an opportune time for me to check in with Helen to make sure I have ticked off all the bits of information necessary for the story so far. We have a little list, you see. I will leave this chapter here, I think.

Helen ended up staying for tea last night. I made chicken tikka masala from a jar, and we chatted about the book, among other things. She told me about her time at the publishing house in London. 'The most exciting time in my life,' is how she described it. And she really did make it sound very glamorous. Fancy dinners with new authors, book launch parties and lots of interesting people. I can tell she misses that world. I even got her talking about her relationship. She never mentioned him on those few times she came to visit Josie and me, but apparently he wasn't someone who wanted to be mentioned. She didn't even tell her work colleagues about him; said they were too up and down. She decided it was easier just to say nothing. Fair enough, I say.

Helen's a bit different from me. She is very outgoing, and I am a tad more reserved, but not shy by any means. What I am trying to say is that I am happy to be around people—that was my job for fifty-plus years—but I also love my own company and I tire easily in loud or particularly busy social settings. Helen, on the other hand, craves social interaction. And she has a lot of stories to share about her time down south. I am sure she won't mind much if I refer to her as a bit of a chatterbox. She is great company for an old soul like myself. If it weren't for Helen, I wouldn't get any social interaction outside of my infrequent visits to the pub with Fiona.

Listen to me, talking like I am surrounded by women. A big part of me misses the company of my mother and sister. My father stole so many potential happy memories away from us.

Tap one. Tap two. Tap three.

It has been a few chapters since I have done any head tapping, hasn't it? Now that we are getting into the sticky part of this story, I fear the tapping may increase in frequency. I hope that doesn't bother you too much.

When Helen was over last night she asked if she could use my computer. Yes, I have a computer. I bought it a while back with the hope of learning how to use it, but I never did. I got as far as setting up an email account—Fiona helped me do that—and that is it. Now it sits upstairs gathering dust. Helen will kill me for saying this, but her telephone died, and she needed to book in to get her greys covered with brown. Apparently you can schedule hair appointments on the internet now. Helen managed to log on with ease and informed me that aside from something called spam, I had one email. It was from American Dave. She wrote it out on a piece of paper for me so I could read it for you today. In your head, you will need to read this in a Texan accent. Helen tried to do her best impression last night but ended up sounding slightly Irish and slightly Russian.

Dear Mr Harrow,

Long time, no speak! As you may or may not know, a production company over here in the States has approached me to make a documentary about the Cavengreen murder. I plan to fly back over to the UK in the coming months to revisit the Dales with the film crew. Since you played such an important part in all this, I would like to ask if you'd be interested in appearing on-screen to tell your story? You'd be paid, of course. I think you'll find £2000 a very generous offer.

What do you say, old friend?

Dave

You can imagine how insulted I was by this. Old friend? We certainly are not old friends. And two thousand pounds! That is considerably less than the book advance Helen is trying to negotiate for me. I will tell you now, I am not going to reply. He can shove his American documentary up his backside for all I care.

Everyone needs my help to tell this story properly. Without me, they are all just guessing at what happened with the scattered jigsaw pieces they have.

Right, I have crumpled up that note. Hold on—I'll have to put it in the bin, otherwise it'll distract me . . . Okay, I'm back.

That squelching noise was the armchair, Helen.

Now I can get into the day I found the body.

Tap one. Tap two. Tap three.

It was just a normal day. Most stories where something unexpected happens start with the words 'It was just a normal day'. Like it was going to be anything other than that. It would be too coincidental if, on the day I found a dead body, my car was also stolen, a man tried to rob me, I nearly got struck by lightning and there was a fire at the hotel. But this was just a normal day.

It started with my usual routine. When I got to work, I was keen to find out if Eric, the night porter, had heard how the wedding went. He had. All the feedback was positive, and the visiting guests were loaded back onto the coaches without a hitch at 11.15 pm sharp. Bruno ordered a bottle of champagne and a club sandwich just before midnight, but there were no other room service requests after that. After he delivered Bruno's order, Eric said there was a brief moment of commotion involving Alec. Apparently, he was drunk and searching for me, but stumbled back to his room once he realised I had taken myself home. I decided that I might need to have a firmer word with him to let him know I couldn't be available in the way he wanted me to be. I was happy to help out here and there, but not if it affected the other guests. Eric told me there was also a complaint from one of the rooms about the bride and groom consummating their marriage somewhat noisily at 11.30 pm and then again at 2 am. There was not a lot we could do about something like that, other than reassure the unhappy guests that we were confident the noise wouldn't last all night. Which it didn't.

Fiona was in a terrible mood that day. That was a bit out of the ordinary, I suppose. She said that guests had been calling the front desk nonstop since the iPads had been placed in the rooms, complaining about unanswered requests and slow service. She had compiled a list that she was going to take to American Dave. Fiona always gets so flustered when she is not best pleased with something. She puffs out her flushed cheeks and faffs about like a headless chicken, not knowing which way to turn. I knew she would be nervous about giving American Dave her feedback, but if there was a chance it would save my job, she would do it.

Mr Potts was uptight that morning too. He had been called back to Cavengreen just after 11 pm by one of the suppliers whose car had been blocked in by the hotel's limousine. It just so happened that Mr Potts had taken the keys home that night by accident. He had dark circles under his eyes and no spring in his step, though he pulled it together whenever a guest walked by. He loitered around my desk longer than normal. The Americans' presence in the hotel had drawn him closer to Fiona and me, as if we had formed an alliance. Mr Potts made it clear that I would not be replaced by an iPad, but he had concerns about the other staff. Everyone working at Cavengreen came from the local area, something I think added to the hotel's charm. But the Americans had plans to fly in the best of the best in hotel management from the likes of Dubai and the USA. Here I had been busy fretting about myself when it turned out the whole team was at risk of being replaced. To say the atmosphere was a little more tense than usual would be true. But we would rise above the disruption and not let our personal problems impact the guests.

None of the wedding party emerged for breakfast. Instead, I sent a room service trolley of eggs, bacon, croissants, fruit and the like, along with some bloody marys, to the bridal suite. The kitchen porter told me that my gesture was greatly appreciated by the groom's somewhat dusty face when he opened the door.

Only the bride's mother and stepfather left their room that morning. They went for a stroll around the garden to take in some fresh air, returning forty-five minutes later with some more colour to their cheeks. They asked if I could make an afternoon tea booking for the whole bridal party, something I had pre-emptively done when they checked in.

Afternoon tea is quite the occasion at Cavengreen. The hotel has won numerous awards for it, in fact, and we would often get journalists and TV crews wanting to experience it for themselves. Afternoon tea takes place at Lavender Plates every other day at 3 pm. Each table is treated to tiered stands arranged with small, triangular sandwiches, homemade cakes and scones with jam and clotted cream. All of it is served with free-flowing champagne, and cigars are available to enjoy on the terrace once all the food has been cleared. It is such a special occasion. During my time, there were some locals who would come every single Sunday without fail. I would always stop by and show my face once all the guests were settled. But that day I didn't get the chance.

At 3 pm on the dot, the iPad on my desk pinged. Suite seven wanted ice; I was to let myself in and put the bucket on the coffee table. It was a simple request. At 3.08 pm I knocked on the door and shouted, 'Concierge,' just as a courtesy. I pressed my ear up against the door and couldn't hear a response, the shower, or the TV. I let myself in and put the bucket down on the table as instructed. When I turned around I saw red smeared across the carpet leading to the bathroom, where a blood-drenched body lay lifeless on the floor.

Tap one. Tap two. Tap three.

It was obvious that they were dead. I remember blinking three times. Three slow blinks. My mind struggled to process what I was seeing. It felt like I was in that room for a lifetime. The mess . . . oh, the mess; it was horrifying. The sight will haunt me for the rest of my days. That dead body was so out of context in my life, in the hotel. It was surreal. Everything at Cavengreen was so perfect. To see pools of blood on the steam-cleaned carpets and carefully mopped bathroom tiles was extremely unsettling.

I didn't get closer; I didn't need to. I could see their face. Their eyes were half open; drooped, you might say. Their expression was vacant, but not peaceful. You always expect dead bodies to look quite peaceful, but this was the opposite. Their mouth was slightly open, as if it wanted to cry out for help. I am sure they tried to in those last moments.

I knew I needed to get help. As I burst out into the corridor, I held my hand over my mouth, trying to hold back the vomit that was creeping up. I could barely draw breath. My skull tingled. Grey clouds muddled my vision. I stumbled down the corridor, running a hand along the wall to help guide my way. I wasn't exactly sure where my feet were taking me, but they were moving fast.

Shamila was the only one behind the reception desk and she was chatting with a guest. She spotted me out the corner of her eye and furrowed her brow as she watched me bulldoze through the lobby. I guess at that point I was probably looking for Fiona. Either her or Mr Potts. I fumbled my way through the lobby, bumping into the centre table, knocking the vase and shaking petals from the display of pink snapdragons.

In a moment that must have shocked everyone, I burst through the double doors of Lavender Plates. Heads turned to look at me. Quite the sight I must have been. The lady at the desk—I forget her name, she was new—held up both hands to try to stop me, but I ploughed on. Waiters dodged out of the way as I staggered across the room to where Mr Potts was standing, following my haphazard entrance with a startled glare. He had just popped a bottle of champagne for the newlyweds and the bridal party; they now sat frozen, eyes wide and mouths agape, as the bottle fizzed in Mr Potts's hand.

I collapsed into Mr Potts's arms and he ushered me to the corridor beside the kitchen. The chefs poked their heads through the kitchen pass to see what was going on; some called out to ask if I was okay, but I couldn't answer. I was in total shock.

Mr Potts upturned a crate and plonked me on it. He asked what was wrong. My ears felt hot and my mouth heavy. That was how I used to feel when my father tried to talk to me.

Tap one. Tap two. Tap three.

I tried to tell Mr Potts what I had seen, but the stammer that had hindered my speech in childhood returned and I struggled to get the words out. Mr Potts told me to take a deep breath. I took three.

Mr Potts asked again what was wrong.

'M-m . . . m . . . murder.' It was the best I could do in the moment.

American Dave and Tanya appeared in the corridor. Mr Potts politely advised them that the area they were in was for restaurant staff only, something American Dave did not appreciate. He reminded Mr Potts that he had free rein over the hotel now that it had been sold. It was neither the time nor the place for him to start throwing his status around, but that is American Dave: tactless and insensitive. He edged around Mr Potts to get a better view of me. 'Has the old man got dementia?' he asked. He came very close and shouted in my face: 'Do. You. Know. Where. You. Are?'

Mr Potts snapped at him to give me some space, then he crouched down to my eye level and told me to ignore American Dave. That was easy enough, since my mind was entirely consumed by the gore of what I had just witnessed.

Tap one. Tap two. Tap three.

Mr Potts spoke so calmly; his face was reassuring in that moment. He needed me to give him more information, and I knew I needed to tell him what I had just discovered. It was just that my mouth and my mind weren't in sync.

'M-m-murder,' I repeated. It took so much energy to get that one word out. I felt exhausted. I rested my head against the wall.

'Who has been murdered, Hector?' Mr Potts whispered. He squeezed my hand and looked intently into my eyes. He had positioned himself in a way that blocked American Dave's line of sight, but I could still see the Yank craning his neck and bobbing up and down to catch a glimpse of me. Behind him, Tanya was trying to look official by extending her arms to block access to the area. Waitstaff were peering down the corridor, wondering what was going on. It must have been quite the exciting bit of drama for those young 'uns.

'Potts.' American Dave grabbed the manager by the shoulder and pulled him backwards. 'Did he say *murder*?'

'Keep your voice down.' Mr Potts jerked away from American Dave's grip. 'If you would just get out the way, I'll be able to find out more.'

'What's taking him so long?' American Dave yelled impatiently. 'Just spit it out, Hector!'

This, of course, only made the matter worse. I knew what I wanted to say. I wanted to tell Mr Potts the suite number and the name of the victim and urge him to call the police. But the thoughts wouldn't translate into words.

With great presence of mind, Mr Potts took a pen and notepad from a stunned-looking waitress and told me to write it down.

Writing isn't something I am good at—you know that—but with a trembling hand I managed to scrawl: *Suite 7. Bruno. Murder.*

Mr Potts seized the notepad and read the words. American Dave lunged forward and snatched the paper from his grasp.

Mr Potts took out his mobile telephone and called the police. I heard him say that one of the staff suspected there had been a murder. I hardly *suspected* that there had been—it was quite clear that a murder had been committed. One of the waitresses offered me a cup of water but I refused it; my hands were shaking so much I wouldn't have been able to grip it.

American Dave sprang into action, shouting, 'Block the exits!' as he stormed past dining guests to the restaurant entrance. He pointed at all the doors and windows. 'No one is to leave!'

The sound of cutlery clinking lightly as it was placed onto china plates echoed around the room. Everyone fell silent and, from where I was sitting, I could see nervous guests sharing confused glances with one another. A few took big gulps of their champagne. Some even laughed, thinking it was perhaps a performance.

'There has been a murder!' American Dave declared. 'Everybody must stay seated until the police arrive.'

Gasps filled the room.

Mr Potts left my side and strode hastily towards American Dave. He gripped the man's shoulder firmly and spoke directly into his ear. I imagine he said something like, 'Stop causing a scene, you American fool.' But that is just speculation. Whatever it was, Mr Potts looked furious. Seeing him take charge filled me with ease, though. My heart rate began to slow. Now that more people were involved, I felt as if the burden of seeking help had been lifted from my shoulders. The tingling in my brain stopped. I put my hands out in front of me and saw that they were no longer shaking. But images of Bruno's bloody body still flashed in my mind, and I sat there tapping my head in repeated sequences of three. To anyone watching, I must have looked crazy. But funnily enough, the tapping helps to keep my mind under control.

'There is no need to be alarmed. The police have been called and are on their way.' American Dave rotated three hundred and sixty degrees as he addressed the room.

Far from acting alarmed, the majority of the guests resumed their afternoon tea. The waitstaff returned to topping up champagne glasses and light chatter filled the room once again. That is one of the things I love about British people; they just get on with it, even in moments of murder or confusion.

American Dave seemed taken aback by the lack of interest in his dramatic announcement. He assured the guests loudly that the police had been summoned, but he had lost his audience's attention.

The floor-to-ceiling windows of Lavender Plates offer a view of the front of the hotel. Through them, I could see four police cars speeding down the driveway, the blaring of their sirens growing louder and louder. They screeched to a halt at the entrance and a swarm of uniformed police emerged. Everyone in the restaurant paused their conversations and turned to watch, some rising from their seats for a better view. A few of the young ones took out their telephones and started taking pictures. I overheard some guests say how exciting it all was, but I doubt they would have said that if *they* were the ones who had discovered a murdered body on a Thursday afternoon. No respect for the dead is what that was.

Meanwhile, Mr Potts had left the restaurant, followed by American Dave, who instructed the hostess not to let anyone else leave. The hostess rolled her eyes but closed the doors behind them and encouraged everyone to continue enjoying their meal.

It felt like an eternity before Fiona reached Lavender Plates. She weaved through the tables as quickly as she could in her heels, her gaze darting left and right as she searched for me. I must have looked a sorry sight, because she gasped and clapped both hands over her mouth when she spotted me. I shuffled about on my seat, straightening my back to try to look less weak and defeated. Fiona tightly embraced my body, then, releasing me, stared deeply into my eyes as if looking for reassurance that I was okay. She shooed some of the nosier staff away and told them to get back to work. Fiona can be very bossy when she needs to be.

She took my hand and pulled me up, keeping a tight grip as she led me through the restaurant, telling me to ignore the stares. As we walked towards the lobby, Fiona told me to prepare myself, that there were a lot of police waiting for me and I would have to be strong. I am not weak, and I wanted Fiona to know that, so I assured her I would be fine.

At the end of the corridor stood a man in a suit. His arms were crossed and he glanced impatiently at his watch like he had somewhere more important to be. When he saw me, he clicked his fingers and a group of policemen appeared behind him. Mr Potts and American Dave stood off to the side; all eyes were on me. Fiona nudged me in the direction of the police. I looked back at her, and she gave me a faint smile and little nod.

The man in the suit stepped forward. 'Right then—Mr Harrow, is it? Show us where you found this body, why don't you?'

It was the longest walk of my life, the walk back to suite seven. My mind was playing all kinds of tricks on me. I could hear my father's voice telling me I was lying, and I could see bloody footprints on the hallway carpet, footprints from when I stumbled out of the room. But there were no footprints, of course. I hadn't got close enough to the body for there to be blood on my shoes. It was all in my head.

The police followed me like I was the Pied Piper, stopping behind me when I nodded towards the door that concealed the deceased guest. I recognised a couple of the officers: Fred and Ellie had worked in the force for many years, and I had seen them around and about my village on the odd occasion. Not that there is a lot of crime around these parts. They would normally be out investigating stolen lawnmowers or missing cats. Mundane stuff. Several of the police looked at me doubtfully, with frowns or single eyebrow raises. Some of them smirked as if they didn't believe me—exactly how my father used to look at me. One of them yawned. Had Mr Potts or American Dave been the one to find the body and report it, then I am sure the hotel would have already been wrapped in police tape, but since it was me, the concierge, the old man, I had to convince everyone I was telling the truth.

When I was younger, my father would always say I was lying about things, even though I never was. Knocks your confidence, that sort of thing. I swear it was just another excuse for the lousy sod to give me a wallop. He owned a panelbeating business: beat by profession, beat by nature. It was very fitting for such a man. He was only ever drunk or hungover, and both versions liked to give me the belt. If I looked at him funny: belt. If I didn't look at him: belt. If I looked at Mum with sympathy after he had beat her: belt. One day, I must have only been about nine or ten, I hid all his belts. In my naivety I thought that would solve the problem. But in lieu of a belt, my father used a plant pot and broke all five fingers on my right hand. He did it in front of Josie, who was only a baby at the time. Mother told the school I fell off my bike. I didn't even have a bike at that point. The purpose of giving you this information is not to forewarn you that I became a violent man because of my father; in fact, I would say I am quite the opposite. I suppose this is just a bit of background that might be useful to explain the little habits that I have—the way my brain works.

In that moment, outside suite seven, I felt like it was me versus everyone else. I could tell what they were wondering: Is the old man cuckoo or is there actually a dead body in there? Their looks of doubt made me question myself, just for a second.

I hung back from the door, not wanting to get too close. That sounds strange, now that I think about it. What was I afraid of? A dead body? There is something haunting about being that close to someone who has been murdered. Bruno's lifeless body was scary because it was unexplained, not because it was no longer breathing.

The unknown is frightening, and there were a lot of unknowns in this situation. I was also afraid that the police would make me go back in there. Once was quite enough.

The officer in the suit asked Mr Potts to open the door. As the rest filed forward, I took a few more steps away, as far as the corridor would allow. American Dave tried to edge his way to the front but was told to stand back, much to his frustration.

Best to introduce the man in the suit now, before I get into what happened next. I had never seen him before, but by the end of this murder hullaballoo, we were very well acquainted. His name is Detective Arjun Raj, and from what I have gathered since, he had been moving quite quickly through the police ranks. He had probably expected to be pushing papers for a couple of years here in the Dales before scoring a plum role back in the big smoke of Leeds—which, for those of you who don't know, is the main city in this county.

His manner was threatening and aggressive; he was not the kind of bloke you wanted to help. He had dark circles under his eyes and a mop of jet-black hair he pushed back out of his face far too often. I would say he was in his early forties, and at one point I noticed he had photographs of two children hanging from his car keys in miniature frames. Not to be rude, but I can't imagine him being a particularly loving father. In fact, I would bet money that his kids fear him, much as I feared my father when he was alive.

Tap one. Tap two. Tap three.

Detective Raj strode everywhere like he was going into battle and had no time for people who he viewed as below him—which seemed to be everyone. There was nothing likeable about him, and in that way, again, he reminded me of my old man.

Tap one. Tap two. Tap three.

Mr Potts unlocked suite seven. Detective Raj pulled on a pair of latex gloves, then opened the door and stepped inside. Everyone's attention was on him as they braced for word that I really had discovered a dead body. Even I held my breath, waiting for confirmation that I had not just gone mad.

Detective Raj came out about twenty seconds later. He peeled the white gloves off his hands and kept his head bowed. We all held our breath. It was uncomfortable. The detective finally raised his head.

'Cordon off the corridor,' he ordered. 'There's been a murder.' Then, raising his voice to be heard above the resulting murmurs: 'The hotel must be put under a full lockdown. No one comes in, no one goes out. Now, move!' Detective Raj clapped his hands together and his officers scattered.

American Dave dodged moving bodies and approached Detective Raj to announce that he had already told the guests in the restaurant that they weren't to leave. I suppose he wanted brownie points. The detective did not respond, instead looking American Dave up and down before concluding that he was not important.

American Dave, clearly desperate to feel relevant, turned to me and told me to go back to the restaurant and await further instruction. Fat chance I was going to listen to him. I started walking towards the lobby to find Fiona.

'Oh no you don't.' Detective Raj gripped my shoulder firmly. 'I've got some questions for you.'

From then on, Mr Potts's office became Detective Raj's office. Mr Potts tried to put up a fight, claiming that the police had no right to take over the hotel in such a way, but he was wasting his breath. Mr Potts was relegated to the holding bay in Lavender Plates for the next five hours, just like the rest of the staff and guests. The only person not in the restaurant-turned-prison was me. Two police officers guarded the door to the library, where I was detained, alone. They were snappy and aggressive, telling me not to try anything. As if I would. I am an old man with a dodgy hip, I was hardly going to make a run for it. Plus, I had nothing to hide. Flashbacks of the body flickered in my mind as I paced up and down.

Tap one. Tap two. Tap three.

I knew I wasn't the murderer, yet I felt threatened by the police. My father's voice echoed in my ears, telling me I was lying and was going to be found out. I feared I was an easy target, and that the police could pin something on me if they really wanted to. I was out of my depth.

Now, I did not know this then, but I do now: while I was locked in the library, the detective was reviewing the CCTV footage of the moment I discovered the body. Obviously, there is no CCTV in the suites, but for safety and security reasons the hotel has cameras in the hallways. I am familiar with the positioning of most of them and can tell you that there is a camera directly above suite six that captures the door of suite seven. The cameras are state-of-the-art and were newly installed at the time, so the picture is really sharp. They would have had a direct view of me letting myself into suite seven and then leaving in all sorts. You would think that would have put me in the clear, but when Detective Raj came back from reviewing the footage, by gum did he give me a grilling.

The detective was just doing his job, I know that. But I am going to say this: there are ways of going about things, and his was the wrong way. Three hours I spent in Mr Potts's office getting interrogated by the detective. I had gone from hotel concierge to prime suspect in a murder case in the blink of an eye. And didn't they just treat me like that! They would not even let me have a glass of water. Stress makes you thirsty, you know? My tongue was practically sticking to the roof of my mouth. I reckon it was dirty tactics to make me talk.

They need not have parched me half to death to do that! Everything I knew I told them in the first two minutes, so why they felt the need to drag me over hot coals for three hours is beyond me. Torture, that's what you would call it.

'What's with the head tapping?' That is the first thing Detective Raj asked me as he paced Mr Potts's office from end to end. He made me sit on Mr Potts's desk chair. It was one of those swivel ones and I tell you what, Mr Potts must sit like a pencil because the back of the chair was as upright as could be. I am all for good posture, but I need a bit of a lean so there is not too much pressure on my hip. That was killing me, in case you are wondering. I must have made too many funny movements in the bother of everything, and now it felt like a dagger had been plunged into my side. And I will tell you what I think of Detective Raj's opening question: rude! That is what I think. Fancy poking at someone's vulnerability as soon as you meet them. His question affirmed that I was not dealing with a nice man.

'It is a nervous thing I do when I have a dark or intrusive thought,' I replied, avoiding eye contact.

'Have a lot of these dark thoughts, do you?'

'Occasionally.'

'And these voices in your head, do they tell you to do bad things?' He had twisted my words.

'They're not . . . not . . . voices. They're . . . they're memories.' I could feel the stammering ghost of my past creeping in. I closed my eyes and lightly tapped the front of my head over and over and over in beats of three. My father's voice yelled at me to stop it. To stop being so ridiculous. To stop being weak.

'What is it that you're thinking about now, then?' I opened my eyes and Detective Raj was leaning towards me, both hands on the desk.

'The blood . . . the b-b-body,' I stuttered.

'Pretty nasty sight, right?'

A nod seemed the only appropriate answer. Looking back, I wish I had been stronger. That is easy to say now that I am out the other side. I don't want you lot reading this to think I'm weak. You have to understand that I had just seen a dead body, a murdered one; I was in bits. At that moment, I was scared. Scared that the memory of all the blood would haunt me forever, scared that I would be blamed for something I didn't do. As this story goes on, I hope you'll see a change in me. This experience has made me stronger, that I know for certain. I don't think you are ever too old to learn, not even at seventy-three. That is many people's downfall in life; they think that they are too old to grow and to change. But not me.

Detective Raj said he wanted to show me something. He opened a laptop and plugged in one of those . . .

Helen, please edit this bit to add in the name of those stick things. They are not something I am overly familiar with.

He plugged in a USB stick *[editor's note]*. The detective pulled up a chair next to me and pressed play on a video. It was me. It was me walking to suite seven, holding the ice bucket. It was strange seeing that version of myself again, the version that had not yet seen a dead body. The version that was just about to have his life changed by a sight that would scar him forever. How innocent I was.

In the video, you can see me knock on the door and then let myself in. Detective Raj paused it there. He got out his mobile telephone and told me he was about to set a timer. He set the timer and then pressed play. My eyes glanced from the screen to the telephone to the screen to the telephone. Ten seconds. Twenty seconds. After thirty seconds,

I knew what he was doing. I knew the point he was going to make. Forty seconds. Nothing. Forty-five seconds. Nothing. Fifty seconds. That is when I emerged from the suite, and that is when Detective Raj paused the timer.

'Obviously, we have just started our investigation and we will need to talk to everyone. But can you tell me why, on entering a room and seeing a dead body, it took you fifty seconds to leave to find help? Seems like something that could have been done in ten, maybe fifteen seconds.' Detective Raj stared at me expressionlessly with his dark eyes. It was impossible to find any warmth in that man.

'Perhaps I should get a lawyer,' I suggested.

'No need for that, Mr Harrow. This is just an informal, off-the-record chat. You're not in trouble.' Detective Raj changed to a more upbeat tone of voice, like he was trying to convince me that what he was saying was true. 'Since you're the one who found the body, we need to get your take on things first.' He bared his teeth in a smile. 'Now, back to those fifty seconds . . .'

'That's just how long it took. I put the ice b-b-bucket down, turned around, saw Bruno, Mr Tatterson, dead in the bathroom . . .'

'You knew he was dead just from looking at him?'

'That amount of b-b-blood . . .' I tapped my head three times. 'It was obvious he was dead. His eyes were open and v-v-vacant.'

'Then what?'

'I was in shock. I stood there in shock. I blinked three times. Then I went to find Mr Potts. To get help.'

You might be wondering about this dialogue; is that how it actually happened or not? But mark my words, this discussion is etched in my memory. It might not be word-for-word accurate, but it is darned well near enough. As much as possible in this story, I will try to re-create the dialogue. In moments where I am unsure of the words, I will just describe what happened in the conversation. I want to be upfront about that because I know you will be wondering.

I asked Detective Raj for some water; he said I could have some once I had explained to him why it took me fifty seconds to find the body and then leave the room. He even timed how long it took him to blink three times. Eight seconds. I told him over and over again, that was just how long it took. The shock of seeing a dead body happened to delay my response—surely that was not too out of the ordinary. But he wouldn't drop it. It was like he wanted this case to be done and dusted as quickly as possible, and that meant extracting a confession from me. I swivelled left and right on the chair as I watched Detective Raj pace the office, telling me I was guilty in not so many words. The hands on the clock jumped like time was flying, except everything felt so slow. I was weary, exhausted, ready to go home. All I wanted was to go back to the day before, when being replaced by an iPad was my biggest problem. Perspective is everything.

'You're lying!' Detective Raj slammed his fist down on the desk after another hour of dead-end questions. He had no idea what he was doing, I see that now. I think he was insecure and desperate for a career win. But in that moment, I thought he was tough and using tactics that he must have learnt from years of experience. In fact, in that moment I thought he was such an experienced policeman that somehow he would get me to break and confess to something I hadn't done. Fear bubbled under the surface, but as Detective Raj continued to provoke me, a side of myself I had not known existed started to emerge. As the clock approached nearly three hours of nonsense, I snapped.

'You're wrong!' I yelled, among other things. I clenched my fists and gritted my teeth. I felt possessed by the spirit of my father; he is the only person I have ever known who would act in such a way. Yet now I understand my father even less than I did before. It took being accused of murder for me to reach the point of losing my cool.

Tap one. Tap two. Tap three.

For him, all it took was looking at my face, it was his own personal worst nightmare. Seventy-three years of life, and I have only just realised that. I still can't understand it, though, and I know I will die wondering how he could have felt that way about me.

When my conversation with Detective Raj finally drew to a close, I felt defeated. I caught sight of myself in a mirror on the wall. I looked hollow, exhausted and hopeless. The detective ordered me to wait in the library on my own. I hadn't given him the easy resolution he seemed to be so desperately craving, and he appeared to resent me for that. That's how I saw it anyway.

The walls of the library felt like they were closing in on me. My hands were clammy and my heart thumped. There was a copy of the Bible on one of the shelves. I have never been a religious man, but I rested my head on the spine of the book and said a quick 'hello' to God, in case He was up there. Religion is not something I was brought up with, but then again, I question a lot of things about the way I was raised. It wasn't my choice not to believe in God; that's just how it happened. If He is up there, I hope He knows I mean no harm. I have always tried my best to avoid trouble. Calmness: that is what I like. And here came murder knocking at my door. And worst of all, the detective was insinuating that I had something to do with it. All I could do in that moment was wait and hope that the truth would come out. Whatever the truth was.

American Dave's voice thundered past the library door, and I jerked my head away from the spine of the Bible. He was telling Detective Raj that he was prepared to do whatever he could to help catch the murderer. Twenty minutes later two police officers came to get me again. They were Fred and Ellie. I have known them for years, just from around and about. Did I say that already? I forget. Anyway, it was nice to see some friendly faces, under the circumstances. They looked sympathetic as they escorted me back to Mr Potts's office for another session with Detective Raj. Fred and Ellie knew as much about me as I knew about them, which was that they appeared to be good people. I reckon you can tell when someone has a good soul; it is in their eyes.

Fred patted me on the back as we walked to Mr Potts's office. It was comforting to know someone was in my corner. At that point, I had no idea where Mr Potts and Fiona were. For all I knew, they had been sent home. Outside Mr Potts's office, Fred whispered in my ear, 'We'll get you out of this ASAP, mate.' I know he meant well, but him saying that put me on edge from the get-go.

Detective Raj made me sit down again even though I would have preferred to stand. There were some notes scribbled on a scrap of lined notepaper that had been ripped unevenly from a pad. The torn edges made me uncomfortable, but it wasn't the time to focus on that. Detective Raj quizzed me on my mood over the last week, claiming that a source had told him I had received some troubling news recently and was, quote unquote, 'angry'. Bloody American Dave and his sodding iPads. The very first chance he got to drop me in it, he did. And now he has the cheek to email me to be in his sodding documentary. You see why I got so worked up about him calling me 'old friend'. And he gets worse as this story goes on. The words that

I can think of to describe that man probably can't be published—as you can imagine, they're not nice ones.

I told Detective Raj that I didn't know what he was referring to, even though I full well did. I added that my mood was fine that week. Yes, it was a shock to hear a new system was to be implemented in the hotel, but I had been at Cavengreen for fifty-odd years; new systems came and went, that was only natural. As the concierge, I had always adapted very well to any changes. I was determined to play down my response to the iPads. Detective Raj didn't need more ammunition.

'You were angry that you were potentially being replaced by new technology.' That is what Detective Raj said. This must have been what American Dave told him. So, the slimy git *was* trying to do away with my job. Those Americans know nothing about loyalty.

'I wasn't angry. I was concerned, but definitely not angry,' I told the detective.

'It's okay if you were angry. We don't use emotions to incriminate people. Sometimes I get angry myself, and that's okay.' Detective Raj attempted a good-cop routine.

The grilling went on for another hour. That makes four hours total, if you're counting. I don't know much about the law, but I am pretty sure he shouldn't have been questioning me for so long off the record. My tongue was like sandpaper the entire time. Detective Raj sipped smugly from a glass bottle of Coca-Cola that he must have taken from my concierge fridge. At one point he even observed that Coca-Cola always tastes better from a glass bottle rather than a plastic one. I haven't touched the stuff since I was a kid. My dad used to mix it with his cheap rum. The smell of it makes me sick, so I could not give a rat's arse about the detective's opinion on the topic. I just wanted to get out of that room and go home.

But the detective informed me that was not going to happen. The hotel was a crime scene and no one was allowed to leave until he had spoken to everyone present. This meant the staff would be required to spend the night. Most of the female employees would share the unoccupied suites; others had to make do with anywhere there was a flat surface to sleep on. But myself and some of the other male staff were told we would be spending the night in the library. It all seemed completely ridiculous. The idea of not being able to leave, not being able to rest my head on my own pillow, in my house, where all my belongings are, a place where I could try to block out the memory of the day . . . It was too much for me to handle.

'This is cri-criminal!' I shouted. 'You let me go!' I stood up and leant forward so we were eye to eye across the desk. I felt myself breathing heavily, glaring at the detective. I wanted to punch him. I have never struck anyone in my life, but I have had plenty of lessons in how to throw a punch, having been on the receiving end of my father's fist many a time. My fingers curled inwards, scraping the desk.

The detective smirked, as if he could tell exactly what I wanted to do to him. But we both knew that would be foolish.

'If you are innocent, then you should have no problem hanging around a while longer to help us solve the case. Isn't that right, Hector?' Detective Raj flashed a nasty grin, his nostrils flaring. He had me exactly where he wanted me: teetering on the edge of a breakdown. And I was so ashamed of my outburst; I was behaving just like my father. Meanwhile the real killer was still at large, and there was a chance they might strike again.

CHAPTER

11

Fiona kindly fetched spare pillows and blankets from the linen room for everyone without a proper bed to sleep in. Myself, Mr Potts, Eric the porter, Dean from the kitchen and Charlie the gardener were consigned to the library. Six-foot-five Charlie took the three-seater, Eric took the two-seater and poor Dean scrunched himself into a ball to spend the night on the armchair. Mr Potts and I did our best to make ourselves comfortable on the floor. Not that the young ones didn't offer the settees up to us. But we both declined, knowing we were unlikely to sleep. Instead, we took the cushions from the window seat and arranged them into two makeshift mattresses on the floor, and tried to make them cosy with blankets and pillows. At the end of the day, though, it was still just the floor, and I was still a murder suspect.

Both still in our work suits, we sat on our makeshift beds, heads and shoulders slumped, defeated by the day. Mr Potts took off his tie and wrapped then unwrapped it around his fingers. He seemed distracted, agitated. Then all at once he sat up straight, as if struck by an idea. He pushed himself off the ground and crossed the room to the globe in the corner. It is one of those old-fashioned ones that spins on its axis and has bumps where the mountains are and dips where there are valleys. He lifted the lid and, careful not to clink anything and wake the others, poured a splash of whisky into two glasses. Like I have said, I am not much of a drinker, but by gum, this occasion called for it.

The snores of the other men were quite soothing. Like there were a few of us in this together. I never went to war, but I imagine what I felt in that room was a tiny fraction of the camaraderie that soldiers feel. At least I was not alone anymore and at least if Bruno's murderer was still in the hotel, they wouldn't risk trying to attack any of us in that room. They wouldn't dare.

From what Fiona has told me since, all the guests were escorted back to their suites. It was their idea to stay in the comfort of Cavengreen rather than go to the police station, at least for that first night, that is. The locals who had just popped by for afternoon tea were eventually allowed to leave around midnight, after it had been confirmed from the CCTV footage that, on arrival, they had headed straight to Lavender Plates with no detours to anywhere else in the hotel. They were therefore off the hook. Recently, there have been a lot of grumblings about the legality of locking down a whole hotel against the will of those inside. The guests had only agreed to stay one night, but remained for four. As it turned out from the report Helen skimmed for me, Detective Raj did put up a sign in an obscure place where no one would see it reading: *Guests are permitted to leave at any point.* That got him out of the woods, legally speaking. The guests may have agreed to stay that first night, but that didn't stop them kicking up a fuss when the police disconnected the Wi-Fi, leaving them with no way to contact anyone outside the hotel. Fat chance getting a telephone signal at the hotel.

Reception is patchy at best all over the Dales. Detective Raj must have been worried about information being leaked to the press. And they were probably trying to avoid the likes of Paula McDavidson snooping around with her notebook of lies before they had a chance to find out who the killer was. Besides, with the number of police roaming the corridors, it didn't feel like we could just casually leave. Cavengreen was like a prison and we were like prisoners. After my interview with Detective Raj, I felt like I was the hotel's most notorious prisoner. Like I was on death row and everyone else was just in for petty theft.

That night, I could tell Mr Potts was consumed with angst. He didn't sleep and nor did I. We didn't speak, though. He leant against a shelf of books—Agatha Christie novels, fittingly. He desperately tried to telephone and text message his wife. He knew she would be concerned when he didn't come home. Quite right. But with no Wi-Fi and no phone signal, there was no way of contacting anyone beyond Cavengreen's gates. We wondered if word had been leaked of my grim discovery, but now I know that it hadn't.

Around 2 am I had to go to the bathroom. Ellie was standing guard outside the library. She must have been dozing off a little because she woke with a gasp when I opened the door. Together, we walked to the bathroom located between the lobby and the entrance to Hugo's cocktail bar. The hotel felt eerily quiet. It had been a while since I had been at Cavengreen so late. Back in my early days at the hotel, I often worked the late shifts. They tend to be the hours that no one wants to do, so the junior staff are rostered on. In those days, there was always a good atmosphere. We would get up to all kinds of mischief, mostly eating leftovers from the fridges of Lavender Plates or racing down empty corridors. There was the odd late-night drink request, and the occasional drunken guest staggering about, but the graveyard shifts were otherwise fairly uneventful.

Ellie was kind to me as we walked the corridor. She and Helen actually know each other from school; Helen told me that earlier. Ellie knew my sister, too, and told me she was sorry to hear about her passing. Ellie would be nearly ten years younger than Josie, but they were friendly nonetheless. Everyone pretty much knows everyone around here. Ellie took a few years off the police force, ended up having five kids. They're all adults now, so I think she picks up the odd shift here and there to keep busy. She's not ambitious, not like Detective Raj, who would be a good few years her junior.

'Make sure you defend yourself, Hector.' That is what she said to me as we headed to the bathroom. 'Make sure no one takes advantage of your kindness, you hear me? You are in a sticky spot, and of course I know you didn't do it, but Detective Raj will be wanting to crack the case, to impress the higher-ups in Leeds. Make sure you don't let him get to you or you'll end up taking the fall for someone else.'

In the bathroom, I hesitated. The bathrooms at Cavengreen are beautiful, but they aren't my cottage, where all my things are, where I have my little routine that I perform every night. I swiped my hand under the tap and water automatically gushed out. And then it stopped. I swiped again, this time filling my cupped hands with water. I felt out of sync with my life. Normally I would be tucked up in bed, a finished puzzle with a pen resting on top on my bedside table, five hours into my nightly eight hours of sleep. I released my hands and let the water splosh into the sink. I filled them up twice more before splashing the water on my face.

I let the water drip off my skin. The man staring back at me in the mirror didn't seem like the same Hector I had known for seventy-three years. The colour had drained from my face, I had dark circles under my eyes, and my hair, which was normally neatly combed, was all askew. As I looked at this different version of Hector, I wondered if his life would ever be the same again. This sort of thing changes people, and I can tell you now, since I have had the time to process what happened, I have been changed forever. The initial shock and pain have eased, but once you have witnessed a murder scene like that, it is like your innocence has been taken from you. I feel I am harder since. Even when I feel happiness or joy, it is more subdued now. Being inside Cavengreen and looking the way I did in the mirror that night felt abnormal. But then again, there was nothing normal about anything that happened over those four days.

Walking back to the library, I noticed the yellow police tape that was cordoning off various corridors. Peering down the hallway, I could see people in white overalls going in and out of suite seven; some held cameras and others had sealed bags, presumably full of evidence. A couple of officers were sitting on the floor, leaning against the wall, typing away on their laptops. The scene was one of organised chaos. You forget sometimes that there are people who see murdered bodies for a living. To me, this was the most out-of-the-ordinary experience, but to them it was just another day. How murder can ever become 'normal' is beyond me, but I suppose it is the same way doctors become desensitised to blood, and I have become desensitised to being treated like a piece of furniture. Even you, the reader, will have a different normal to my normal. Sorry—that was a tangent.

Ellie kindly let me linger long enough to take all that in. Part of me thinks she wanted to have a nosy too and knew I wouldn't mind a quick look at what was going on. As we watched, several men exited suite seven carrying a stretcher with a body bag on top. They were escorted down the corridor by a convoy of police officers. There was a swoosh of air when they walked by; the body bag was close enough for me to touch, had I wanted to. Ellie bowed her head, but I kept staring at that white bag. It was surreal to think that a man who had been alive twenty-four hours earlier was now in a bag. It seemed like an undignified end to his life, being carried out in plastic by strangers. But then again, being murdered was hardly dignified either.

Detective Raj appeared as if out of nowhere. He must have been trailing behind the police officers, out of sight. He clocked me and Ellie and his usual frown scrunched into an even more severe scowl. He carried a takeaway coffee cup which he threw at the wastepaper basket behind my desk, not noticing or caring that he had missed. Ignoring Ellie, he drew the back of his hand over his mouth, wiping away some but not all of the brown stains that had folded their way into the dry cracks of his lips. His teeth were coffee-stained too and when he spoke the smell of stale breath laced with caffeine turned my stomach. He demanded to know what I was doing in the lobby. He appeared dissatisfied when I told him I was on my way back from the bathroom. It was as if he wanted me to tell him that I was returning to the scene of my crime. Ellie corroborated my story but the detective ignored her.

'How convenient,' Detective Raj hissed. 'One last look at the body, eh?' He wanted me to be the murderer and he was acting like I was. It was terrifying to think he was wasting so much time focusing on me when the real killer was potentially still roaming the hallways. When I said as much to Detective Raj, he told me not to worry, that a thorough search of every suite would take place with every guest interviewed over the next couple of days. A couple of sodding *days*? It was about bloody time they got down to business, I thought. The sooner they did that, the sooner they would work out I wasn't the culprit. Although, as you will find out, things would get much worse for me before they got mildly better.

Morning crept in slowly. I hadn't slept, not even for one minute. Mr Potts eventually drifted off around 5 am, but the sound of a horde of police cars pulling up on the gravel outside woke him at six. Ellie said her goodbyes; she was heading home to sleep. Thankfully she made sure that Fred took over her post. It was good to see him.

It wasn't long after Fred arrived that there was a call to his radio from Detective Raj. He barked orders that were hard to decipher. Fred looked confused and held the radio right to his ear to try to work out the detective's instructions. He needn't have bothered, as before long Detective Raj appeared at the door to the library.

'Did you not hear me? I said take this lot to Lavender Plates. We need to use the library for a briefing,' he barked.

Those of us who had spent the night in the library gathered up our few belongings and I put all the cushions back on the window seats. As we tried to leave, dozens of police officers barged into the room. It was like when you try to board the London Underground just as crowds of people are getting off. Not that I bother much with London. Went there once or twice to see what all the fuss was about. Overcrowded, unfriendly and expensive. That is what I think.

No offence, Helen, I know how much you miss it. You're far more cosmopolitan than me, though.

My opinions on the UK's capital aside, it felt good to be out of that library. I heard one of the police officers comment on how the air smelt of disgusting stale breath. Just like school bullies, a bunch of them turned and laughed at us. I want to make this clear: the treatment we received from *most* of the police was nothing short of disgusting.

Lavender Plates felt bleak. It was normally one of my favourite places in the hotel. Even at 6 am, there would be plenty of activity, with the chefs busy preparing breakfast and a few early risers already getting their morning coffee and reading the newspaper. The hotel will pretty much make anything you want for breakfast, as long as they have the ingredients. Even then, if a guest had a particular request and they gave me that information in advance, we would arrange it. Lots of people enjoyed oysters and champagne for breakfast in my day. There is no reason why you can't rise and shine with a little glamour. That is what Cavengreen is all about. But there were no clinks of champagne flutes that morning.

Mr Potts flicked the lights on and brought us out of the depressing shadows. It felt strange to be basking in the glittering light of the chandelier, but then again it felt strange to be anywhere in Cavengreen during such a time. That place is too special for the horrors it endured.

Mr Potts fetched everyone orange juice and bottles of cold water. Then, without even asking for Fred's permission, he started up one of the cooktops and shouted out for us to give him our egg orders. That small action reminded me for a second that we weren't prisoners; we didn't have to ask for permission in *our* hotel. Not that Fred minded, of course. Had any of the other officers been watching us, I am sure they would not have allowed it. Starvation felt like one of their tactics to get us to talk quicker. Or to get *me* to 'confess' quicker, I should say. Mr Potts insisted on making me scrambled eggs and bacon even though we both knew I would not be able to eat. He even made Fred some. It was a funny old sight, seeing Mr Potts with his shirt all wrinkled and his top button undone. His hair was messy, and he was yawning every couple of minutes. This was quite a different man from the one who normally fussed around the hotel making sure everything was spick-and-span. It was nice to see this more human side of him.

Rain pelted down outside, and our small group sat silently by the windows. The three young lads knocked back their food as if they had just returned from being lost at sea. Mr Potts took a few bites, and I politely ate half of mine, despite the knots in my stomach. Fred moseyed around the restaurant, stroking the wallpaper and having a gander in the china cabinets and wine room. I think he was trying to give us some space. Not wanting to sound like a gossip, I chose not to share my experience of seeing the body being taken out at 2 am. Whatever I did or said, I was aware that Detective Raj might find out. So, I kept my head down. Not that I would be able to do so for much longer.

From outside Lavender Plates, I could hear Fiona shouting. She was telling whoever was guarding the door to move out of her way. Fiona's good like that. She's a strong woman who doesn't take any nonsense. The double doors to the restaurant swung open and Fiona scanned the room before beelining towards me. She flung her arms around me and then held my cheeks in her hands, surveying my face for any signs of distress. It was nice to know someone had been worrying about me.

'Ridiculous! All of this is ridiculous!' she shouted. 'Mr Potts, what are you doing about this? Keeping us locked up like wild animals—it's barbaric!'

The young lads held back laughter. I must say, Fiona looked quite the sight shouting at Mr Potts while dressed in one of Cavengreen's bathrobes with her hair in a messy bun on top of her head. I could see the long grey pencil skirt she had been wearing the day before sticking out beneath the hem of the robe, but she had swapped her high heels for a pair of white Cavengreen slippers. Mr Potts was taken aback, to say the least. An angry Fiona was not the kind of wake-up call he needed that morning.

'I'm afraid this is out of my hands, Fiona,' Mr Potts replied meekly—uncharacteristically so.

'Well, whose hands is it in, then?' Fiona waved her own hands impatiently from side to side.

'Perhaps the Americans can advise us on what is going on,' Mr Potts replied. 'They are technically the new owners of the hotel, after all.'

'The Americans! Pfft. They are just a bunch of good-for-nothing—'

'Howdy, everyone!' American Dave waltzed into Lavender Plates, his mistress and two minions following him like disciples. He tipped his cowboy hat in greeting. 'What a day. How did y'all sleep? Fiona?'

Fiona lifted her chin, made a dismissive noise and turned her head away, her arms folded, just like she always does when she's annoyed.

'Any coffee going?' American Dave took a seat and fanned a linen napkin onto his lap. He removed his cowboy hat and placed it on the table. I remember wondering why he was so relaxed about everything. It was almost like he was enjoying the goings-on, unfazed that there was still a murderer on the loose. He bored us with details of the hotel's plans to 'step into the future' and how he was going to suck the soul out of the place. Not that he used those words, of course. He said he wasn't at all worried about how the previous day's incident might impact the hotel's brand because by the time he was done with the name change and renovations, people wouldn't even know it was the same place. Eyerolls swept across the room when he said that. Cavengreen meant a lot to the rest of us, even though it was just a workplace. We were a family and, to me, Cavengreen was like a second home.

Once American Dave had finished his monologue, he turned his attention to me.

'What's the deal with you and that detective, Hector?' he probed. 'Y'all were chatting for a long time yesterday. You're not a suspect, are ya?' He twirled his cowboy hat on his fist.

I chose not to answer and sipped on the cup of tea that Mr Potts had kindly placed in front of me. I avoided eye contact but could see

Mr Potts and Fiona glaring at the American. A very clear line had been drawn.

'I've seen you do this bizarre head-tapping thing a couple of times,' American Dave was snarky in his observation. 'When I asked one of the young guys here in the hotel about it, he told me you do it whenever you have a bad thought. So, would tapping your head three times stop you from murdering someone? Or is it not that powerful?'

His American mistress laughed, and his two minions followed her example.

'No more, Dave.' Mr Potts kept his voice low, but he was firm.

'What?' American Dave scoffed. 'We know someone in this joint is a killer, why shouldn't we suspect him? Just because he's old doesn't mean he didn't do it.'

'You'd better watch yourself, you low-life . . .' Fiona began.

'Or what?' American Dave tilted his head, awaiting a response.

'Or else you'll have me to deal with,' Fiona finished.

The Americans all laughed like hyenas.

'I've changed my mind.' American Dave took a bite of a bread roll and spoke with his mouth full, crumbs flying. 'Hector couldn't have killed someone. Not when he needs some middle-aged broad to fight his battles for him.'

'That's enough!' This was me speaking now. I had stayed quiet long enough. Heat radiated through my hands and that's when I noticed that I had slammed them onto the table and broken a saucer. Blood trickled down my left hand and onto the wooden parquetry.

Fred rushed over from the window. He grabbed my wrist and ushered me towards the door.

'I'll be telling Detective Raj about this. He'll welcome my help!' American Dave bellowed after me.

I turned around and saw him place his cowboy hat onto his head smugly, only for Fiona to knock it to the floor with a quick swipe of her hand as she marched by. She and Mr Potts followed me, Fiona channelling her rage into huffing and pulling her dressing-gown belt into a tighter knot. Things were going downhill swiftly.

We sought refuge in Hugo's.

Hugo's didn't have quite the same feel as Lavender Plates, but the enemy—that is, the Americans—had called dibs on the restaurant, so the moody ambience of the cocktail bar would have to do for our small army.

'Best we don't mention this to the detective, I reckon,' Fred said, nodding at my hand.

'I don't believe we'll have a choice,' I replied. 'The American has probably already told him. Sucking up; trying to feel important. He's all ego that sodding Yank.' I rinsed my wrist in the sink behind the bar, watching the blood swirl down the drain. Flashbacks of Bruno's dead body clanged around my mind. I tapped my head three times with my dry hand.

'I'll tell them that it was an accident,' Fred reassured me.

'But you were looking out the window,' I reminded him.

'I saw what happened.' Fred tapped his nose and nodded his head. 'It was an *accident.*'

I'm not entirely sure why he emphasised the word 'accident' when it truly was an accident, but his support was appreciated. I have never in my life dealt with such conflict. Well, not since my father dropped dead. Although I would hardly describe getting belted every other day as conflict.

By the time I was sixteen and working, my dad left me alone. I had reached an age when I was starting to think about defending myself, and Dad was getting weaker by that point. Then, by the time I was twenty, my father was housebound due to deteriorating health. You might find this odd, but I looked after him. I used to bring him food and turn his chair around to face the TV. Sometimes you just do what you have to do. I arranged for the panelbeating business to go up for sale and used the money to pay for food and bills and so on. Despite my father being a complete prick, he was good at what he did, and the money was enough to last until well after his death.

Tap one. Tap two. Tap three.

But I couldn't just close my eyes tight and count to three over and over until this conflict at the hotel came to an end. As Fiona said, I would have to be strong.

We were in Hugo's for six hours. Mr Potts sat on the floor behind the bar, sneaking swigs of whisky whenever Fred turned a blind eye. I was starting to think he might have an alcohol problem, but that was none of my business and I wouldn't want to start any rumours that might damage his reputation. Lots of people use alcohol as pain relief in dark times.

Fiona paced up and down and got me to repeat my account of what had happened until she was satisfied that the police wouldn't be able to break me. Every so often Fred would swap out with another officer and then return half an hour later with little snippets of information. He told us that Detective Raj was interviewing the guests suite by suite and each room was being thoroughly searched. Nothing of note had been discovered yet, though. He said that a pair of twins were up next.

That reminds me, I must tell you about the fallout from the twins' newspaper article. Paula McDavidson has continued to harass me for my side of the story. If I go to the supermarket, she's there. If I pop out for some milk, she's there. If I am withdrawing money at the bank, she's there. It really is getting quite bothersome. She tells me that the impact of her story with the twins wasn't as powerful as she thought it might be and the feedback from her superiors is that she needs my take on events. I have told her on multiple occasions that she isn't getting it. But it has been uncomfortable to say the least. I have noticed people in the village giving me little looks. Couples nudge each other when I pass and people that I haven't spoken to since school have started coming up to ask how I've been and then grilling me about Cavengreen. The cheek of it! But I keep my mouth shut. And I haven't told anyone about this book. Helen told me not to until everything is signed off and we get a publication date. To be honest, I thought you just wrote the words and then off you go, but apparently there's a whole process of editing and cover design before that. I did get one useful nugget of information from Paula McDavidson. She told me that American Dave has booked his flights and will be landing in ten days. She was very smug when she told me that he had asked her to be part of his documentary. She probably thinks she's going to become a big star in America. Deluded old bat.

Back to the twins. Fred was radioed with instructions to escort them down to Mr Potts's office for questioning. An officer named Tyrone took his place in Hugo's. Tyrone was particularly unfriendly; he had a scowl like one of those ferocious dogs that are illegal in the UK. He looked like a right thug with his shaved head, and I caught a glimpse of a neck tattoo poking out of his collar. I've never understood why someone would want to doodle permanent drawings on their skin. Not that I judge anyone for doing so. Do what you want with your own body, I say. It's just not for me. Tyrone sat in one of the booths and glared at us, biting his fingernails and spitting them onto the ground. It made me sick to my stomach. Fiona was livid; she kept saying, 'If he does that one more time, I'm going to snap.' But she didn't snap. I think it just made her feel better to say that she would.

Fred returned an hour later. Tyrone refused to swap out with him; he was enjoying taunting us with his homemade lunch of sausage rolls, complete with excessive amounts of ketchup. Fiona watched him eat, clearly disgusted by the way he chewed with his mouth open and licked his fingers before pressing them onto the fallen crumbs on the table and sucking them clean. The memory of the sound of meat getting broken down in his mouth is enough to make me never want to eat a sausage roll again. Which is a shame really, because Maude's Bakery does a belting one with a mix of pork and lamb mince.

To get rid of Tyrone, Fred pretended that Detective Raj had specifically requested his assistance on something that seemed important. That got him up and moving. Flakes of pastry fell to the floor as he leapt to his feet and virtually sprinted out of the room, saying, 'See ya later, knobheads.'

We all huddled around the bar, waiting for Fred to share any updates. This might look bad—a police officer sharing confidential information—but Fred was on our side. He knew that we were the good guys and he kept saying how he wanted to go out on the right note. That makes sense now, since he resigned from the police force right after Cavengreen. Swanned off on a round-the-world trip the week after. He sent me a postcard from the Taj Mahal the other day. I have never fancied India; too busy for me.

When Fred had knocked at the door of the twins' suite, they told him they were in the middle of a pamper session and he should come back later. They tried to shut the door in his face but he shoved his steel-capped shoe in the gap so it couldn't close all the way. He told them that it was urgent, and they had to follow him right away. The twins whined shrilly about how ridiculous the whole situation was, how they couldn't check their social media accounts because the Wi-Fi had been disconnected, and how they were one more inconvenience away from calling their lawyers. Detective Raj had no idea what he was getting himself into with those two. We laughed as Fred told us how the detective had looked pale and broken when he finished questioning them.

Fred said he'd had his ear pressed up against the door the whole time. He couldn't tell which twin was saying what, but one was definitely more vocal than the other. That would probably be Ruby, from what I've experienced. And didn't they just have a few things to say about me! Of course, they didn't use my name. That would be beneath them. Instead, they referred to me as 'that old concierge' and 'the old man behind the desk'. Any of you reading this who are around the same age as me, don't be offended by all the references to age that are being thrown around. Some of these young 'uns will label you as 'old' as soon as they see a grey hair. But they'll be seventy-three one day and then they can decide just how 'old' they feel. Personally, I feel a million bucks. Minus a few for the dodgy hip.

Having established that I was the 'old man' in the twins' story, Detective Raj quizzed them on what exactly I had done to get them so riled up. The twins told the detective how, on their way to Olive's wedding, they were ambushed by a drunken guest on the staircase. That would be Alec, in case you need reminding. They complained that 'the very rude old man at the desk' did absolutely nothing to stop the attack and that, on the contrary, it seemed almost like I was encouraging it. What a load of nonsense! You'll recall from my account of the scene that I did nothing of the sort. The incident was over as soon as it had begun, and everyone was sharply on their way.

Fiona huffed in frustration. I peered over and saw her shredding a drink coaster into tiny pieces. Meanwhile, Mr Potts was resting his forehead on the counter and shaking his head in despair. At the time, it was hard for me to process what the implication of the twins' lies might be. Detective Raj had already put me through the wringer and I had come out the other side—or so I thought.

According to the twins, they went back to their suite to change their shoes during the wedding dinner, and they saw me and the victim arguing in the lobby. You and I both know that is not what happened. They described how Bruno was flailing his arms erratically in what appeared to be anger, when in fact, as I've told you, he was just apologising for being rude when I had approached him at dinner earlier. The twins said I grabbed my car keys and stormed out the front door mid-argument. Lies, lies and more lies from that meddlesome pair of rotten brats.

They repeated these falsehoods in their interview with Paula McDavidson. Despite it being proven that I was not involved, those twins are still trying to drag my name through the mud as if I have a case to answer. Having an argument with someone who turned up dead the next day hardly paints me in the best light. When this book is released, it'll be their word against mine. But I've got more of this story up my sleeve than they do.

Fred said he heard Detective Raj tell the twins that he had seen the footage of a heated discussion between me and Bruno, but that even though it looked like an argument, there was no audio to back up their claims. Finally, Detective Raj had said something sensible. However, don't expect much more of that from him.

～∿∾～

Detective Raj wanted to see me again. The call came through on Fred's radio. This time, I poured myself a glass of water to take with me. Fred gave me a minute with Fiona and Mr Potts before I left. He must have thought I needed a pep talk. Mr Potts said nothing, instead taking a swig of whisky and then grimacing as it hit the back of his throat. He patted me firmly on the back and then slumped down into one of the booths. Fiona was fiddling with her mobile telephone. She put her finger up to her lips and then slipped the telephone into the inside pocket of my suit, mouthing, 'It's recording.'

I have never been much of a rulebreaker, and Fiona's bold move made me nervous. It felt dangerous, and I am almost certain it was illegal. But then again, as Detective Raj told me, these were just 'off-the-record' conversations. One man speaking to another man, casually. Now that I am writing this book, let me tell you, I am so thankful that Fiona pulled that move. It isn't half useful having a recording of that conversation with Detective Raj to go off. Best thing to do, I reckon, is to get Helen to transcribe that recording here and then I will pick things up a bit later. We will probably have to change Detective Raj's name—for legal reasons, that is—but Helen can advise me on that next time we catch up. This will be the first time I'm listening to it myself, so I am interested to hear just what was said.

Detective Raj: Take a seat, Mr Harrow. Some things have come
　　to light since we last spoke and I'd like to get your thoughts.
　　Two witnesses have come forward with information that

links you to the victim. They claim you were seen arguing with said victim at approximately 7.30 pm the night before you found the body. Now, I just want to make one thing clear: there's a lot of *you* interacting with the victim going on, and not a lot of other people interacting with him. Funny that. So, tell me, what were you and Bruno Tatterson arguing about that night?

Hector: W-w-we weren't arguing.

Detective Raj: Don't give me that, Mr Harrow. We have CCTV footage of you and Mr Tatterson arguing in the lobby before you rush off. Here, I'll show you.

[A few minutes pass in silence.]

Detective Raj: Looks like an argument to me.

Hector: It . . . it was a discussion. Mr Tatterson, B-B-Bruno, was apologising to me.

Detective Raj: And why would a hotel guest that you met hours earlier need to apologise to you, the concierge?

Hector: I in-in-interrupted his dinner and he w-wasn't happy about it.

Detective Raj: Why not?

Hector: He was busy on his telephone.

Detective Raj: Busy doing what?

Hector: No idea.

Detective Raj: And for that he felt the need to apologise to you? It's your job to cop it a bit from the guests, is it not?

Hector: That's called customer service, yes. Bruno did not need to apologise to me, you're right. But he did. You can see him doing so in the video. And I accepted, graciously, and then went home for the evening.

Detective Raj: That's not how it looks. Right, moving on. How do you explain this then? The same witnesses said you allowed a guest to attack them on Thursday afternoon. Is this true?

Hector: Not in the slightest.

Detective Raj: So, what happened with . . . Mr . . . I can't read my own writing . . . Maclean.

Hector: Alec. He'd had a few drinks and interrupted the bridal party's photographs on the stairs. It was just a one-minute interaction and then he was on his way.

Detective Raj: And by the looks of the CCTV footage, you did . . . nothing?

Hector: It is not my job to get involved in such things. Alec did not attack the bridal party; he wanted to talk to me, and they were just in his way, I suppose.

Detective Raj: What did he want to talk to you about?

Hector: His book.

Detective Raj: What book?

Hector: The book he is writing. Is this relevant?

Detective Raj: I'll ask the questions, Mr Harrow. And you're saying he was drunk?

Hector: He'd had a couple of drinks.

Detective Raj: How many is a couple?

Hector: I'm not sure. He was in his room.

Detective Raj: We've got CCTV footage of you going into his room.

Hector: I go into a lot of guests' rooms. I am the concierge.

Detective Raj: So I've heard. You've got access to every suite then?

Hector: I'm not the only one. But yes, I do.

Detective Raj: Hmm. And you didn't see Mr Maclean drinking when you went into his room?

Hector: He was having a glass of whisky.

Detective Raj: How many?

Hector: Just the one glass in his hand that I saw.

Detective Raj: You know what I mean.

Hector: There's no way of knowing if he had drunk a glass before or after I went in.

Detective Raj: We're going in circles. I think it's best we keep you separate from the rest of the staff for the time being.

Just until I get all my ducks in a row. Fred—get in here!
[A pause.] Take Mr Harrow to the gardener's shed out back.
He's not to leave until I say so.

Fred: The shed? I heard there's a free room upstairs. I'll take
him up there.

Detective Raj: I need that room.

Fred: Um, perhaps back to Hugo's then?

Detective Raj: No, his friends are in there and I don't want
them setting him up with stories. The shed is the only place
where I can be sure he will be isolated.

Fred: We can keep him in the hotel, and I'll make sure no one
talks to him.

Detective Raj: No, that's too risky.

Fred: I'll take him down to the station.

Detective Raj: I can't be here and there at the same time. The
shed is the best option. It'll just be for a few hours. You
understand, don't you, Mr Harrow?

Hector: Okay.

Listening to the exchange now, I can't believe I heard myself agree to
go out to the shed. I don't remember that. I must have been completely
consumed by panic. It's not in my nature to disobey authority, it never
has been. That must be why I just heard myself agree to ill treatment.
I feel sad for the man who said 'okay' at the end of that recording.

He was scared. Like I've said, I am stronger now. I should have said no. I should have stood up for myself, like Fred was trying to. But I was overwhelmed.

You might be wondering why I didn't tell Detective Raj the truth about Alec's drinking. Well, I didn't believe Alec killed Bruno, so I saw no reason to fuel the fire by explaining just how much alcohol Alec seemed to have consumed that evening. If Alec had drunk too much and somehow ended up killing Bruno—which, mind you, seemed very unlikely to me—then I was sure that would come out eventually. If he was innocent, then I didn't want to get him in hot water by telling Detective Raj that he had drunk at least a bottle of whisky, likely more. I am glad Fiona had the foresight to get that conversation on tape, or on telephone, whatever you want to say. It jogged some memories that will help with the book.

Fred escorted me to the gardener's shed. On our way, I asked if we could stop by Hugo's. Fiona flung her arms around me as soon as she saw me and asked if I was alright. I was not alright, but I told her I was and I slipped the telephone back to her.

She looked at Fred, wanting reassurance that nothing bad had happened to me. He told her about the shed. She kicked off, of course. But he told her his hands were tied.

'It's just for a few hours,' he said.

She is such a mother hen, is Fiona. She quickly grabbed some linen from the staff storage room opposite Hugo's and slipped it into a Cavengreen tote bag. It was just a thin sheet and pillow, but it was better than nothing. She also stuffed some of the minibar items that we put in the suites into the bag. Then she handed Fred two bottles of water and a kettle to carry. Fred was under strict instructions from Fiona to make sure I had food and plenty of cups of tea, as it gets a bit nippy down in the gardener's shed, even during the warmer months. When I looked at her face, it was like I was boarding a train off to war, and she was worried she might never see me again. Mr Potts gave a grave nod of his head. Their attitudes were not exactly reassuring.

CHAPTER

The gardener's shed is about the only place in Cavengreen that is not suitable for spending the night. A night on the library floor was sheer luxury in comparison. The shed itself is about as nice as sheds get, but that doesn't change the fact that it is still a shed. It is made of wood and the floor is covered in soil and green clippings. Worms, some alive, some dead, made for unsettling company.

Fred sat on the floor next to me for the rest of his shift. He radioed Detective Raj a couple of times, asking if we could go back inside yet, but the response was always, 'Not yet—soon though.' He didn't go willingly, but ultimately Fred's shift had to end and a new officer took his place. He left me with one of those keyring torches and wished me well. His face when he left was full of sorrow; he knew I was in for a rough night.

And rough it was. The days might have been warming up, but it was bloody freezing out there. My teeth chattered uncontrollably, and I had to resort to warming my hands over the steam from the kettle, which I flicked on at least ten times during the night. The young officer—one I hadn't seen before—who replaced Fred, sat on a wooden stool complaining about how cold it was. He lasted all of eight minutes or so before taking himself indoors to keep an eye on the shed from the warmth of the function room. I asked if I could go inside with him, but he said no. It was only his third week on the job and he was too scared to rock the boat.

Torture is the only word for what happened to me that night. I tell you what, if Fiona hadn't stuffed that sheet and pillow in a bag then I reckon I would have frozen to death. I'm hardly skin and bones, but there's not a lot of fat on me either.

As someone who lives a life of diligent cleanliness, you can imagine the constant state of discomfort and angst I was in that night. My work suit was filthy with dirt and all sorts. I couldn't complete my nightly routine. All I wanted was to read a good mystery book in my armchair and then head up to bed with a puzzle. I felt like my skin was infected with some sort of disease after not being properly washed or in a clean set of clothes in two days. I hadn't even brushed my teeth. Somehow, though, I must have nodded off, or perhaps passed out. One of the two. I awoke to a boot lightly kicking me in the side.

Right-ho, I need to leave it there. Fiona will be here any minute, so I need to get the kettle on and put out some chocky biscuits. She's popping over to help me fill in some of the blanks in the book; things that happened when I was in isolation. This is my story, but it will be helpful for you to have all the information from that evening, as I am told there were quite a few disturbances. I trust Fiona. I trust her to give her voice to my story and that it will be the truth. You should trust her too.

～ぃ～

Fiona just left. She wouldn't let me record our conversation on the dictaphone. She said she would have done it if it were just for me to listen to, but she wasn't comfortable with Helen being the one who would transcribe it. They have never met, Fiona and Helen. Hopefully they will one day. They are both very important ladies in my life. But Fiona didn't want Helen to listen in on our conversation; she said she wouldn't be able to be herself knowing that someone she wasn't familiar with was privy to our chat. And I respect that. It does make my job that bit harder, though. My brain is so full of her words. By 'eck she is a fast talker; even with a pen and paper I wouldn't have been able to keep up. So, I'll quickly need to regurgitate it all for you.

Fiona told me that right after Fred led me away, American Dave appeared in the hallway, wearing his cowboy hat. Fiona described the way he strutted down the corridor with his shoulders back and his feet seemingly too far ahead of the rest of his body. Like a rooster, she said. He was cocky.

'Look, no policemen,' American Dave said, doing a quick spin with his arms outstretched. He then went on to bragging about how he had been given full access to the hotel and no longer had to be escorted around. Apparently, he had a solid alibi for the time of the murder. Since then, we've found out that his alibi involved sneaking into the plunge pool at the hotel spa with Tanya, and then stumbling back to her suite with her, wearing nothing but towels. I have heard that a gallery of timestamped photographs on her telephone revealed that they were very busy, only taking a break to order room service for breakfast and then eventually emerging at 3 pm for afternoon tea. Apologies in advance to American Dave's wife. I am sure you deserve better.

Next, Fiona described how, at around 11 pm, she heard a Scottish man—presumably Alec—shouting that this lockdown was preposterous and demanding to leave the hotel. Fiona said he was slurring his words and when she popped her head out of the cocktail bar, she saw him swaying and stumbling through the lobby. As I said before, *technically* anyone was allowed to leave at any time. Not that they made that clear to us when they kept us under police guard and told us not to move from where we were. But Alec was fighting back. He had his car keys in his hands and an overnight bag flung over his shoulder.

'Move out of my way!' Alec repeated, over and over, Fiona said.

Two officers tried to block his exit, but Alec was determined to leave. The officers tried to tell him he had to stay in the hotel until the police had finished their investigation. Alec barged past them and out of Fiona's sight. She could still hear them.

'If you start that engine, we'll have no choice but to arrest you for drink-driving,' the police shouted. 'Come back inside, sir.'

Fiona hoped that Alec would at least decide to leave on foot, to be the first to take a stand against the police handling of the situation. The Scots are known for their defiance. When I asked her if she would have followed him, she said no, not without me. But to her disappointment she saw Alec plod back through the lobby, dragging his bag behind him. The police confiscated his car keys. Fiona said he mumbled something incoherent, staggered behind my concierge desk, took a bottle of water from my fridge and then wandered off down the guest corridor. Alec might have failed in his quest to get out of the hotel, but it was obvious that unrest was bubbling.

After that, Fiona said various guests were paraded through the lobby on their way from Detective Raj's interrogation room, formerly Mr Potts's office. Most grumbled and complained but were compliant, and many were carrying glasses of wine. Fiona said Patrick's two groomsmen were interviewed together and she overheard them talking on their way back to their suite. They were whispering about whether or not they should have confessed that they were both unconscious the night before the murder, having smoked 'a lot of weed' in the hedge maze after the wedding. As it happens, they decided not to and instead flushed the rest of their stash of drugs down the lavatory to hide the evidence. Not that I have ever touched drugs in my lifetime, but I can imagine the sort of impact something like that would have on the brain. Innocent or guilty, I probably wouldn't have mentioned it to the detective either. Fiona joked that a bit of marijuana from time to time might help with my intrusive thoughts, but that's not something I plan on trying tomorrow, or the next day for that matter.

The last thing to note would be the mental state of Mr Potts. It was bad, Fiona told me. Sleep deprivation and the stress of the investigation had really started to get to him. He sat slumped in one of the booths in Hugo's, only looking up occasionally when Fiona huffed and puffed. I'm not telling you this to embarrass Mr Potts or make him look weak. Stress affects everyone differently. I lose my ability to speak properly, Fiona gets all huffy-puffy, and Mr Potts internalises everything. That is just how it is. Before the murder, Mr Potts gave off the impression that he was a strong, confident gentleman. I mean, he would have to be to run an establishment like Cavengreen.

While patchy, Fiona's recollections are relevant to the story, so thank you to her for popping by. It is always nice to see her. Now, let us go back to my point of view.

After spending the night in isolation, I was relieved when Fred turned up with a takeaway cup of coffee, two slices of buttered toast and a change of clothes. I can't say I have ever worn tracksuit trousers and a hooded sweatshirt before, but at that point I had to take what I could get. At least they were clean. I must say the trousers looked even more ridiculous with my polished work shoes. Not that I wasn't grateful; I am just setting the scene.

Fred told me I would need my energy because Detective Raj wanted some of the hotel staff to help move sandbags from the gym. I was horrified. Some of those things are packed with ninety or even one hundred kilograms of weight. The hotel has a personal trainer service that can be booked on request. I've seen muscly blokes lug those bags up and down the gym, biceps bulging and the veins in their temples pulsing. Back in my youth I would keep in fairly good shape, but not now, and especially not since I've done my hip in. But Fred said Detective Raj insisted we meet him in the gym, so after my coffee and a quick lavatory break, we headed there.

Expecting to see some of the young 'uns from the hotel staff, I was surprised to find it was just myself, Fred and Detective Raj. Our voices echoed off the polished floors and bounced off the mirrored walls. All the equipment had been stored away and the room was empty except for a few tumbleweeds of fluff that blew across the floor and, of course, the sandbags that needed to be moved. Raj told me that the other blokes were changing and would be along soon, but I was to get started in the meantime.

'This one,' Detective Raj said, kicking a big black bag with *90 KG* written in white on the side of it. 'Come on then. Move it from there to there.' He pointed from one side of the gym to the other.

The hotel was turning into some sort of prisoner-of-war camp. Fred gave me a look that seemed to say, *Pick your battles,* so I moved around to one side of the sandbag and leant my good hip against it to try to shift it with my body weight.

'No, don't push it—drag it,' the detective ordered.

So, I moved to the other side of the bag, grabbed the handle on top and pulled it towards me. It wouldn't budge. And I am not surprised. I am a hotel concierge, not a bloomin' bodybuilder. I gave it a good go, though, gritting my teeth, grunting and everything as I pulled hard on the handle. A little too hard, it seemed. My dodgy hip cracked, and heat rushed through it. It felt like a forest fire was spreading through my bones. The pain was so excruciating it brought me to the floor. My hands clasped my hip as if it was crumbling apart and they could hold it together. I was howling in agony and angry that some detective had pushed me that far. It felt criminal.

Fred rushed over, telling me to breathe.

'It hurts!' I gasped through gritted teeth.

Fred begged Detective Raj to call an ambulance.

Instead, the detective walked towards the door. 'Take him upstairs to rest—suite two is free,' he said over his shoulder. And then he was gone, slamming the heavy door shut behind him.

Fred squatted down next to me on the floor. He breathed along with me to try to help calm my frantic, pained breaths. Inhale, exhale. We did that for a minute or so and it helped, somewhat. He gripped my hand tightly and told me to focus on his grip. I looked at our clasped hands, noticing how wrinkled mine was next to his. Even now when I look at my hands, sometimes I can't believe they are mine. They are older than me, that is how I feel. Fred's effort to distract me worked and I was able to control my breathing. The pain subsided enough for me to shuffle over to the mirrored wall and lean up against it. In a weak voice, I asked Fred what that was all about. It was obvious that none of the other staff members were coming to help. This little game of Detective Raj's had been designed for me alone.

'The dead man,' Fred began. 'He was in the bathroom. But that's not where he died. There was blood smeared across the floor as if someone dragged him from the bedroom. I'd guess he weighed about ninety kilos.'

CHAPTER

A letter arrived with today's post. There is something so special about a handwritten envelope nowadays, when everyone communicates via email or telephone. The only other post I get is bills, bills and more bills, all of them with a printed address in a clear window. A computer most likely autogenerates them. But this letter is special. Someone has taken the time to write my name and address on an envelope, lick two stamps and stick them in the top right corner. There is only one person that this could be from.

Note to Helen: Can you please type out the contents of the letter for the readers?

Dear Hector,

I'm sorry I haven't been in touch sooner. As you can imagine, things have been difficult and I've been focusing on making sure my family is okay. But I wanted to write to you to make sure you are doing well. It was awful what you went through at Cavengreen, and I am so sorry for my

part in that. I am doing okay, all things considered. Hopefully you'll come
and visit me soon. I'd like that.
Regards,
T. Potts

The letter is short yet it says everything I wanted to hear. I'm glad
he's doing well. It is always a worry when you suddenly lose contact
with someone. We formed a sort of bond during our time locked
inside Cavengreen. Little did I know how brief our friendship would
be. I do plan to visit him soon, though; I need to know why he did it.

Let me tell you everything I know and believe to be true about
Mr Potts. It will be useful for you to have some background information
about him. His first name is Toulouse and I believe his mother is of
French descent and his father is English. His wife's name is Isabella,
and I think I heard Mr Potts mention once that she is Italian. They
have a fifteen-year-old son named Anton. Isabella and Anton visited
the hotel once for afternoon tea, but unfortunately I didn't get a chance
to say hello. Had I known of the bond that would ultimately form
between myself and Mr Potts, I would have taken the opportunity to
get acquainted with his family. A man's family says a lot about him
and perhaps I would have spotted some red flags if we had met sooner.
Although I am not sure what my lack of wife or children says about
me. Perhaps that I am unlovable.

Tap one. Tap two. Tap three.

Sometimes I wonder who is going to bury me when I die. It is
a luxury to have a family who care for you. If I had my time over,
I think that is something I would have prioritised. But time went so
fast for me and here I am. Alone.

Mr Potts lived ten minutes from Cavengreen in a renovated
farmhouse. I know that because I dropped him home once when his

car was having engine problems. It was a lovely house with tall gates and climbing ivy. It is a shame they aren't able to live there anymore. That was the extent of what I knew about Mr Potts before the murder. During the lockdown at the hotel, I learnt that he doesn't manage stress particularly well. Mr Potts might have had silver service and hotel manager training, but there is no manual for how to deal with a murder.

Mr Potts was the first person to come and see me when I was allowed out of isolation and taken to rest in suite two. He burst through the door just as I was getting out of the shower. Luckily I had a towel wrapped around my waist, or he would have been in for a fright.

He wrapped his arms around me, undeterred by my hairy chest pressing against his bedraggled suit. His face was red and sweaty, and the dark rings around his eyes had deepened. He smelt like whisky and peanuts.

He walked over to the minibar and rummaged inside, eventually pulling out a beer. After cracking it open, he told me that according to Detective Raj I'd said that the police should look closely at him, but that he didn't believe a word of it. I couldn't fathom why Detective Raj would resort to such dirty tactics as turning the staff against each other. He told Mr Potts that I said I'd overheard him threatening Bruno the day before he was murdered. If you've got this far in the book, I'm sure I do not need to tell you that I heard and said nothing of the sort.

Mr Potts was horrified when I told him about the sandbag incident. Surely anyone would be horrified on hearing such a story. Although I imagined American Dave would have a good laugh at my expense if he ever heard what I had to endure. Nevertheless, as far as I knew, the sandbag incident had proven my innocence. If Bruno's body hadn't been dragged across the floor after the murder, then I am not sure where I would be now. The sandbag test would not have helped rule out many others. Most able-bodied adults could probably drag ninety kilograms if required, Mr Potts included.

After getting dressed, I joined Mr Potts in the suite's living area. He playfully mocked my overly casual attire, but it was nice to share a laugh in such a moment. Seeing a concierge in a tracksuit is like seeing a fish in a top hat. Mr Potts was sitting on the sofa and had made himself a coffee, but his shaky hands caused liquid to spill over the rim of the mug whenever he tried to take a sip. Clearly, he needed some rest. I suggested he lie down, but first he wanted to tell me about the interrogation he'd been subjected to by Detective Raj. Apparently, the forensics team had found faint bloody footprints on the carpet. Detective Raj said that it wouldn't take long for them to find out who they belonged to. He even insinuated that if Mr Potts wanted to come clean at that moment, then it would save everyone a lot of time. Mr Potts didn't, of course; why would he? We would spend two more nights in the hotel before anyone left in handcuffs.

Mr Potts slept for nearly seven hours. That time flew by. In between cups of tea, I sat in an armchair staring at the puddle of spilt coffee on the table. In seven hours, it did not get any smaller. In any normal circumstance, I would have had to clean the spill up straight away, its very existence making me twitch with discomfort. But I left it because I wanted my mind to focus on something other than my current predicament. While that pool of coffee was in my sight, it was all I could think about. It was a welcome break from wondering who the murderer might be.

As soon as I heard Mr Potts stirring, I grabbed a tissue and mopped up the mess. Mr Potts stretched and yawned, then he swung his legs over the side of the bed and stood up, scratching his head as he walked over to the minibar. He took a bottle of beer and packet of wasabi nuts. He offered me a drink, but he was just being polite. We both knew I wasn't going to crack a cold beverage with him.

It was golden hour at the hotel. That is how wedding photographers refer to the time just before the sun sets. An orange hue lit up the suite and beamed onto Mr Potts's face. Even with seven hours of sleep and good lighting, he still looked weary.

'Who do you think did it?' Mr Potts asked me after a slug of beer.

'No idea,' I replied.

'What do we know so far? We know it wasn't you.'

'And we know it wasn't you.'

'How do you know that?' Mr Potts looked me right in the eye. 'I mean, it wasn't me, but you're just taking my word on that.'

'Your word is good enough for me,' I told him.

'Thank you, Hector.' He swigged his beer. 'We know that Eric, the night porter, saw Bruno when he dropped off champagne just before midnight, so it couldn't have been a wedding guest, because they all left at quarter past eleven. And then the next time anyone saw Bruno that we're aware of was when you found the body just after three the next afternoon. That's a long window of opportunity.'

'I'm the only person that the CCTV shows going into the room. Could he have done it to himself?' I asked.

'And then dragged his dead body across the floor? Unlikely.'

'He could have done it and then tried to crawl to the bathroom.' But a flashback of the body reminded me that there was no way a man could have perpetrated such horrors to his own flesh.

Tap one. Tap two. Tap three.

'Hector!' Mr Potts leapt up with an energy I didn't know he had. 'The terrace doors. There's no CCTV on the terrace doors. That's how the murderer got in undetected.'

'Of course.' It was so obvious. I am not sure why we hadn't thought of it sooner.

'The murderer had to have known that there was no CCTV out there. Hector, it could have been a staff member.'

'Or a guest who didn't care if they were caught.'

Cavengreen has never had CCTV on the terraces; it was always considered an invasion of privacy, which is fair enough. We'd never needed it until then. There are no cameras in the gardens either, but there are a few on the external building, pointing into the car park and onto the restaurant terrace. Inside, there are cameras everywhere. You can't sneeze without someone watching. This is all information that I am sure the police had at that point. Mr Potts said Detective Raj had covered one of the walls in his office in sheets of white paper with names, alibis and question marks all over, just like in the movies. When I quizzed him on what was written down, he said he could not recall. Absolutely useless.

There was a knock at the door that startled us both.

'Move aside, you big oaf,' snapped a familiar voice.

My hip twinged with a lightning bolt of pain as I jumped up faster than I have moved in years. I am very glad Detective Raj did not see that momentary boost in agility or he'd have had me lugging sandbags again.

Tyrone the pit bull was patrolling the hallway, and he scowled as I opened the door and ushered my dear friend Fiona inside. She had a black smear on her face and was still wrapped in a Cavengreen dressing-gown. Her slippers were gone, and she marched around the suite barefoot in search of another pair. Mr Potts and I exchanged glances as we watched a flustered Fiona open up all the cupboards. When she finally found a pair, she slipped them on then slumped in an armchair and rubbed her temples, asking for painkillers, which we did not have to hand.

Fiona was agitated and muttering to herself about how she should have gone for one of the voluntary redundancy packages offered the year before. But she had kept working because she feared loneliness after the death of her husband. There is no feeling worse than loneliness, in my opinion. Loneliness consumes you. It encompasses sadness, shame and regret all in one. Loneliness makes you question your purpose in life. Because if you have no one to share life with, then what is the point? Loneliness digs into your brain and makes you feel unworthy. Once you let it in, it is like a fog that won't lift. And then you find that your physical health starts to suffer along with your mental state. That is why my job at the hotel meant so much to me. The guests, Fiona, Mr Potts—all the staff, really: they gave me the energy I needed to get through each day. Even if I had been given the green light to leave the hotel during the lockdown, I wouldn't have left until everyone else had been allowed out first. This book is giving me purpose now that I am no longer working there, but once I have finished, I will need to fill the void in my life. That is something I am still working on, don't worry. I have not come this far to just give up and start digging my own grave.

That was a bit of a sidestep; let us get back to Fiona. She was questioned during the night, along with the other reception staff. As you can imagine, it was a hostile experience for all involved. Fiona recounted the conversation she'd had with Detective Raj, mimicking his voice and facial expressions for our benefit. At one point she even managed to get Mr Potts to crack a smile when she told of how, when asked to put her finger in some black ink and provide her fingerprint on a piece of paper, she instead smeared a penis and testicles. Needless to say, that did not go down well with the detective, she said.

Detective Raj ended his questioning by granting Fiona permission to move around the hotel as she pleased but not to leave the premises.

If Fiona had been given the freedom to wander the hotel, then Mr Potts and I assumed we had too. In my borrowed hooded sweatshirt and tracksuit trousers, I opened the door to the suite. Tyrone barked at me, asking what we thought we were doing.

So I told him straight. 'We're going for a walk around *our* hotel.'

And that's what we did.

CHAPTER

15

It would seem that we were the last to know that guests and staff had been given permission to move freely around the hotel, including the gardens. Suite seven was still sealed off by yellow police tape, but aside from that and Mr Potts's office, nowhere was off limits. We wandered by Lavender Plates, probably looking like the walking dead. The exhausted chefs were firing up the ovens, promising to do their best with the supplies to hand. Surveying the room, I wondered if the murderer was still sitting among us and if perhaps I could do my own investigating to help solve the case so everyone could go home and I could get back to my puzzles and routine.

The newlyweds, Olive and Patrick, looked tired and despondent. They were sitting at a table with her parents and his groomsmen, no one speaking. They had dressed for the occasion, whatever they thought it was. There was an upside-down champagne bottle in an ice bucket on their table and another, almost empty, in front of the bride. I am sure this was not quite the honeymoon they had envisaged.

Knowing I looked unkempt and unprofessional, I was hesitant to approach them, but I decided that it was the right thing to do. I advised Mr Potts to hang back. He hadn't showered and his eyes looked bleary, not to mention the fact he smelt of alcohol. It was hardly the image we wanted the guests to see, so he opted to go out onto the terrace to try to telephone his wife.

Olive and Patrick feigned delight when they saw me. There wasn't much to be said other than to issue apologies and well wishes. They were very polite and told me they were glad they at least got to enjoy their wedding day. They asked me if I knew anything about the investigation; I told them I didn't.

Olive's mother, Sue Bainbridge, had been frowning at me as I talked; I could see her in my peripheral vision, her arms crossed and lips pursed. Her husband put his arm on her shoulder and quietly advised her to relax but she was a bull, and I was the colour red. You will have to excuse me, because I don't remember the conversation word for word, and I don't want to go putting words in mouths, but Sue seemed to be under the impression that this was all my fault, and that I should just confess so everyone could go home. Considering she believed me to be a dangerous murderer, she was acting rather bossy.

All the other tables of guests had started to look over. A few nodded their agreement. Others rolled their eyes and offered me sympathetic smiles. I had to remember that I was the concierge and confrontations with the guests were not appropriate, but this woman was getting on my last nerve with her accusations. As I indicated earlier, a different version of myself had started to emerge during that time in the hotel; one that resembled my father. My usual approach to customer service had been replaced with a determination to defend myself.

As bluntly as I could, I told Sue and everyone else who was listening that I had been proved innocent and she was more than welcome to ask Detective Raj to confirm that if she did not want to take my word for it.

Sue immediately stood up. Her daughter, Olive, tugged at her blouse, urging her to stop causing a scene, but Sue wafted her away. She strode out of the restaurant, turning to bark her husband's name, snapping her fingers. He scrambled from his seat and followed, clutching her handbag in one hand and a half-eaten croissant in the other.

Olive shook her head and sighed. For a second, I thought she was going to apologise for her mother's behaviour but instead she picked up her mobile telephone and appeared to be absorbed in whatever she saw on the screen.

I raised my hands to straighten my tie, only to find the two dangling tassels of my borrowed hooded sweatshirt. It felt ever so strange to be dressed so casually at the hotel. It's like when you see your local doctor or an old schoolteacher at the supermarket and the context seems wrong. That was me at that moment: completely out of context.

The peace was disturbed moments later by those wretched twins. Ruby and Oksana nearly accidentally-on-purpose knocked me over on their way to exchange air kisses with the bride and groom.

'What is *he* doing here?' the louder one, Ruby, asked as she flung a napkin over her lap and poured the last few drops of champagne into her glass. She clicked her fingers in the air and demanded that another bottle be fetched for her. Not that any staff were officially on service nor paying any attention to her. 'Shouldn't he be in prison or something?'

I remember those words so clearly, and I remember the hatred with which she looked at me as she said them.

Olive must have kicked Ruby under the table then because she yelped and shouted, 'What was that for?'

Through gritted teeth, Olive whispered that they would talk about it later. Everyone at the table looked at me as if I were an annoying insect that they wanted to swat away. It was time for me to exit.

Alec was sitting in a corner of the restaurant, twirling a spoon around a teacup, and chewing the end of his glasses. It was nice to see him drinking tea and not whisky. As it happens, he had added a splash of brandy to his tea, but I was none the wiser until he told me.

He greeted me with a firm handshake that seemed genuine. He thanked me for my book ideas and said that, as a result of my help, he had finished a first draft. There was just one problem: he had misplaced his laptop. We both knew it couldn't have gone far, but Alec couldn't remember a thing about the previous night. He didn't even remember trying to leave the hotel or the police confiscating his car keys. The look of horror on his face when Fiona briefly swooped by to remind him was a picture. That is one of the reasons why I have never been a big drinker. Fancy waking up and finding that hours of your life are missing from your memory. My mother used to try to tell my father off the morning after big night. She would tell him how he hit me, or how he had broken a picture frame or scared Josie, but he would always say, 'I don't remember doing that,' putting a swift end to the discussion. My mother knew better than to argue with a man who was good with his fists but bad with his words.

Alec invited me to join him and, since I wasn't on the clock, I thought, why not? Fiona and some of the other female staff were sharing cake over at the chef's pass, and Mr Potts was still outside, so I saw no harm in sitting down for a warm brew, minus the brandy.

Alec and I speculated over where his laptop could be. He even considered that someone could have stolen it, although he couldn't see why anybody would. There was a moment when I saw in his eyes that he had come to terms with the fact that it was lost. His shoulders dropped and he puffed out his cheeks. He confessed that he hadn't yet backed up his story.

That reminds me, Helen, can you please make a note to back up my book if you haven't done so already? I am sure you have, being a professional at this business, but on the off chance you haven't, please do. I am sure the last thing you want is to have to retranscribe these tapes all over again. What a nuisance that would be.

Alec kept twirling his spoon around his teacup, seemingly mesmerised by the mini whirlpool the movement created. He must have been relaxed, because he chose to open up to me. As I have said before, lots of people confided in me during my time as a concierge. They might have seen me as a free therapist, knowing I would be too polite to tell them to stop talking. It was my job to cater to the guests' every whim, and if that meant listening to them talk about themselves, then so be it.

It was different with Alec. His company was pleasant, and I found what he had to say very interesting. He was someone I would have chosen to be friends with, had the opportunity arisen. Alec told me about his wife, whom he'd had to have put into full-time care when she was paralysed from the neck down after a car he was driving skidded into an embankment one evening. He was consumed by guilt and sadness, mourning the loss of his old life and living with the pain of having destroyed his wife's future. There was no use comforting him by telling him it wasn't his fault, because I didn't know if it was or wasn't. Perhaps it was. Perhaps they were arguing and he took his eyes off the road, or he was otherwise distracted or tired. Without the details, there was no way of knowing. He made it clear several times that he was sober when he was driving. People cram in all sorts of details out of fear of judgement. Sometimes it is better to say something for clarity, rather than sit there wondering what the other person makes of you.

As interested as I was in what Alec was saying, I became slightly distracted by the sight of Mr Potts, climbing from one of the outdoor chairs onto the concrete ledge of the terrace. Jumping off would do nothing but scrape his knees so I did wonder why he was up there until I saw him shaking his mobile telephone up to the high heavens, presumably in an attempt to get signal. It seemed to work and moments later he was talking, or rather, shouting, to someone on the other end. I turned my attention back to my Scottish friend.

Alec had a son named Joseph and a daughter named Hailey; both had children of their own. Neither of them were able to spend much time with their father after blaming him for the car accident. Alec told me he was lonely, something I understood. You can have a family and friends but still feel lonely—for example, you might spend all day surrounded by people but get into bed at night feeling as if you weren't able to have a meaningful conversation or you weren't given the affection you craved.

From that conversation with Alec, I knew he would never get used to feeling lonely. He said that was why he started writing, because when he was writing he felt like he was talking to someone. I understand that now. Even recording this, I feel like I am chatting away to people. Even though you don't know me now, you will soon. I have been as open and vulnerable as I can be in this book. That is a scary but rather exhilarating thing.

Back to Alec; we had a grand chat. We spoke about Scotland and the places he likes and the places I have always wanted to go. He said that after all this was over, he would invite me to visit the Loch Ness Monster. That was the nickname of the landlord of his local pub rather than a mythical sea creature, he added. We had a right laugh about that. Who knows if it was a genuine invitation, but had things turned out differently, I would have made the effort to get up there. One day I will go on my own.

At that point Mr Potts banged on the window and indicated that he wanted me and Fiona to join him outside. He didn't half make me jump. Mr Potts had lost all sense of self and had clearly forgotten he was the hotel manager. Instead of his straight posture and neutral face, he was hunched, frowning and frantic. However, it wasn't the time to remind him of how he should be acting. I mean, there I was in a hooded sweatshirt and tracksuit trousers.

Mr Potts wanted to tell us that, according to his wife, the press had got wind of something happening at Cavengreen. He said he only got to speak to her for a minute before the telephone signal dropped out, but it was enough time for her to tell him that the six o'clock news had announced that Cavengreen was under police guard and an investigation of the staff and guests was taking place. That was all they knew. There was no mention that a man had been killed or that a crazed detective was holding everyone against their will. It wouldn't be long before Bruno's face would be plastered across the newspapers and television, but that wouldn't be until after we all got to go home. Well, most of us.

Fiona grabbed her mobile telephone out of her pocket. She said she was fed up and wanted to tell the media exactly what was going on at Cavengreen. I remember her asking for the number of the TV news, like I would know. I didn't even know it was possible to simply telephone the news with updates and the like. It didn't seem like a good idea. If Detective Raj got wind that the staff were campaigning against him then who knew what horrors he would conjure as punishment. Rumour had it he was close to breaking point and forcing his staff to work eighteen-hour shifts until they solved the case. But Fiona was determined to have her say.

Her long pink fingernails tapped against the telephone screen, and she made an impatient clicking noise with her tongue. Unable to connect to 'the TV people', as she called them, she turned to go back inside to ask one of the young 'uns if they had managed to get their telephones to work. But then she paused. She took a few cautious steps forward and knocked on the glass. Then she knocked again. I turned around, but I could not yet see what she saw. If I had seen, I would have moved faster.

Fiona knocked again, then she ran inside.

Once she had moved out of the way, I could see exactly what had so alarmed her. Alec was slumped against the window, his face slowly sliding down the glass, leaving a smear. One hand gripped his chest.

Mutterings of a man being poisoned spread around Lavender Plates. Patrick, the groom, lifted Alec from his chair and laid him on the floor. He started performing CPR. The chest thumps were particularly violent, but I am told that's normal. Detective Raj, followed by several officers, barged through the crowd. The detective pushed Patrick aside and took over the CPR himself. He desperately exclaimed that another man could not die, especially not on his watch.

After a couple of minutes it became painful to witness. Some of the younger staff moved away and others were crying at the back of the restaurant. Patrick knelt at Alec's side and checked his wrist for a pulse. Then he checked again. He told Detective Raj he could stop the CPR, but the detective only pumped Alec's chest harder. There is no doubt that some ribs would have been broken. The police officers exchanged glances, as if wondering whether to intervene. It was left to Patrick to seize Detective Raj and pull him away.

'He's dead,' Patrick announced, checking his watch, presumably to record the exact time.

My initial thought was of Alec's wife and children. How he never got to say goodbye. How his children might forever regret not having been on good terms with their father in the end. You can say sorry to a dead person, but they won't hear you.

I am not a crier by any means but Alec's death really got to me. The post-mortem would ultimately determine he'd had a heart attack, most likely brought on by stress. He'd had plenty of that to deal with.

Alec Maclean was the second guest to leave Cavengreen in a body bag in forty-eight hours. It was frightening for the guests. We didn't know at that point how Alec had died, so theories of a serial killer on the loose circulated quickly. Most of the guests made a quick exit from Lavender Plates and locked themselves in their suites. Some of the staff started to turn on each other, asking questions that they would never have asked before, like, 'Where were you in the hours before Bruno's murder?' and, 'Did you put anything in Alec's drink?'

Detective Raj stepped outside onto the terrace. We could only see his back. He kicked some gravel and held his head in his hands. He crouched down to a squatting position and then shot back up with a loud expletive. He turned and stormed back inside, pausing in the doorway to look around fiercely at the remaining staff and guests, who stared back wide-eyed. Alec's death had made Detective Raj—

CHAPTER

Right in the middle of my train of thought, you will never guess what happened. Just now, I heard some voices out the front of my cottage, so I went to look. I opened the door but no one was there, though a large box with a red ribbon around it was sitting on the mat. An early birthday present was my first thought. Perhaps Fiona or Helen had dropped it off in a hurry. It is my birthday this coming Sunday, so it would not have been completely out of the blue to receive a present, although I cannot say I expect them. But I have got the box here now, and after I describe its contents to you it is going straight in the bin.

So, picture this: I am on the doorstep with a parcel, and seeing as it is a lovely day, sunny and not too warm, I decide to open it there and then. I untie the ribbon, lift the lid of the box and see a card sitting on top of a second box. Written on the card is a single word. It is a word that haunts me and has ruined a whole genre of movies. As soon as you read it, you will know what's coming:

Howdy.

That was the word. In this context, it feels threatening, intimidating and sinister. As soon as I read it, I looked left and right, suddenly feeling unsettled. Then there was the box. This big bloomin' box. Inside it is a tan cowboy hat.

You can imagine what happened next, and if you could hear this audio recording, you would know how flustered I am still. Out from behind the limestone wall next to my house popped American Dave, followed by a grinning Paula McDavidson. They were clapping like seals, so pleased at the execution of their surprise delivery. American Dave was wearing the same cowboy hat he'd worn at Cavengreen. He was dressed in blue jeans and some clunky black boots. This is the Yorkshire Dales, not a ranch, buddy!

Paula McDavidson looked at American Dave in awe as he fired his cowboy jargon at me. I am not even sure what half of what he said meant. And then—you will not believe this—I noticed a man with a camera on the far side of the wall recording our interaction. Here I am, minding my own business in my own garden, when the American and the local busybody appear out of nowhere to ruin my day. I held my hand up to block my face, shouting that I did not give them permission to film me. They will probably just blur me. I have seen clips of those American cop shows before. Everyone from around here will know it is me; even with a fuzzy blob concealing my identity, I still walk, talk and stand like Hector.

As I shouted at him to go away, American Dave smirked. He's obviously had his teeth whitened because I was nearly blinded. He hooked a thumb through his chunky belt buckle and propped a foot up on my wall. All he needed was a piece of straw in his mouth and he would look just like the cowboys in the movies. He introduced his cameraman and producer to me. I don't care to remember their names.

Some local schoolkids cycled by and shouted a very fitting 'Wanker!' at American Dave, which caught him off guard. I'm not one to encourage children to curse, but it was more than appropriate in that moment.

'I know your parents, Joel Umbridge!' Paula McDavidson shouted after them, only to be met with a middle finger, presumably belonging to Joel.

Paula was in her element, enjoying the limelight with an American. She is the type of woman who thinks Americans are all glitz and glamour, and I bet she's thinking that she'll hit the big time after this documentary. I tell you what: there is no way they will make anything half decent without my side of the story. Where was American Dave when Alec died? In his suite with his American mistress. He was not part of the action; he was too busy getting some!

'We need you to appear on camera,' American Dave told me. 'It won't take long. We just want to ask you some questions about Cavengreen.' He explained that some company is interested in streaming the documentary when it is completed. Apparently that means the whole world will see it. I am certainly not going to support the whole world seeing his pack of lies so I replied sternly, 'Fat chance.' He persisted, of course; told me there was big money to be made and maybe even an all-expenses-paid trip to America. I am not interested. And I think I made that very clear by slamming the door in his face, something I am sure will make great footage for their documentary.

You would think I would be used to these bothersome pop-ins by now, but they seem to get worse every time I open my front door. That won't be the last I'll see of American Dave, I would bet money on that. Now he knows where I live, I am sure he and his cameras will be back. They will be sniffing around Cavengreen too, no doubt. Nuisances, the lot of them. Surely I could get them done for harassment.

Well, there's no use getting worked up. That is exactly what he would want. There is a story that I need to tell, so I will fetch a brew, calm down a bit, and resume recording. I really want to finish this part about Alec. And get this bloody great big hat out of my sight!

A cup of English breakfast does wonders for the temperament. I am like a new man after a warm brew. American Dave is not going to throw me off. Him being in the village has lit a fire in my belly. It is a race to see who can get their story out first. And it *has* to be me.

Let us get back to Alec. We all saw him die; there was no obvious foul play at work. It would be up to a post-mortem to conclude if he had been poisoned, like some of the guests were speculating.

While most of the guests had rushed back to their suites, fearful of further attacks, Olive, Patrick and the twins lingered in Lavender Plates, giving me funny looks and pointing out that I just so happened to be the last person who spoke to Alec. The twins made that very clear to Detective Raj. They were like schoolkids telling tales.

Detective Raj was having none of it. He covered his ears with his hands and closed his eyes. The twins clicked their fingers in his face and shouted, 'Hello?' but Detective Raj seemed determined to block them out. They thought this was an appropriate moment to demand the Wi-Fi be turned back on. The detective turned away, ignoring them. The twins stormed off, taking a bottle of champagne with them.

Olive pressed herself against Patrick and he tenderly comforted her by stroking the back of her hair. At that moment, American Dave and his mistress walked into Lavender Plates, their arms around each other's waists. Their timing could not have been worse.

'Who died?' American Dave asked jovially when he spotted our glum faces. He smiled broadly.

Detective Raj looked at him and then tilted his head back, directing an exasperated sigh towards the heavens. Patrick was the one to announce that Alec had died.

American Dave's smile turned to a look of shock. 'Fuck!' he mouthed as he caught sight of Alec's body.

He disentangled himself from his mistress and put his hands on his hips.

'What the fuck is going on here, y'all?' he demanded, his voice raised to a volume not appreciated by those of us who had just been through a traumatic experience. But he was right, it was time to try and get some answers.

We sat around for a few hours, the sky darkening as we sunk deep into the night, waiting for Alec's body to be taken from Lavender Plates. It was a solemn time. May he rest in peace.

Once Alec's body had been collected, Detective Raj and some of his officers, American Dave, Fiona, Mr Potts, and I gathered in the library. American Dave's mistress tried to join us, but he slammed the door in her face, leaving her in the corridor. We each took a seat and looked expectantly at the detective. (Except Mr Potts, who was in the corner of the library, his back turned to everyone. Nobody else noticed, but I guessed what he was up to, and the ever-so-slight clink of the lid being placed back onto the whisky decanter confirmed my suspicions.)

Detective Raj took his place in front of the unlit fireplace. He seemed drained. His eyes begged for sleep and his facial hair, which had been neatly groomed, now looked patchy. There were coffee stains on his white shirt, which was wrinkled and untucked. He agreed to answer any questions we had, as long as his responses stayed in that room. I think he could sense that we had the potential to become a troublesome bunch and that keeping us on side would help maintain control.

Fiona went first. 'Are you any closer to finding out who killed Bruno, and now, potentially Alec, so we can all get the hell out of here?'

'We're slowly ruling people out, so yes, we're getting closer,' Detective Raj responded.

Fiona followed up with: 'Do you think the killer is still in the hotel?'

'Yes. Looking at the CCTV footage, we are positive that the killer is still among us.'

It was my turn. 'Do you realise that there's no CCTV facing the terrace doors of the suites?' I asked.

'We are aware of that and assume that is how the killer gained access to Mr Tatterson's suite.'

'What about the murder weapon?' American Dave leant forward in the armchair, resting his elbows on his knees and twirling his hat in his hands.

'Missing.'

'But it has to be somewhere in the hotel?' American Dave persisted.

'Presumably so.'

'Well, let's all get off our asses and look for it!' American Dave sprung up.

'Oh, sit down you great *arse*!' Fiona snapped. 'We don't even know what we're looking for.'

'A knife, we think,' said Detective Raj, adding: 'We are still waiting for forensics to confirm.'

When you work in a hotel, you have a fair idea of the sort of inventory stored within the building. And knives, well, we had plenty of those. Sushi knives. Steak knives. Fish knives. Gardening knives. Letter openers. Butter knives (although I am fairly certain one of those wouldn't break the skin). I am sure American Dave's documentary will paint him to be a hero because he happened to be the one who eventually found the murder weapon. We will get to that later.

The clock above the fireplace chimed eleven times. We were to spend our third night in the hotel, and we all agreed that perhaps it was best for everyone to get some rest. It was clear that the killer, whomever they may have been, was still hiding in plain sight within the hotel. Either that, or they had just been taken away in a body bag.

Everyone dispersed back to the suites, myself and Mr Potts agreeing to share suite two, him on the sofa and me in the bed. He was very kind to offer me the bed. It is one of the benefits of being classed as an 'old man', even though that is not how I feel. But I accepted gratefully. I was in desperate need of a long rest if when I woke I was to put my energy into helping solve the case so we could all go home.

On the way back to the suite, we stopped at my concierge desk to take a few bottles of water from my fridge. Nothing on my desk was where it should have been. My hands throbbed, desperately wanting to sort and tidy everything. There were empty bottles of water, sweet wrappers and crushed cans of soft drink strewn across my files. The telephone was off the hook and Cavengreen pens were lying lidless all around. Something sticky had collected fluff and dust in a little patch. It was the stuff of nightmares—to me, that is. Of course, being locked in a hotel with a murderer was bad, but it didn't itch at my brain in the same way as a messy desk.

As I surveyed the damage I could sense that Mr Potts was growing impatient. I knew that I would have to clean up another time, though denying my urge to tidy caused me great discomfort.

Tap one. Tap two. Tap three.

Instead, I took a deep breath and bent down to open the fridge. I was surprised to find a black satchel inside. It wasn't mine and I hadn't the foggiest idea why it was in the fridge of all places. I checked over my shoulder; Mr Potts was flicking dead petals off the floral display. I pulled the satchel out and, peering inside, I knew immediately what I had found. It was Alec's lost laptop.

I took it. Part of me felt like I needed to protect it now that its owner was no longer with us. Alec was so passionate about his work. The other part of me was overcome by curiosity. I wanted to read what was on there. In that moment, for all I knew, Alec might have been murdered too, and maybe that laptop held some answers. Mr Potts didn't even notice I was suddenly carrying the satchel as we walked back to our suite. Soon enough I would tell him I had it. Indeed, I would need his help to access its files.

CHAPTER 18

A change of scenery is required for today's recording. Helen's idea. We spoke on the telephone yesterday and I told her all about how I was ambushed by the American and Paula the busybody. Helen thought it was rather funny and told me it would make great content. 'Anything for a good book,' that is what she always says.

I invited her along to Cavengreen with me, so she could see the hotel for herself, to get a sense of the setting. I thought that might help her with the editing. She said she was too busy. Something about paperwork, forms to fill in and all that. I didn't pry.

Fiona was more than happy to set up a little space for me in the gardens at Cavengreen. It feels peculiar coming back here. The last time I was here was the day we were all finally allowed to leave. Well, most of us. A couple of months have passed since then and, while I no longer work here, Cavengreen will always be my second home. Coming up the driveway and seeing the hotel brought back so many good memories. I will never tire of the sight. I mean, in fifty-odd years, I never did. Even after all that has happened, she's still my Cavengreen.

When I arrived, there was quite a bit of hustle and bustle going on out the front. Fiona greeted me with a warm hug and orange juice in a champagne flute. I felt like a guest, and I knew that was Fiona's intention. Isn't she lovely?

I pointed out some scaffolding around the main archway outside the front of the hotel.

'They're changing the sign,' Fiona told me with a sigh.

I'd known this was going to happen, though I haven't mentioned it to you lot. Part of me hoped it might never come to pass. The Americans have officially taken over Cavengreen and given it a new name. With the name of the hotel being plastered over the news the last couple of months, they have decided to rebrand. Fiona said the hotel has been busy enough, but instead of the normal clientele, they have been taking bookings from ghost hunters and those with a morbid fascination. What an odd thing to have as a hobby, visiting murder sites.

The new sign for the hotel was resting against the back of a truck when I arrived. I had to tilt my head sideways to read it. Fiona rolled her eyes and tutted at it. As of today, the hotel is named The Lavender. It is a nice name, I suppose. The Americans have planted lavender in terracotta pots all along the driveway and the front of the hotel. I must admit, it looks lovely—though a nightmare if you have allergies, of course. Still, this place will always be Cavengreen to me, and I'm not about to start using its new name in this book. Not only would that be confusing, it just wouldn't feel right.

The name is not the only thing that has changed around here. Most of the staff are new too. The Americans only kept on Fiona and the kitchen staff. Fiona laughed when she told me that; she was surprised since she had given American Dave so much grief during the lockdown.

He had described her as 'fierce' and 'just like me', which she found highly insulting. She only agreed to stay on because they gave her a generous pay increase. But she did note that the soul of the hotel is missing now that the staff have changed over.

'Ninety-nine per cent of us aren't even from round here now,' Fiona said with a frown. 'There are accents from London, America, all over the place. Not another Yorkshire voice outside of me and the kitchen.'

Inside the hotel, things are different. My old desk is blocked from view by what Fiona called 'touch-screen kiosks', and I saw a man pressing his finger on one to bring up a map of the local pubs. The floral display in reception is larger and more elaborate, and the butlers' uniforms have changed. Instead of classic navy suits and white shirts, the butlers now dash around in pale lavender linen. They look a bit like they're working at an asylum, but that seems to be in keeping with the Americans. It wouldn't be classy of me to criticise too much. But The Lavender does not have the same five-star feel that Cavengreen had. There, I said it.

Fiona led me out into the gardens, where I had requested she set me up for the day. It is still one of my favourite places, despite everything that happened here. Fiona has prepared a table for me with an umbrella for shade. There is a jug of iced water with orange wedges floating in it, and she brought over a plate of tomatoes, mozzarella and basil that I have already eaten most of. The sun is shining, a breeze is blowing lightly through the trees, and I feel calm. A brand-new team of gardeners are busy snipping at stray twigs on the outside of the maze.

I must say, I was not entirely sure how I would feel coming back here for the first time. When I left, I was frazzled, exhausted and numb. But Fiona has made me feel welcome and relaxed. Regardless of the unfortunate goings on here, I have fifty years of happy memories from this place—I'd best not forget those.

The reason Helen thought it might be a good idea for me to write here, and I agree, is because I need to refocus. A big chunk of the story is now out of my head and into this dictaphone, and I have touched on pivotal moments like Alec's death and my experience of being a suspect. But things are about to get more intense. Coming back to Cavengreen today, my mind feels invigorated and ready to tell the next part of the story. Even just sitting here in the garden, I am starting to remember more about how I felt in certain moments.

You might be wondering why I chose this spot and not somewhere a more private. But for this next part of the story, the garden is key.

The garden smells like freshly cut grass and lavender. It didn't that evening, though, on night three. When I got back to the suite with Mr Potts, he sank onto the settee and sat with his head hung low. He told me that the police had decided to turn the Wi-Fi back on to placate the increasingly anxious and frustrated guests. The press had already caught wind of the situation so there was no use keeping it off any longer. A text message had come through from Mr Pott's wife. She was angry because he still wasn't home and she didn't understand what the hold-up was. That seemed fair. From the outside, it must have sounded very strange: a bunch of staff and guests kept under police guard in a hotel where not one but *two* people had been carried out in body bags. Mr Potts had missed his son's football match, apparently, and the lad had scored the winning goal. Not having kids of my own, I couldn't tell him I understood what it was like to miss those key moments in their childhood, but I did tell him that there would be plenty more to come and he would be present for those.

Mr Potts still hadn't noticed the laptop, which I had placed on the bed. He finally took himself off for a shower, with a little push from me.

I sat in a chair next to the bed and stared at the laptop warily. I had seen plenty of people use them around the hotel, but I had never used one myself. Edging closer, the first thing I did was lift the lid, if that is what it is called. The machine whirred and screeched and then a picture of a rocky landscape popped up. It seems safe to assume that it was somewhere in Scotland. A little box appeared asking for a password. That was an obstacle I hadn't anticipated. Was Alec hiding something?

If anything, the need for a password made me even more eager to see what was on the computer. I knew about the book, but what about other notes? Alec told me he often documented interactions with people or descriptions of events, just in case he wanted to use those moments in his work. He had written about me, so perhaps he had observed others around the hotel and written about them too. Clutching at straws, you might call it, but the laptop was the only straw I had in that moment. As soon as I heard the shower stop, I slammed the laptop shut and slid it under the bed. I wasn't quite ready to share my discovery with Mr Potts. I wanted more time to consider if withholding the laptop from the police was the right thing to do.

Around 3 am, I awoke to the sound of voices on the terrace outside our suite. I got up and peered between the curtains, and sure enough there were two people having an argument. Both of them were wearing Cavengreen robes and I had to squint a little to make out who it was in the darkness. Two women, that much was obvious from their hushed shouts. I recognised Olive's blonde curls first and then I identified her mother Sue, short in stature and yappy in voice. Olive kept having to shush her as her volume increased.

I glanced over at Mr Potts on the sofa—he was fast asleep—then carefully opened the terrace door a smidge, just enough to hear what the two women were saying.

'Nobody can know,' Olive said in a sort of shouted whisper.

'Just tell me the truth, Olive,' her mother replied. 'I can help you.' She clutched at her daughter's arms, only to be shrugged away.

'I didn't do it, Mother.'

'You know it doesn't look good, though, don't you?'

'Yes, Mother,' Olive hissed. 'I know exactly how it looks.'

'Let me help you, Olive,' Sue urged again.

'I don't *need* help. I told you: it wasn't me.'

That was all I caught of the conversation before they moved off into the garden. I watched them pace up and down the lawn, their abrupt hand gestures making it clear they were still arguing. So many possibilities rushed around my head, as I am sure they are doing for you right now. When I thought about suspects, I considered staff members, even Mr Potts or, at a stretch, perhaps more so before his death, the drunken Alec, but I'd never considered the bride. Then I remembered the noise complaints from the wedding night; they placed the bride in her suite at 11.30 pm and 2 am. But there were plenty more unaccounted for hours between then and me finding the body. What was the bride hiding? I had to know, and I imagine you lot are pretty keen to find out too.

In the morning, I told Mr Potts what I had seen and heard. I sprang the information on him almost as soon as he opened his eyes; the poor man was quite taken aback. I had been waiting since 3 am to tell him. He rubbed his face as he tried to process the information.

'Coffee,' was his response.

He poured a splash of brandy into the coffee I made him. I was not pleased. I needed Mr Potts to help me decipher the information and crack into the laptop that day; if he was drunk, he'd be useless. He was an adult, though, and my boss, so there was nothing I could say to stop him.

That first sip seemed to revive him, and he asked me to repeat everything I had just told him, but a little bit slower.

I started with the laptop. He didn't share my optimism that we would be able to guess the password of a man we barely knew. He also didn't share my shock that there was a password to begin with. I'd thought that was a sure sign Alec was hiding something, but Mr Potts told me that it was commonplace for people to protect their devices with a password for the purpose of keeping their contents private.

Then I told him about Olive and her mother. He agreed that the conversation sounded suspicious, but it didn't actually prove anything. Looking back, it was obvious he wasn't as keen as I was to find Bruno's murderer. He was too consumed by whatever demons he was fighting in his head. Not that he didn't provide some assistance, it was just that I could have done with a bit more help. Nevertheless, it was his idea to keep what we had discovered to ourselves for the time being. I agreed this was sensible. Going to Detective Raj with a few small pieces of a puzzle would only have angered him. He was already drowning in question marks, and in my opinion, he needed our help. Otherwise, who knows? We could still be stuck in that hotel today.

Mr Potts and I sat in front of the laptop for an hour typing potential passwords. *Alec.* Incorrect. *Scotland.* Incorrect. *Celtic.* Incorrect. *Rangers.* Incorrect. *Author.* Incorrect. *Password123.* Incorrect. We exhausted our options quickly. Not knowing much about a person makes it a million times harder to try to guess their password. Mine is always just my birthday. Although I might have to change it now that I have shared that with you. Mr Potts was getting frustrated by the *Incorrect Password* alert on the screen. He saw the whole exercise as pointless, reminding me that even if we did happen to get into the laptop, the chances of us finding something relevant were close to zero. But the only other option we had was to sit around waiting for the answers to come to us. Fat chance of me doing that, I can tell you that for free.

I don't believe it. Two guests from the hotel just came over and ambushed me with a barrage of questions about the murder. They said they recognised me from the newspaper and wondered what I was doing sitting in the garden talking to myself. I didn't tell them about the book. I don't care if they think I'm barmy; I can't risk American Dave finding out about my secret project.

One of the guests, a man, swung a bottle of red wine in one hand and sipped from a glass in the other. He asked me if I had been to the prison to visit the murderer. I told him no, not yet. The other guest, a woman whose teeth were stained red from the wine, asked if I was going to be in the American documentary. Surely word of American Dave's film couldn't have spread as far as Cavengreen's guests. Trying to sound casual, I asked how they knew about it.

'They're here now filming. We saw them in the lobby.'

Can't a man enjoy his tomatoes and dictaphone in peace? (That wasn't my first thought when I heard of the potential interruption, but it sounds mildly humorous for the book.)

As if on cue, American Dave appeared.

'Hector, my friend! Just the man we're looking for. Let's talk.' American Dave strode towards me across the lawn, his camera crew following behind and Fiona anxiously teetering over the grass as quickly as her heels would allow.

'I had no idea they'd be here today,' she said apologetically.

'Fiona here tells me you're writing a book. Well, fancy that.' American Dave chewed a piece of gum aggressively; seeing it swivel around his mouth made my stomach turn. Never have I ever chewed a piece of gum, and it is one of my pet peeves when people do so, especially when talking. Not that I would expect American Dave to have manners. He sticks out like a sore thumb in this part of the world.

'No,' Fiona began, 'what I said was, Hector has been approached by a publisher to write a book.' Fiona grimaced at me awkwardly, her eyes wide, I could tell she regretted letting the cat out of the bag. She mouthed, 'I'm sorry,' over American Dave's shoulder.

The camera was pointed right at me, so I reminded American Dave's posse that I did not give my permission to be filmed nor for any sort of fuzzy blur to be used to conceal my identity. They kept filming, I expect they wanted to frustrate me so much that I would launch myself at the camera. That would make great footage, wouldn't it? Instead, I started to pack up my belongings. I didn't even manage to get to the part of the story that I wanted to. But there is no use trying to go on with that fool dancing around me with his cameras and loud voice.

'And who gave you permission to sit out here? This area is for paying guests only,' American Dave said with a smirk and a cocky tilt of his hat.

'I invited him to sit out here,' Fiona said, her voice firm.

'Is that so?' American Dave took my napkin off the table and spat his gum in it. Then he put it back, right in my eyeline. 'With all due respect, Mr Harrow, you are not a paying guest and it is not Fiona's place to invite non-paying guests into private areas of the hotel. Please leave.'

❧

Can you believe it? He kicked me out! That Yankee Doodle sod booted me out of Cavengreen. I'm recording this from my car. The bleedin' good-for-nothing is still watching me from the window of Lavender Plates. His cameraman is still filming. I CAN SEE YOU. This is just what they want. *Get the old man all riled up and see his reaction. That'll make great TV.* That swine. He had security escort me to the door. And the icing on the cake: he banned me! He stamped me with a lifelong ban from The Lavender.

He's still standing there. He's shooing me away. Alright, I'm going, I'm going. Squeeze the steering wheel one, two, three times. Sod. Go back to America, why don't you? Swine. I can't believe this is the last time I'll be driving down this driveway. My last time through these gates.

Let me look back at her one last time; a beauty of a building, she is.

Sorry about all that huffing and puffing. I forgot you lot were still there. Not that you're here, but you are there. The dictaphone is on the passenger seat, so I guess you're along for the ride back to my cottage.

You too, Helen.

I am lost for words, to be honest with you. Cavengreen means so much to me. That place rescued me from the darkness of my home life. It taught me that there was good in this world. I have seen more people go in and out of those doors than anyone else and I never thought for a second that one day I would be told that I can never go back. It is my hope that the Cavengreen family read this book and see what monster has taken over their once-beautiful hotel. What a shame. What a damn shame.

Let's end it there, Helen. Any mutterings you hear after this are for my ears alone. I'm driving so I can't turn the tape off. Oh, Cavengreen.

CHAPTER

Helen got a right earful when I got home yesterday. She ended up coming for tea. Pie and mash. I told her all about how American Dave banned me from the hotel. Helen has such a rational head on her shoulders, it took her no time at all to convince me that it was okay.

'It is not about the hotel,' she said, 'it is about the memories.' And do you know what? She is absolutely right. All of the good memories I have from my time at Cavengreen are stored in my brain, and all of the bad ones are in this book, to be banished from my mind as soon as the publisher clicks print.

Tap one. Tap two. Tap three.

It is a pity I will never get to take Helen to the hotel. I had planned to take her to Lavender Plates for afternoon tea as a thank you for helping me with the book, but I will have to think of some other fancy place now.

Helen had a listen to some of the audio I have recorded over the last few days. She thinks I should slow down, pad a little. That was an interesting thing to hear, because I feel like all I have done is waffle.

All the interruptions from American Dave and the like have thrown me for a loop, and I feel like I've done a lot of complaining about that and not an awful lot to push this story forward. There is still a lot to be told. It might turn out, when Helen writes all this up, that the murder happens in the first few pages and then you spend the rest of the book trying to decipher my gibberish. If that is the case, then you may as well flick through to the final chapter.

Helen might take that part out. I am sure professional authors don't tell their readers to skip to the end. Fingers crossed Helen salvages some content for the bits in between the murder and the finale.

Beans on toast is my favourite way to start a day. One can of beans, two pieces of toast cut into triangles—never rectangles—and enjoyed with a nice hot brew in my big, comfy armchair. Good old beans on toast picked a peck of pickled peppers.

Sorry, Helen. Just warming up the vocal cords. Feel free to cut that out if you wish.

This morning's newspaper arrived with a thud. I was just having a quick glance when I came across a write-up about you-know-who. COWBOYS AND MURDERERS is what they have gone with for the headline. There is a picture of American Dave, cowboy hat and all, with his arm around Paula McDavidson, who has also donned a Stetson for the shot. His teeth glow even in the grainy black-and-white photo, and Paula certainly looks like the cat that got the cream. The caption underneath reads: *Texan Dave Cleesey stands in front of his newly purchased hotel, The Lavender, with renowned journalist Paula McDavidson.*

Renowned?! Bloomin' renowned? The woman's never written a decent thing in her life. Back in the day she used to do the weekly horoscopes and now she's done one interview and suddenly she is *renowned*. Purely because of her nonsense articles, I learnt that I am a Leo. Paula always predicted I would be coming into a spot of bother soon. It only took ten years for her prediction to come true. Useless good-for-nothing. Maybe she should have read her own horoscope to see that she would become a terrible journalist who should find a new career path.

Right, Helen has just opened the gate. I'd best let her in.

For the sake of the dictaphone, Helen has arrived, and she has brought chocolate éclairs. Perfect timing, I have just brewed another pot. While we get stuck into these, I will tell you the next part of the story. Helen is listening in today. This is an important part, and she wants to make sure I don't miss any of the details.

So, where were we? Mr Potts and I were failing to break in to Alec's laptop. Olive and her mother were hiding something, but what? It was suspicious to say the least.

I put the laptop in the suite's safe, code 1608, the day and month of my birth. (Must remember to update my debit card's pin code soon.) We didn't know it at the time, but that would be our last full day at Cavengreen. Everybody would be going either home or to prison the following day.

We headed down to Lavender Plates just after seven, wondering if there would be anything left in the fridges for breakfast. The chefs were busy defrosting lamb stew, and Olive and Patrick had donated their wedding cake. Cake for breakfast. I suppose it was better than listening to my belly grumble all day. The kitchen's supply of eggs, bacon, and sausage were long gone. The head chef complained that if he had known how long this lockdown was going to last then he would have rationed the food.

The sound of Fiona's heels clip-clopping on the parquetry announced her arrival before we could even see her. She looked like regular Fiona again. She was no longer in a bathrobe and slippers. Her uniform was fresh and pressed, her hair in a slicked-back bun, and her face had a nice glow. She smoothed her skirt with her hands, and then greeted those assembled in the dining room with a 'Good morning' and a smile. She told me she had found a fresh uniform in the laundry room, and she had done what she could with the hotel's amenities and dribs and drabs of make-up that she found at the bottom of her handbag. Fiona was optimistic that we would be let out that day, and if there happened to be media outside the gates, then she wanted to look professional.

I hadn't even considered that there might be media waiting. Cavengreen has such a long driveway, it is impossible to see anything beyond the grounds. Mr Potts had an idea. The hotel is just two storeys high, but above the suites on the first floor is an attic space used for storing Christmas decorations and antiques. The attic is the only place in the hotel high enough to see beyond the gates.

The on-duty police had grown restless and spent a lot of the day outside the front of the hotel kicking gravel, smoking and making jokes. It made roaming around the building much easier. Fiona was reluctant to come at first, but when the twins waltzed into Lavender Plates wearing matching pink tracksuits, she changed her mind and followed myself and Mr Potts, bringing along a piece of wedding cake wrapped in a paper napkin.

The attic was accessible by a narrow staircase tucked away behind a door marked *Staff Only*. I had been up there many a time. Back when I was doing odd jobs at the hotel, I would often be asked to fetch and carry things from storage. It is full of old paintings, sculptures, mirrors, and the like, most covered in white sheets. Many of the items up there are worth a fortune. The ceiling is high enough in the middle that you can stand up, but you have to crouch down as you get closer to the sloping edges. There is a huge arched window at one end of the room where light floods in, revealing tiny dust motes that hover like glitter.

The attic is actually the place where I had my first kiss. Her name was Penny Duckford and she was a maid at the hotel. We were both sixteen—or she might have been seventeen. Well, we were around the same age. Penny had lovely long red hair and cherry-coloured lips. When she spoke, her nose scrunched up, and when she felt shy, she couldn't look me in the eye. There was something special about her.

We were up in the attic one day looking for the Christmas chinaware. It was freezing up there, so cold we could see our own breath. We were pretending to be dragons breathing fire when I puffed out a gust of foggy breath and, on my inhale, she kissed me. Her eyes were closed; it was romantic. It only lasted a couple of seconds. When she pulled away, I was hoping to ask her on a date, but she ran off downstairs before I could. It was a hard knock for a young lad. Worse still, Penny avoided catching my eye after that and we never spoke again. I tried, but she always walked away. Maybe it was me, maybe it wasn't. The moment was nice, nonetheless.

Fiona sucked in her stomach and carefully slid between the dusty boxes, not wanting to soil her fresh uniform. Mr Potts reached the window first and gasped. When I caught up to him, I could see why. Outside the gates at the bottom of the driveway was a crowd of thirty or so people and about half-a-dozen parked cars. We squinted, but it was hard to make out much detail.

Fortunately, I had a solution. Next to me there was a tall object with a sheet over it. If my memory served me correctly . . .

I pulled the sheet off to reveal a telescope that had been at the hotel since before my time. It was old and dusty, but by 'eck, it still worked, and that was all that mattered. We took it in turns to survey the scene.

When it was my go—after Fiona and Mr Potts had each had a good gander—I saw that the media had arrived in force. There were people with cameras around their necks and video equipment set up on large tripods. Some of the journalists sat slumped in those fold-up camping chairs. They must have been there a while.

Then I spotted a man holding up a white sign with a telephone number on it. The others had seen it too. We debated for a minute whether or not we should call. And then we did.

Mr Potts took his mobile telephone from his pocket and dialled, and I watched through the telescope as the man with the sign put his arms down and scrambled for the phone in his pocket.

'Hello?' he said when he answered.

'We saw your number on the sign,' Mr Potts told him. 'We're in the hotel.'

Mr Potts and the journalist discussed what the media knew already about what was going on inside the hotel. They knew someone had been murdered and that another man had died from a suspected heart attack. That was the first we were hearing of Alec's potential cause of death. Thankfully—although that seems an odd choice of word—we were back to having just one murder to solve. The media knew the murder victim was a man. They knew that the killer had not yet been identified. And they knew that all the guests and staff who were present in the hotel at the time of the murder had volunteered to remain locked down until the culprit was found.

'Volunteered?' Mr Potts said, frowning.

The man on the phone—Mick I think his name was—confirmed that the police had released a statement saying that while those in the hotel were permitted to leave at any time, we had chosen to stay. We were flabbergasted to hear this. Three nights we had spent in the hotel by that point, one of which I spent on the floor of the library, one in the gardening shed and the other . . . well, the other was in a lovely suite with Mr Potts.

Mr Potts told the man on the telephone in no uncertain terms that the guests and staff had *not* been given the option to leave and were being held against their will. I watched through the telescope as the man on the other end of the phone moved away from the crowd and into the privacy of his parked car. He offered us money to stay and leak information to him. It would be easy to do with the Wi-Fi back up and running. He wanted videos of the detective, recordings of conversations and pictures of the crime scene. Even hearing the offer made me feel filthy. Not in this lifetime would I ever be someone's rat. But there were three of us, and he only needed one person to agree. Fiona pondered the deal for a minute or two. She needed the money, I knew, especially since her husband's death. I told her I wouldn't judge her if she agreed to the deal, but she might judge herself. Her answer was no. Sweat dripped from Mr Potts's forehead as he grappled with the decision. To be a rat or not to be a rat. He squinted into the sun for several seconds, then he sternly told the man no, that as hotel manager it would be utterly disgraceful for him to act in such a way.

'A hypocrisy,' he said. Then he hung up the phone.

We spent some time up in the attic, sitting on upturned buckets by the window. Fiona ate her cake, offering to share it out of politeness, even though I knew she wanted it all for herself. There were a lot of long sighs. I could tell Fiona was thinking about how the money might have changed her circumstances, but I know her: her soul is too pure to do such a thing. Mr Potts was tapping away on his phone, as usual.

His wife wanted regular updates. I had seen over his shoulder some of the long messages she had sent him.

It was a moment of peace. Some of the old boxes up in that roof must have been there since I'd first come to Cavengreen as boy. I had a rummage, looking for any old bits of uniform or lost property I could change into. Everything smelt musty, but I found a box with one of the old butler uniforms inside. It was a style from maybe a decade ago, when the hotel trialled an olive-green hue. It wasn't a popular colour with the staff, but I didn't mind it. I pulled out a blazer and pair of trousers in my size and thought they would do quite nicely. It might not have been the correct uniform, but by that point the rules were out the window. I mean, some of the staff were still wandering around in Cavengreen robes like they were at a day spa.

We left the loft after an hour or so. The day had only just begun, but the weight of the circumstances were dragging us down already. Fiona peered out from the door at the bottom of the stairs and ushered us out when the coast was clear. She had been staying in suite fifteen, right next to the stairs on the first floor, and she wanted to duck in to grab her telephone. We followed her, and Mr Potts immediately went to the minibar. Behind his back, Fiona rolled her eyes.

Everything in Fiona's suite was neatly folded and organised in logical spots. It was a much calmer place to be than the room I was sharing with Mr Potts, which was littered with empty beer bottles and used towels. The view of the garden from the upper level is nice too. (The gardeners make sure that the maze hedges are high enough that those staying on the first floor of the hotel can't see any of the pathways.) A flock of birds flew in murmuration up above; it was a beautiful sight, the way they created waves in the sky. It was one of those rare events that I wished everyone in the world was able to see at that moment, but while Fiona and I were fixated on the sky, Mr Potts alerted us to some goings-on back on the ground.

American Dave and his mistress were standing at the entrance to the maze, and we had a clear view of him kissing his lover's neck, mouth and chest before, giggling, they slipped between the hedges.

'Our new boss, everybody.' Fiona stuck out her tongue in disgust.

God knows what they intended to do in there. Seems a bit prickly, if you ask me.

Fiona distracted us with a rant about how inappropriate American Dave's conduct was. But whatever it was that the pair of them went into the maze to do, I am sure they had barely got started before American Dave's lover ran from the greenery, screaming. American Dave followed, waving his hands and shouting, 'Help!'

Squads of trained police officers had searched the whole grounds of the hotel over and over by this point. So how was it that, all of a sudden, the murder weapon happened to appear in the centre of the maze?

CHAPTER

The maze at Cavengreen has been a feature since the 1970s. A gardener from Spain was flown in to transform the grounds. Her name was Elena, and you might be shocked to hear that, during her time at the hotel, we had a bit of a dalliance.

Helen has just choked on her éclair. Is it so surprising that I might have had a few love affairs in my day? I have been single for seventy-three years, so believe you me, I have got some stories. Helen is blushing; I don't think she has ever thought of me like that. But back in the day, I was quite the looker, and on occasion I would find myself temporarily involved with a member of the opposite sex. Never a guest. I want to make that clear. Not that some didn't try, but I would never have done anything that put my job at risk. That is not to say that when a guest stopped being a guest there were not interactions. But definitely nothing untoward happened in the hotel.

Elena was a beautiful woman from a small town called Cudillero. I believe it is quite the tourist trap now. She had long brown, almost copper hair and her skin was golden. Around here, she stood out. Elena had a gap between her two front teeth, which made her smile all the more alluring. I was drawn to her love of plants and gardening; she knew so much and was happy to share her knowledge with me. She was the one who suggested creating a hedge maze, and I helped her plan the route. I could find my way to the middle with a blindfold on. One day, when we were sketching some potential layouts, our hands touched and then I kissed her. That was the start of something special that ended as soon as she went back to Spain. Postcards were sent back and forth for the next few months, but they gradually were few and far between. Her final message told me she had met someone.

Helen looks sad for me, but it's okay, these things happen. There have been many times in my life where potential love has slipped away. I know Helen understands that, having recently ended a relationship herself. She's looking away.

I didn't mean to upset you, Helen.

She insists I haven't, but I know she is only being polite.

That story sent Helen into a bit of a tailspin. She scrolled through the contacts on her telephone, offering to set me up with this woman or that woman. Set-ups aren't for me. If love is supposed to come my way, it will come. But for now, I have chocolate éclairs, my puzzles, my mystery books, and great conversations with my dear friend. What more could a man want?

Back to the hotel. There was pandemonium after the murder weapon was found. American Dave alerted Detective Raj to his discovery and within ten minutes the entire maze was wrapped up in yellow police tape like a Christmas present. Myself, Fiona and

Mr Potts went downstairs and lingered on the patio, trying to pick up pieces of information from the conversations that rushed by. American Dave did his best to shoehorn himself back into the action; the police had thanked him for alerting them to his discovery but said he was no longer needed. Even after he was dismissed, Detective Raj had to repeatedly tell him to move back so his team could do their job. He ended up being ordered to stand with us and not stir from that spot. His ego took a bit of a bruising, and for a few moments there he was the quietest I had ever seen him.

When he eventually piped up, American Dave told us that in the centre of the maze he had found a steak knife covered in dry blood, one of the new concierge iPads and a pair of women's boots. Everything was bundled up in a Cavengreen bath towel. He described how he'd scrambled to get out of the maze after his discovery, only to get lost in dead end after dead end. I knew exactly where he would have gone wrong. He would have exited the centre of the maze on the opposite side from where he came in. We designed it so that the middle of the maze was perfectly symmetrical, meaning that if you lost your bearings, there would be a chance that you wouldn't know which way was which. Part of me felt smug for having helped design a maze that American Dave had struggled to escape, but I didn't let on.

Helen just told me it is unlikely we will be able to insert a photograph of what was found in the middle of the maze. Apparently, that will increase the book's printing cost too much and requesting permission to use the image from the police could take months. I haven't seen the photograph yet. It is probably being kept in evidence until the trial.

Tap one. Tap two. Tap three.

The good thing about American Dave loving the sound of his own voice so much is that he did an excellent job of describing exactly what he found in the maze. We asked him how he knew they were women's boots and he said it was fairly obvious from their small size. That changed everything for us. I guess we had all assumed that Bruno's murderer was a man, especially since they'd had to drag his ninety-kilo body along the ground. Not that women aren't strong, but—oh, you know what I mean. It just never crossed my mind that the killer might be female.

The police erected a white tent over the centre of the maze, as the evidence couldn't be moved until it had been properly photographed and examined. Prints were taken of the bottoms of American Dave's shoes to rule him out. His mistress, Tanya, was also invited to provide shoe and fingerprints; her hefty size nines quickly cleared her of suspicion.

Then it became a game of Cinderella. Everyone, men and women, were told to meet at reception, where they would have to remove one shoe and prove their shoe size for the police. It was chaos, having everyone in the lobby at once. People leant on the furniture, leaving grubby marks on the wood. Mr Potts helped me empty the dead flowers into bin bags. I had never seen the entrance table look so bare. A queue of guests and staff were ranged around the room. Detective Raj sat in an armchair and invited each person to step forward one by one and have their shoe size recorded. If they passed the test, they were free to return to their room. If further questioning was needed, they would be escorted into the library.

As it turned out, the blood-covered boots were a women's size five. Helen tells me that is quite small, with a size six being considered the average for women in the UK. As you can imagine, all the men were ruled out. Even if they curled their toes, there was no way any of the males could squeeze their feet into the boots.

The first woman to be pulled to the side was one of the receptionists, Shamila. And by God, she looked like she was going to pass out from fear.

Fiona rushed straight over to stand by her side, but two police officers extended their hands to keep her at a distance. I saw Shamila gulp and look plaintively at Fiona, who mouthed, 'It will be okay,' then gave her a reassuring smile. Shamila was led into the library. I can imagine her sense of relief when more suspects joined her, including one of the other reception girls, Chloe, as well as the bride, the bride's mother and the twins. Mr Potts looked at me with raised eyebrows when the bride was taken away. She was fast becoming our prime suspect, but we needed more evidence before we could share our suspicions with the police.

The girls were in the library for an hour. During that time, Mr Potts went to our suite for 'a lie-down', which I think was code for a top-up, leaving me and Fiona to wait anxiously behind the reception desk. We ducked down whenever one of the police officers walked by, not wanting to be ordered back to our rooms. Fiona printed off the reception roster, which proved that neither of the girls was working the day before the murder and both had just started their shifts when I found Bruno's body.

Fiona knocked on the library door, but a voice within shouted, 'Go away!' We both recognised the voice as belonging to Detective Raj. Fiona slid the roster underneath the door.

Behind the reception desk, Fiona nervously wrapped an elastic band around her finger, only stopping when the tip turned a hue of reddish-purple, and then beginning the process again on another digit.

I've always thought Fiona would make a great mother; she is fiercely protective of the people she cares about. Sadly, it wasn't to be. I will get her permission before we put this next bit in the book, so if it makes it into the final copy that means she said it is okay.

I have known Fiona a while, so I was there when she was working through her infertility struggles with her husband. They tried for years to conceive, with no success. We would take tea breaks together and she would cry. The days when a pregnant woman would check in or one of the female staff would announce they were expecting were the worst. Then, when IVF first came about, Fiona and her husband saved every penny they could to have a go. She was working double shifts and I know her husband had two or three jobs at the time. They had their go, it worked . . . and then it just went away. Fiona took a month off work after that, and when she came back she was a much harder, more rigid version of herself. That sort of pain can change someone forever. They didn't do another cycle.

Sixteen minutes after Fiona slipped the roster under the library door, her two receptionists were released. Fiona greeted them with comforting embraces. She told the police that she had the telephone number of a journalist, and if they didn't let the girls go home, she would contact the media and expose exactly what was going on inside Cavengreen. In the end, Detective Raj reluctantly agreed to let the girls leave, but their departure was a strictly confidential exchange to placate an irate Fiona. They left at noon, just before everyone would start causing a fuss about wanting lunch. It all happened very fast. The girls were bundled into the back of a police car and asked to duck down as they passed through the gates, so as not to be seen. From the entrance of the hotel, we could hear the distant eruption of the media shouting as the police car sped by.

You might be wondering why we didn't try and leave too. I guess it is like how a captain will never leave his sinking ship, not until all the passengers and crew have disembarked. Plus, Detective Raj made it clear that wasn't an option for us.

Detective Raj, after seeing off the two receptionists, snapped at Fiona and me to return to our suites and refrain from meddling. His tone was hostile bordering on vicious. That man had not only reached the end of his tether but had gone way beyond it. His determination to solve this case had made him even more impatient, and when he returned to the library, we could hear him shouting at the remaining suspects.

'If you're not guilty then you should have nothing to be afraid of!' he yelled.

Those twins can give as good as they get. They shouted back just as loudly, telling the detective that they came from a very rich and powerful family, that their lawyer was on his way and that they would sue both the police force and him personally. It was nice to hear someone fight back, even if it was the loathsome twins. They burst out of the library shortly after that, demanding lunch and insisting that housekeeping be sent up to their suite *immediately*.

The bride, too, was released from the library, though she looked anxious and tired. I wondered if I should tell Detective Raj about the conversation I had witnessed between Olive and her mother. I told Fiona what I knew but she advised me to hold on to that information a little longer. And so I did.

That was going to be it for today's chapter, but I have a small update to give you. Helen is in the kitchen cooking bangers and mash for us. We are going to have a late night, reviewing some of the pages she has already transcribed. She has a few questions for me on what I meant here and there. While I was waiting for her, I turned on the 6 pm news. That is not something I always do. Quite often I like to read a book or do my puzzles of an evening, but I saw no point starting a crossword only for Helen to interrupt me. So, the news it was. After a story about the royals and rising petrol prices, the anchor announced something that might be of interest to include in the book. I recorded what she said for Helen to insert here.

The Yorkshire Dales will soon feature in a new documentary set for a global release across multiple streaming platforms. The Lavender Hotel, formally known as Cavengreen Hotel, will take centre stage in the documentary, which will include exclusive interviews with some of the staff and guests who were inside the hotel at the time of the murder of Bruno Tatterson earlier this year. The documentary will be hosted by Dave Cleesey, General Manager of the Sapphires Group, which acquired the hotel shortly before the murder took place. Local journalist Paula McDavidson will also appear, as will the hotel's former concierge, Hector Harrow. [Name omitted by editor] confessed to the crime four days after the murder, and it was announced today that they will face trial on the fourth of next month.

This is just getting ridiculous. The Americans know full well I am *not* featuring in their documentary. There is no convincing me. What I really want to focus on is that trial date, which is less than three weeks away. I'll need to get a move on with this book. I want to get most of it onto the tape before the trial starts, because I am not going to have much time to record once it's all go, go, go. It is my intention to head to the courtroom every day, even the days when I'm not standing as a witness. Have I told you about that yet? Well, yes, I'll be giving evidence at some point, unsurprisingly. The courthouse sent me a very official looking letter telling me I was required by law to appear as a prosecution witness—date to be confirmed. Although that is now confirmed by the news report. I am not looking forward to seeing some of the other witnesses take the stand, but I need to see Bruno's killer punished for what they did—to him, to me, and to everyone else involved.

Helen has just come in with the bangers and mash, so I will sign off for the evening. There is a lit candle in the middle of my mashed potato.

That is something new. I have also just noticed a gift tucked under Helen's arm and a cheeky grin on her face. I am not normally one for birthdays, and seventy-four certainly isn't a milestone, but it is nice that she remembered. It is tomorrow, mind you, and I intend to spend the day like I do every year: alone, thinking about my father.

Tap one. Tap two. Tap three.

CHAPTER

21

Helen bought me a book for my birthday. She knows I am not much of a reader of anything other than murder mysteries, and she didn't want to risk getting me something I have already read, so this one is mostly pictures, or photographs to be exact. It is called *Around Australia* and is a collection of lovely snaps from various photographers. The gift someone chooses to give says a lot about them and even more about what they think of you. Although I am not entirely sure why Helen got this for me, I appreciate it nonetheless. The acknowledgements section thanks her for being the *Commissioning Editor*, so she must have had something to do with it. But I don't believe I have ever mentioned wanting to go to Australia; in fact, I think Helen is aware that, as far as flying goes, I prefer to stay within a two-hour radius of the UK, no further. That rules out such places as Australia, which I have heard is a twenty-four-hour journey. How people avoid a blood clot on those long-haul flights is beyond me. And I am sure the price of the fare is through the roof. And that is just for economy. Anything else would be too flash for me, even if I could afford it.

Some of the places in the book look very nice, but it's not my sort of landscape. I prefer rolling hills and big lakes, and Australia is very beachy with big patches of dusty red in between. Tasmania looks more my thing, but I wouldn't go that far to see a place that looks quite like the Lake District. Come to think of it, I remember Helen visiting Australia a few years back, not long after Josie's funeral. It's hard to keep up with all the places she's been. The stamps on her passport would be inked in like sardines. She used to go for work trips all the time, finding new authors and this and that. Always went alone, as far as I know. I daren't ask if she went with her ex-partner. Not after the other night. It wasn't on tape, but I probed her on her relationship—a touchy subject, I know—and she got very snappy with me when I asked if she still kept in touch with him, shouting, 'Absolutely not!'

Sorry, Helen, but you practically bit my head off. I'm not one to take offence, though, so don't worry about me. He must have been rotten to you. I won't ask you any more about him; I don't need to be told twice. Perhaps you gave me the book because you're thinking about going back to Australia and you're subtly trying to convince me that I want to go too, so that I'll visit you.

Helen is always saying she would love to go and live overseas soon.

Don't be going that far, Helen! Even if I make a bob or two from the book, you won't catch me flying twenty-four hours to Australia. Anywhere a bit closer to home and I'll be there to visit you at the drop of a hat.

You might recall me saying yesterday that I always spend my birthdays alone, thinking about my father.

Tap one. Tap two. Tap three.

I can't help that. He ruined birthdays for me. It's all bad memories and intrusive thoughts. The first time he gave me a hiding was on my birthday, like turning eight suddenly made it acceptable. Don't think he always marked my annual milestone like that, as if it was some kind of ritual, because he didn't. But he did make every birthday miserable. He didn't believe in presents. My mother used to hide little gifts wrapped in tinfoil or baking paper behind the bedhead. When my father nipped out to get the paper or more alcohol, we would sit on her bed with my sister and unwrap them. Those are some of my happier memories. It would just be silly stuff, like a wrapped-up onion or chalk, but she loved seeing the look on my face when I got to experience something normal. As soon as my father got home, we would scramble to hide everything and get out of his and my mother's bedroom.

My father made a special effort not to speak to me on my birthday, maybe because it reminded him that he never wanted to be a father. He was much the same with my sister, except that, as far as I know, he didn't lay a hand on her. Josie surely would have told me if he did, and when I asked her again on her deathbed, she still said he never had.

I haven't told you much about Josie, have I? I loved her so much. She was much better at school than I was and used to take part in every extracurricular activity she could. Mainly because she didn't want to come home, I suspect. When our mother died, she took over all the household duties, but when she turned sixteen she moved out with her boyfriend. Freedom at last. Just like her mother, she ended up marrying a not-very-nice man, only Josie divorced him in the end. Two kids; we speak occasionally but I guess they're busy. I understand that. And then Josie died of breast cancer. It happened so fast. I was there when she slipped away. Helen planned the funeral; I think I mentioned that.

Even though Helen was living down south, she came up every weekend to visit my sister in hospital. Helen understands the pain I feel. That is a bond we will always share.

So, happy birthday to me. Later today I will go by Josie's grave with some purple tulips. When I purchased Josie's plot of land, I knew she would want to be next to our mother. It is just unfortunate that our mother is next to our father. At the same time as purchasing Josie's plot, I organised one for myself next to hers. Her two children spent far too long considering if they want to reserve a spot too, so I just went ahead and locked mine in. One less thing to worry about. I may not be close to many people right now, but I know I will rest with my beloved mother and sister forever.

By gum, I didn't intend for the book to take such a depressing turn, but this is just how I get on my birthday. I keep reminding myself that this birthday is different. I am writing, or narrating, a book. Fancy that. It wasn't exactly a birthday wish of mine to be involved in a murder investigation and then write a book about it, but the unexpected twist in my life has brought with it something different to break up the monotony. Not that I want to be disrespectful. I would much rather Bruno was alive than have my name on the cover of a book. On that note, let's get back the story.

Fiona and I went to Lavender Plates to ask the chefs what they could offer the guests for lunch. It turned out Fred and Ellie had brought in some bread rolls and enough ingredients to make a huge pot of pasta. Fred said the other police officers weren't best pleased with them for helping us out. For some reason, the police were acting like we were the enemy and needed to be punished. It was nice having Fred and Ellie around to dilute their us-versus-them mentality.

Fiona donned a hairnet and apron and was straight in the kitchen asking how she could help. It was her job to divvy up the portions. Fred took me to one side and asked if I had heard anything that I wanted to report. Lying to him felt terrible, but I wasn't ready to bring the police in just yet. Fred told me that Detective Raj had been ordered to let everyone go home tomorrow, regardless of whether the case was solved or not. Apparently, the police had been inundated with legal letters from the guests' lawyers. Why they weren't letting us go then and there is beyond me, but I suppose finding the murder weapon that morning had bought the detective a few more hours. No wonder Detective Raj was so frantic.

Fiona pushed the trolley from room to room and I handed food to the guests. We were both enjoying being back in service. During our rounds, Fiona told me that she missed her husband; that she felt lonely not having him to telephone during all this. She just wanted to hear him say that everything would be okay and there would be a nice roast dinner waiting for her when she got home. That is a familiar feeling: not having someone to share things with, whether happy or sad. I told her that she always had me, but I knew it wasn't the same.

The groomsmen didn't want their pasta. One didn't eat carbs and the other was gluten-free. A huge waft of stale air escaped when they opened the door to their suite. From what I could tell, they had spent the last three nights draining their minibar and watching movies on the loudest volume. One of them was doing sit-ups on the floor. The other closed the door in our faces with a rude grunt.

'More for us,' Fiona said with a smile.

We took the lift upstairs and started at the far end of the corridor: the bridal suite. I raised my hand to knock on the door, but Fiona quickly ushered me aside. She put her finger to her lips and then we each pressed an ear against the door. I am not normally one for snooping, but Olive was someone to whom we had to pay special attention. She and her husband were arguing.

'What the fuck, Olive?' Patrick shouted at his bride. 'You've made things so much worse. We could have just explained what happened and it would have been fine. Now you look guilty!'

'Keep your voice down!' Olive yelled back. 'I panicked. I had to get rid of it. You know I had to do it—for Mum.'

'I need to speak to her,' Patrick said.

The suite's door swung open abruptly and me and Fiona smiled like we had heard nothing.

'Pasta?' Fiona offered.

'Just leave it on the side.' Patrick gestured for us to enter. 'Actually, let me take it.' He snatched the bowls from our hands, a blob of bolognaise sauce almost spilling over the rim.

I caught a glimpse of Olive. She had black make-up smeared down her cheeks, and her eyes were red. As soon as she saw me looking, she walked away into the bedroom. Their suite was unusually tidy, I noticed—like housekeeping had been, except the hotel was not offering this service at the time.

Patrick stormed off down the corridor, presumably to speak to his new mother-in-law. We desperately wanted to follow but couldn't risk being caught nosying. Patrick was angry, that much was obvious. My mind immediately went to the murder weapon. Could that be what he and Olive were talking about?

We finished delivering the food and Fiona went to her room for a rest. I returned to my own suite to find Mr Potts in the bathtub, bubbles and all. He was slurping wine from an overfilled glass and seemed to be in an uncharacteristically good mood. He told me that his wife had convinced him to change his outlook and that he had decided to embrace the experience. It was quite the shift in attitude.

Clearly the change in mood meant instead of seeking solace in alcohol, he was now celebrating with it. I filled him in on everything that had happened since the morning, which felt like a lot. I told him how the two receptionists had been sent home and suggested that, if he pushed hard enough, then I was sure he would be allowed to leave too.

'I think I will wait this thing out,' he said. 'No point leaving before the finale.'

It was an odd thing to say, that much was obvious. But I am not one to judge, because I stayed too. Only, I did it because of my dedication to Cavengreen. I knew I was on to something with Olive. My gut told me to stay. Plus, I had no one to go home to. Everyone I cared about was in that hotel.

Except you, Helen, of course.

Meanwhile, Mr Potts had been drowning his sorrows the whole time and calling his wife. So, yes, it immediately struck me as strange that he wanted to stay. Stronger alarm bells should have been ringing about what he could have been planning, but I was too distracted.

I told Mr Potts what we'd overheard outside Olive's room. Rightly so, he said they could have been talking about anything. But when this exchange was set alongside the conversation in the garden, it was as clear as day to me that both Olive and her mother were involved in the case somehow. It was time to tell Detective Raj what I knew.

CHAPTER

22

Mr Potts and I waited in the lobby for Fred to fetch Detective Raj. He appeared from the hallway eating a sandwich. A smudge of mayonnaise sat on his upper lip. It was distracting, but we weren't on good enough terms for me to embarrass him by pointing it out, so I spent the whole conversation trying not to look at it.

'Just the fellas I wanted to see. Where's the third musketeer?' Detective Raj laughed. We ignored his question and his snigger trailed off into a sigh. 'Come to my office.'

We followed him to Mr Potts's office. I have entered it many times before, but on this day it felt unfamiliar. Mr Potts's office was not really Mr Potts's office anymore and, as it happened, it never would be again. Pinned to the wall was a large sheet of paper covered in all sorts of scribbles with various names, including my own, crossed out. Seeing that was a big relief. A few names were circled: Mr Potts, the twins, American Dave, the groomsmen, and Fiona among them.

Detective Raj made us sit with our backs to the wall so we couldn't study the list for too long. He offered us tea and sandwiches from a platter that had obviously been delivered by an outside catering company. We both accepted and thanked him. Then Detective Raj paced up and down behind the desk without speaking while Mr Potts and I exchanged confused glances.

'Here you go, boss.' Tyrone the pit bull entered the room and handed Detective Raj a newspaper. He left, flashing his sharp-toothed grin on the way out. Detective Raj studied the paper for a couple of seconds and then took a long inhale.

'What do you call this?' he asked, slamming the newspaper down on the desk. It was a copy of the *Yorkshire Sun*. The headline read HOTEL OF HORRORS.

'Read this bit out loud,' Detective Raj said sternly.

I put my sandwich down and leant forward to see the paper more clearly as Mr Potts began to read.

'*Cavengreen guests and staff kept prisoner until cold-blooded murderer found,*' the article began.

I was glad Mr Potts had taken it upon himself to do the reading, as I knew I would be unable to do so without stuttering.

'And what's that?' Detective Raj indicated a different part of the page.

It was a photograph of me, Fiona and Mr Potts in the window of the attic. Neither of us answered Detective Raj's question.

'Tell me what you were doing up there,' the detective said. 'And how did you access it?'

'We went up there to get some respite,' Mr Potts informed him. 'And the staircase is behind a door on the first floor marked *Staff Only*. It's hardly hidden. I'm surprised you've not been up there yourselves. No wonder you've got nowhere in this investigation.'

I remember gulping nervously, then reminding myself that there was nothing to be nervous about. The big red line through my name proved that.

Detective Raj summoned Tyrone back into the room. The two of them huddled in the corner, whispering. I could feel anger building up inside me at the police's incompetence, which was stopping everyone from getting to go home. By the time Detective Raj had sent Tyrone off to find the not-so-secret staircase, my cheeks were hot with rage, which in my childhood had signalled I was about to stammer. Except at that moment, the words came easily.

'When will this bleedin' nightmare be over?!' I shouted. My breathing was loud, my chest rising and falling. My top teeth sank into my bottom lip, just as my father's used to do.

Tap one. Tap two. Tap three.

'Calm yourself, Mr Harrow.' Detective Raj leant forward, gripping the edge of the desk with both hands and looming over me, trying to establish his dominance. But instead of finding him threatening and powerful, I saw him as weak and scared. The man in front of me was crumbling, unable to do his job properly and losing control. My temper might have got the better of me, but Detective Raj was in a much worse fix.

'Why should I?' I spat back at him. 'This whole investigation has been a joke since day one. Someone died here, Detective! And you have the murderer at your fingertips but not the competence to find them. How about the bride? How closely have you looked into her?'

'The bride was with her husband the whole time.' Detective Raj folded his arms and turned to look out the window so I couldn't see his face.

'Says who? She and her husband? Because all we know is that they were together at half past eleven and again at two am. And, oh yes, that she and her mother have been having some intense three am conversations in the gardens. But that's what all innocent people do, isn't it, Detective?'

'You're just mentioning this now?' Detective Raj rubbed his temples in frustration. I had planned to tell him more about what I had overheard, but after he made me so angry I didn't feel like helping his cause. 'But Olive's husband places her in bed, asleep, at the time we suspect the murder took place.'

'A husband will lie to protect his wife, Detective.'

Detective Raj turned to me with a pensive look on his face. He called for Fred and ordered him to fetch Olive and Patrick and escort them to Lavender Plates. It was time to get forensics to take a closer look at their suite.

By 2 pm, the hotel bridal suite was completely taped off. The other guests peered out from their doors, gossiping about what could be going on. Olive and Patrick were silent and solemn as they followed Fred down the corridor, like they were walking to their own execution. The bride reached for her husband's hand, but he pulled away. Everybody saw it. Patrick's groomsmen walked on either side of their friend, leaving Olive to continue down the hallway alone. Her mother cried as she watched them descend the stairs into the lobby. To all of us, this felt final. It felt like the police might be on to something. And as you know from my storytelling, there is only one more night in the hotel left to go until someone confesses.

CHAPTER

23

Unfortunately, I was not privy to what happened when forensics swept the bridal suite. Nor could I tell you what sort of conversations were had in Lavender Plates while the married couple and groomsmen waited there. I imagine that there was a lot of tension and probably not a lot of truth-telling. Myself, Fiona and Mr Potts lingered in the lobby, watching a steady flow of police and forensics officers march up and down the stairs like worker ants. Fred was acting coy with me. He didn't pass on any information, either because he didn't know anything, or because what he did know was too grim to share. I tried to gauge which it was from his face, but his expression gave nothing away.

Sensing that our time in the hotel might be coming to an end, Fiona, Mr Potts, and I started tidying up the lobby. We needed something to keep us busy. There was rubbish everywhere and both the reception and concierge desks needed a good wipe down. We got bin bags out of the cupboard and Mr Potts filled them up while

I polished. Fiona logged in to her computer to start issuing refunds to the guests. It felt good to wipe away some of the chaos, and I could tell Fiona was feeling a little more relaxed too as she worked her way through some of her admin tasks.

I took the vase from the centre table to Hugo's to give it a rinse in the sink. The lights were dimmed, as always, and it wasn't until I'd finished rinsing the vase and turned around that I noticed the shadowy outline of a cowboy hat in the back corner of the bar. His head was tilted down and he slowly rotated a whisky glass in his hand. The door was just a couple of metres away, but he uttered a soft 'howdy' before I could make it out into the corridor. A conversation with American Dave was not something I was in the mood for, so I found myself politely saying a 'howdy' back and then taking a few more steps towards the door.

'You know,' American Dave began, his voice still low, 'I kind of hoped you were the murderer. It would have made you more exciting.'

'Sorry to disappoint,' I told him, although I really should not have bothered engaging with such a fool.

'But now, I bet you're going to come out of this looking like the hero. And who am I to you? The big bad American villain who cheats on his wife and doesn't care.' He drained the last few drops of whisky from his glass.

I didn't know how to respond. I was no hero, and he was no villain. I was just a man who tried to do good things, and he was a man who didn't care if he did bad things.

'My wife is going to hear about this somehow, isn't she?'

'Secrets never stay secret for long,' I told him.

He sucked at his top teeth. 'You know, Hector, I'm not really a cowboy,' American Dave said. I thought this might be the start of a monologue about why I should feel sorry for him. Turns out, it wasn't.

He rose to his feet and took a few steps towards me. 'I am a cow*man*. And you'd better stay out of my fucking way.'

He pushed me lightly in the centre of my chest, just enough to make me stumble backwards. It was a coward's move.

'*I'm* going to be the hero of this story,' he said. 'I'm going to solve the case. I'm going to be famous all over the world.'

He threw his whisky glass towards the counter; it skidded across the bar and smashed on the floor behind. He wiped his mouth on his sleeve and then left. He was about as unpleasant a man as they get. But he had achieved one thing: he had further fuelled that fire in me to solve this case before he could.

Back in the lobby, I had an idea. Fiona was still tap-tapping away on her computer. She was focused on the screen, but this couldn't wait. I asked her to pull up Alec's reservation. As I have told you, after anyone made a booking at Cavengreen, I would always telephone them to gather additional information. As soon as I hung up, I made sure to tell one of the girls behind reception what the guest had told me, and they would add it to their file. I figured there could be something in Alec's file that might help us work out the password to his laptop. It was a long shot, but it was all I had.

Fiona did as I requested. She printed out everything on Alec's record and then we went through it together, highlighting key points in yellow. There was plenty to work from and it couldn't wait. With Mr Potts, we headed back to suite two to start punching words into the laptop. We had his address, so we tried the words *Paisley* and *Glasgow*. Neither of those worked. We tried his birthdate in different combinations. Mr Potts worked out what day of the week Alec had been born, so we tried *Monday*. Working our way down the printout, we tried his favourite food, *scallops*, and then *fishing*, *whisky* and *pottery*. Still nothing.

At the bottom of the page was a section for extra details. I'd ask the guests questions about their family or if they were celebrating any special occasion, and we would use this information to personalise their check-in experience. There was a note with Alec's children's names, Joseph and Hailey. Of course. My heart thumped. It felt like the key. First, we tried *Joseph*. Denied. Then we tried *Hailey*. Denied. Then we tried *JosephHailey*. A spinning coloured wheel appeared on the screen. I had no idea what it meant but Mr Potts pumped his fist in the air and Fiona shouted, 'Yes!' We were in.

The screen opened on a white page full of type. There were all sorts of dot points and unfinished sentences, about twelve pages' worth. Fiona elbowed Mr Potts aside and sat in front of the screen, declaring herself a fast reader.

'There are a few bits about you in here, Hector,' Fiona said. 'He describes what you look like and then labels you a "kind man".'

Fiona continued scrolling down the page, sighing when she didn't find anything of use.

Then she cried, 'Aha!' and moved her head closer to the screen. There was a whole paragraph about a bride and her mother having an argument in a garden. Fiona read it aloud, and while I can't remember the exact wording, it was an exchange between two women about an affair one of them was having. It wasn't clear who was the guilty party, however. At one point the bride said, 'He'd better not spoil my wedding,' and her mother replied, 'Don't worry, darling—I won't let him.'

Surely it couldn't just be a coincidence!

There was more, though. In the scene Alec recounted, the mother decided to go and speak to the man, to persuade him not to reveal the affair. She argued with her daughter over whether that was the right thing to do. The discussion became quite heated, with the bride telling her mother to just leave her alone and the mother apologising as her daughter ran away.

If what we were reading was based on events at Cavengreen, which, since Alec told me he was writing about people in the hotel, I believed it was, then we could narrow the killer down to one of just two people: the bride or her mother. One of them was having an affair with Bruno, and one of them committed the murder to prevent him from ruining the wedding.

The scene ended there. Mr Potts poured a drink, while Fiona sat at the end of the bed, recapping what we had read and piecing it together with what we had overheard ourselves. It all fit together so neatly. Bruno was killed because he was going to expose an affair. But who was the murderer?

Laptops, gadgets, and the like are not really my thing. I don't trust them. I keep all my bills and important documents in a locked cupboard, and I use my puzzle book or a good murder mystery for entertainment rather than those video games that the kids are hooked on. Nevertheless, I had a go and clicked just off to the side of the page we were looking at, which made the screen behind it pop in front. It was the *Yorkshire Sun*, but an online version. I had no idea that they had gone on the web. Not that I will be switching from paper to screen anytime soon. Although, saying that, it was a lot easier for me to read the words in the larger font on the laptop. Normally it takes me quite some time to read the articles in the paper.

Mr Potts leant over me and hit a button that refreshed the page. He used that word: 'refresh'. A new selection of articles popped up. At this, Mr Potts panicked suddenly and slammed down the lid of the laptop. He picked it up and insisted that we should go and tell Detective Raj what we knew without delay. Fiona marched towards him. It was clear that there was something on there that Mr Potts didn't want us to see. Of course, that meant we had to see it.

'Give it here, you silly man,' Fiona demanded.

Mr Potts dodged from side to side, as Fiona snatched at the laptop. She was able to grab it, and there was a bit of a tug of war, but Fiona eventually managed to wrest it from his grasp, with a heave that made Mr Potts overbalance and tumble to the floor.

Fiona raced into the bathroom and I followed. We locked ourselves inside as Mr Potts hammered on the door. We punched the password in again and clicked on the headline article. There was a video. Fiona pressed play.

There was a lot of movement, and the view wasn't great, but I recognised my green uniform immediately. And then I recognised the room. It was Mr Potts's office. I heard myself shout, 'This whole investigation has been a joke since day one.' It was a video of my exchange with Detective Raj from only a couple of hours earlier. I looked angrier, more like my father, than I had remembered being. My face was red, my jaw tense and my fists clenched, just like his used to be. I was shocked at the sight of myself.

Whoever had made the video had a perfect view of me, as if they were sitting right by my side. Every so often a finger or smidge of jacket covered the screen. It was clearly filmed by someone who didn't want to get caught. Someone sitting right next to me. And that person could only have been Mr Potts, also known as the man who sold out his friend for a bit of fast money.

There is no point hanging on to ill feelings; I am not like that. Mr Potts did what he felt he had to do in that moment, for reasons I am sure I will never understand. But just because you don't understand someone's actions, doesn't make them wrong. Personally, I am not motivated by money, but then again, I only have myself to spend it on.

One day I hope to visit him and ask questions about a few things he did over those four days, not just about the video.

Now, those are my feelings about the situation *today*. But let me tell you, when me and Fiona first realised what was going on, we were not so forgiving.

'You drunken idiot!' Fiona shouted when she stormed out from the bathroom.

Mr Potts was sitting on the end of the bed with his hands supporting his slumped head. I am not sure if it was the shame or the alcohol that made him look so pathetic, but for a second I pitied him. Fiona, on the other hand, walloped him across the back of the head with one of the bed cushions and demanded he explain himself.

It wasn't much of an explanation. At first, he claimed it wasn't him, but he quickly backtracked when he realised how stupid that sounded. Then he offered to split the money from the newspaper with us. The cheek of it! I wasn't going to give up my morals for a measly few thousand pounds. And any interest Fiona might have had in the money beforehand had gone out the window. She made it clear that even if she needed the money desperately, she would never betray her friends.

I felt sick to my stomach. Mr Potts had been my comrade throughout the whole ordeal. I trusted him. I thought we were a team. Clearly the friendship I thought we had meant nothing to him.

Mr Potts scooped up the few belongings that he had. He told us he was going to ask Detective Raj if he could leave. A single tear dripped from his eye as he apologised. He said he wished he had never done it. But judging by the sound of a fist banging on the door to our suite, the damage had already been done.

'Hector Harrow, you get out here RIGHT NOW!' the bride shouted.

CHAPTER 24

Helen has been thinking about the trial date and says the publisher wants the book ready to go by the time the jury give their verdict. She said that would be best from a marketing perspective, and I suppose that makes sense. I'd better shake a leg then. Especially now that I've been prepped to be a witness. I met with the prosecution team yesterday; didn't think it appropriate to take the old dictaphone along. First up, they reckon I'll be. We went through what they'd ask me and potential questions the defence team might throw my way during the cross-examination. It's a lot more rehearsed than I would have imagined. I've got the list of questions here, and notes for my responses. Like a script.

I telephoned Helen after the session. She's not best pleased that I've been called as a witness, mind you. It means that I can't watch the trial until after I've done my bit in the stand, and even after I've given my testimony I have to get the judge's permission before I can return to the viewing gallery. And that permission might not be granted. It is all such a kerfuffle, but there's not much that can be done about it. Best not to think about all that right now though, eh?

Fiona knows I am not a birthday person, which is why she dropped round a belated 'just because' lemon tart this morning on her way to work. It is always nice to see her, although now I am worried that she is not being treated well by American Dave. Fiona told me that he plans to hang around until after the trial has finished. That could be months! She says he is making her life a living hell, bossing her around and insisting she perform menial tasks like making him coffee and tidying his desk. He's redecorated Mr Potts's old office. Fiona laughed when she told me how he has nailed a hook to the wall just for his cowboy hat and put up photos of himself riding a horse in just his jeans, no shirt. A topless cowboy is not quite the look that Cavengreen used to go for, but I suppose it is The Lavender now.

A lot has changed at Cavengreen since it traded hands, and now that American Dave is in town, Fiona said the hotel has turned into a film set. All staff were sent an email saying if they weren't happy to give their permission to appear in the background shots of his documentary then they had to stay home and miss their shifts. Fiona can't afford not to work, so she has resorted to dodging the cameras as much as she can. The producer has been badgering her for an interview, which she has been avoiding like the plague. But I am not sure how much longer she will be able to get away with that. I advised her to do the interview but make herself seem so incredibly boring, with short, vague answers, that they can't use it. She is not a woman you can dull down easily, but when she left here she was quite giddy about her potential acting role.

But back to talking about Cavengreen, not The Lavender. You will remember me describing how the bride was hammering on the door.

Mr Potts opened it, with Fiona quickly snatching his telephone from his hand before he could take any more secret videos.

Olive stood there, arms folded, tapping one foot impatiently. She looked tired. Her mother was by her side, seething with rage. Their husbands had accompanied them, but seemed content to remain in the background. The twins and groomsmen, all dressed in Cavengreen robes and carrying glasses of champagne, rounded out the party. It was quite the ambush.

Mr Potts snatched his phone back from Fiona and slipped through the crowd and out of sight. I squinted to see if I could see him filming from the back of the group, but it seemed he had learnt his lesson.

'You made it look like I'm the murderer!' the bride shouted, her voice shaky and face tense. She looked like she was holding back tears.

'My daughter did not kill anyone!' her mother added.

'You're a liar!' the twins joined in. 'You're probably trying to cover up your own actions.'

Fiona looked at me. This was a battle I had to fight myself, and she knew that. I took a deep breath. I explained how I had overheard Olive and her mother Sue arguing the previous night, that Olive had claimed she didn't do it, but that her mother had sounded unconvinced. I watched the faces of their husbands change when I mentioned the note on Alec's computer. This was the first they were hearing about it.

'You were sleeping with the dead guy?' the bride's stepfather shouted at his wife.

'No—I swear I wasn't,' Sue replied.

'Then what? Olive was?'

'This is nothing to do with me,' Olive interjected.

'Then what is this old man talking about?' Patrick demanded.

'He's lying!' Olive answered defensively.

'Yes! The old man is lying!' piped up one of the twins—Oksana, I think. 'He's the murderer and he's making up stories to frame you.'

'How do you explain the women's shoes in the maze with the murder weapon then?' Fiona interjected.

'He planted them there to throw the police off,' the other twin said dismissively.

The conversation went round in another circle or two. Each husband quizzed his wife on the bomb I had just dropped. The other guests began to poke their heads out of their suites to see what all the fuss was about. One of them used his camera telephone to film the argument, the footage ultimately ending up on the news.

[Editor's note: The following content has been inserted during editing and was recorded out of sequence.]

Hector here. But you know that. Helen suggested we revisit this part of the book. She said it would make a great scene if we went back and found the footage that ended up on the news. She's here now, laptop open and all. She picked up some raspberry cheesecakes from Maude's Bakery on her way over. I can't say I would normally opt for a cheesecake but this one looks delightful. First bite. Yes, delicious. Thank you, Helen.

Right, Helen tells me this website she is on stores videos from all around the world. Somehow, she has managed to find the footage of the argument in the hallway. I haven't seen it since it was on the news, and even then, I half-hid behind a pillow, not wanting to relive the moment. Now that the dust has sort of settled, I will watch it again, for the sake of the book. The video is titled 'Posh people gone wild after

Cavengreen Hotel murder'. I am sure they aren't referring to me with the word 'posh'.

Right, I'm ready, Helen. Should I talk over the video, or should we watch it first and then I'll make my comments? Okay, I'll tell you when to pause. It looks like it's only a twenty-second clip anyway. Press play.

[The video plays.]

Right, pause. See there, you can tell from the angle that it was filmed from the door of one of the suites. They got a good view, mind you. That's Patrick you can see. Do you hear how he is yelling at Olive? Because they're all shouting over each other, it is hard to make out what they're saying. Then that is Olive's stepfather, there, and her mother Sue. I remember he was telling her off about the affair. That was the most I heard him speak the whole lockdown. Press play again.

[The video plays.]

Pause here. Those two gormless puppies there, those are the groomsmen. They're just standing to the side watching things unfold. And those two girls are the twins. That one is Ruby, and that's Oksana. Press play.

[The video plays.]

Pause. We just saw Patrick grab Olive by the arm. It was a bit rough, wasn't it? Much more so than I remember. Then again, there was a lot going on. He's started dragging her down the hallway, in the direction of the camera. He hasn't seen the camera yet, but from what I remember, he will in a second. Press play.

[The video plays.]

Pause. See how close they are to the camera? The man filming was obviously trying to hide it; you can see his hand smudge across the lens a few times. The sound is a bit muffled, but you can just about hear Patrick demanding—quite aggressively, I must say—that Olive tell him the truth. He is looking intently into her eyes, one hand gripping each of her shoulders so she can't get away.

In the background, you can see the twins moving in and out of the shot, trying to get a better view of Olive and Patrick. Nosy parkers. If you look closely, you can see they're smirking. Rotten, the pair of them! Press play.

[The video plays.]

And that's it. Not long, was it? In the end, Patrick spots the camera and lashes out at it, his face filled with anger. The video ends on a freezeframe of his hand, complete with a shiny new gold wedding band, about to snatch the telephone from its owner.

Thank you for that, Helen. You can insert this bit in just before Fred appears saying he'd been looking everywhere for us.

[Editor's note: End of out-of-sequence scene.]

'There you all are,' Fred puffed, his cheeks red. 'I've been looking everywhere for you. I turn my back for one second and you're all out of Lavender Plates like the clappers.' He smiled, completely oblivious to what was going on. 'What's everyone doing up here?'

The argument erupted again as everyone spoke over each other, trying to explain what was going on and whose fault it was.

Fred looked stunned, to say the least. He glanced over at me, and I shrugged, not knowing how to begin to describe the situation. Turns out, I didn't need to. Detective Raj came storming down the corridor, four police officers marching behind him.

'QUIET!' he ordered.

One of the officers accompanied this demand with a loud whistle, one of those ones you make with your fingers in your mouth. I have never quite figured out how that is done. Nevertheless, it worked. Everyone stopped shouting.

'Library,' Detective Raj barked. 'All of you. NOW!'

The atmosphere in the library was tense. Fiona and I sat in the window seat. That was our territory. The husbands both sat in silence on one settee, while their wives whispered to each other in the corner of the room. The twins were glued to their phones, their fingers frantically tapping the screens. The two groomsmen, meanwhile, were sniggering by the bookshelves.

Detective Raj paced back and forth, his hands thrust into his trouser pockets, glaring from the window seat to the sofa to the corner to the bookshelf. 'I don't know what that commotion was all about, but you're going to tell me—no lies, no cover-ups, no evasions. You first, Harrow.'

So, I told him what was on Alec's laptop, about the conversation on the terrace between Olive and her mother, and the fight I'd overheard between Olive and her husband. The detective wasn't impressed. I had discovered more about this murder case in one day than he had in three. He threatened to have me arrested for withholding evidence, but I assured him that Alec's laptop had only become evidence about half an hour earlier, when we'd managed to crack the password. That shut him right up.

Fiona's version of events was the same as mine, but things took a turn when he asked the others to give their account. In fact, the twins kept saying 'no comment' to every question, even if it wasn't directed at them. As soon as they'd done that a couple of times, everyone else followed suit. Detective Raj clicked his neck from side to side in frustration. No one was going to talk. And it was my word versus the rest of the room.

We had reached a stalemate when there was a rap on the library door.

'Enter!' Detective Raj snapped.

The door opened and a man with a briefcase walked in. His name was Leon Black, he informed us, and he was the twins' lawyer. He thanked the detective for giving him the clearance to enter. Detective Raj replied that after the threats he received from Leon's employer, they didn't give him much choice. Leon looked very young. My guess is that their family's regular lawyer was unavailable, so the firm had sent this guy instead. He had a flop of brown hair and bushy eyebrows. His teeth were crooked and his belt struggled to contain his belly. He was already flustered, sweaty, red, and wide-eyed when he entered. I could tell he was out of his depth.

He pulled Detective Raj to one side and they had a muttered conversation, Leon umming and ahhing every so often. I heard the lawyer ask if detaining guests in the hotel would be classed as 'normal protocol' or not. By that point we were all aware that there was nothing normal about the situation. Detective Raj instructed Leon to take a seat.

As if we didn't have enough egos in the room, American Dave chose that moment to barge in. He wanted to know what was going on; in his words, it was his hotel and therefore he needed to be across everything. He looked most put out on spotting me among those present, clearly miffed that I was involved and he wasn't. I would have gladly given my place to him. I was being dragged into this ruckus from all directions, when all I wanted to do was help find out who the murderer was so I could go home, have a brew, and get into bed with a puzzle. Yet there I was.

Never in my life has anyone been jealous of me. I mean, why would they be? What is there to be jealous of? I live a simple life. But American Dave has always had a bee in his bonnet about me, because I was on the inside of the investigation and he was left on the sidelines. I tell you where I would rather be and that's nowhere near the action. I'd rather have been ten thousand miles away. American Dave would have loved to have been the one to find the body.

Tap one. Tap two. Tap three.

He wouldn't even be scarred by that memory; he would probably use it as an anecdote to pick up women in one of his cowboy bars.

American Dave elbowed his way onto the sofa, taking the position next to Leon the lawyer. They shook hands. Then everyone looked towards Detective Raj as if he were teaching a class.

'Does anyone want to confess so we can all go home?' Detective Raj wearily drawled.

'No comment,' the twins replied in unison.

Even their lawyer looked embarrassed at this. Glances were exchanged between everyone else in the room. Someone in the group was going to leave in handcuffs very soon.

American Dave took it upon himself to go around the room, staring us all in the eye one by one and asking if we were the murderer. I must have blinked when he asked me because he declared that I looked guilty. This was enough to start the twins yapping on about my supposedly threatening behaviour towards them. Their lawyer pinched the gap between his eyes and raised a hand to shush them. He had only been at the hotel for ten minutes, yet already he seemed more exasperated with the situation than the rest of us.

'Get fucked,' Olive said when American Dave asked her the question.

'We got a live one here, Detective!' he called, pointing at Olive.

Olive slapped his hand away and spat in his face. American Dave wiped the saliva from his cheek and called her a bitch. Olive lurched forward to hit him, her mother grabbing her arm and her husband coming forward to intervene. The situation was deteriorating, fast.

Olive sobbed into her husband's chest, seemingly ashamed of what she had done. I can't imagine she had ever spat in someone's face before. I am not trying to defend her, but that hotel was a pressure cooker, and as I have admitted to you, at times even I acted in a way I am not proud of. Besides, I was quietly pleased that someone had put American Dave in his place.

American Dave demanded Olive be charged with assault, but Detective Raj only rolled his eyes. He said that he hadn't seen what happened, and everyone else in the room nodded their agreement. For the record, the twins' lawyer didn't nod, but he genuinely hadn't seen, as he'd been staring at the floor in despair. American Dave tried to hire him to sue Olive, but Leon declined, claiming it would be a conflict of interest.

Meanwhile, time was creeping on. It was 11 pm; by midnight the murderer would declare themselves. So, I think I will pause here. For dramatic effect. By all means, go to sleep, make some lunch, whatever it is that you need to do. I will see you back here soon.

CHAPTER

25

For those of you who moved straight from the last chapter, I am glad that you are still interested in what I am saying. I do worry. I know I waffle and ramble; it is the only way I can get the story out. It is down to Helen to tidy it up, but then again, I have told her to leave it as close to my original words as possible. I am still hoping that the final version of the book, the one that you're reading, is a little less all over the shop than what is on this dictaphone. Perhaps I will release the audio tapes one day. If the book sells well and people are interested, that is. Helen says that would be called an audiobook. I have made a note here to record one of the editing sessions with Helen, if she'll let me. She hasn't been too keen in the past. That way, you can hear, see, whatever, for yourselves just how that process works.

But I am sure you are not interested in that right now. You are here because you want to know who the murderer is. It is time for the big reveal. I am not sure if it is a good or bad thing if you guessed it right. I mean, there were clues along the way, so those of you who got it right did well to pick up on those little breadcrumbs. But Helen also said that, for the sake of writing a good book, it can't be *too* obvious who the murderer is, so I've tried to throw you off here and there. Maybe when the book comes out, I will do a bit of a book tour. Then you can all tell me if you guessed right or not. I would like that.

Returning to the hotel. As you can imagine, by this point everyone was growing tired. American Dave was going on and on about how the murderer needed to confess. His tactic was wasted on this lot. In *Cluedo*, you don't see one player simply shouting in the others' faces until someone owns up to being the killer. This was much the same. We had most of the pieces of the puzzle. The crime was committed with a knife, in suite seven. We just needed the who.

As it turned out, the forensics team had already decided the who for us. A sweaty man in one of those plasticky suits entered the library. He gestured to Detective Raj to join him out in the lobby. They must have found something in the bridal suite. Patrick placed his arm around his wife, pulling her close. Despite everything that had been said, he still wanted to protect her.

Detective Raj re-entered the room, some of the colour having returned to his tired, washed-out face. He stood in front of the fireplace and slowly pulled a set of handcuffs from his back pocket. Two officers stood like guard dogs at the entrance to the library. All eyes were on Detective Raj. He didn't say anything. He just held up the handcuffs, taunting us. And then suddenly he turned his head in the direction of his target.

'Olive Nixon, I am arresting you on suspicion of the murder of Bruno Tatterson. You do not have to say anything, but it may harm your defence if you do not mention when questioned something which you later rely on in court. Anything you do say may be given in evidence.'

Olive was handcuffed. She screamed that she didn't do it. Patrick had to be held back by his groomsmen; there was no rescuing her. Olive cried out for her mother, who looked panicked, as though a million thoughts were racing through her mind. Detective Raj held Olive's forearm and escorted her into the lobby. Olive kept looking back. We all stood at the library entrance and watched her leave. Her mother cupped her hands over her mouth. She kept looking between her husband and her daughter. Her feet edged forward. And then she went for it.

'WAIT!' her mother shouted, hurling herself into the detective's path. 'IT WAS ME! I killed him.' She spoke through tears. Her hands were shaking as she held out her wrists for the handcuffs. Then she lifted one hand to her daughter's cheek and stroked it tenderly. I couldn't hear her words, but I could tell by the movement of her lips that she said, 'I'm sorry.'

'Mum, no,' Olive sobbed.

Detective Raj looked taken aback. His gaze kept shifting from one woman to the other. American Dave laughed and called out, 'Oh, boy,' before opening the globe bar and pouring himself a whisky. He smiled into his glass as he took his first sip. Then he raised his glass to Olive and tilted his cowboy hat down, saying, 'Well played, y'all.'

Detective Raj didn't know what to do, that was obvious. But there had been a confession. He gestured for the two police officers to restrain the hysterical Sue. They used what I would call unnecessary force to drag her away from her daughter. It was painful to watch how she wailed, her heart breaking as she confessed to being the one who killed Bruno, knowing that her life and family would never be the same again. Her husband, Martin, looked on in disbelief.

'How could you?' he asked quietly. Pulling a handkerchief from his pocket, he dabbed his eyes. Sue mouthed, 'I love you,' to him, but he turned his back on her. She called his name as she was handcuffed. She fell to her knees and the police forced her back to her feet. Olive tried to reach her, to help her, but her husband held her back. She buried her face in Patrick's chest again and he stroked the back of her head, watching, gobsmacked, as his mother-in-law was taken away. So there you have it: Sue killed Bruno. I wonder how many of you guessed that.

Blue lights flashed across the front of the hotel. We followed the procession outside and watched the police escort Sue into one of the cars. Her terrified face peered out from the window. Olive broke free of Patrick's hold and ran to the car. Sue placed her palm against the glass, Olive doing the same from the outside. Then the engines started and a convoy of whirring vehicles headed down the driveway. We could hear shouting and see camera flashes from beyond the gates, before they closed again.

Olive sunk to the ground and knelt in the gravel. Patrick crouched down and cradled her. American Dave yelled, 'Yeehaw,' as he tossed his hat up into the air. Classless. Fiona leant her head on my shoulder and linked her arm through mine.

It truly felt like the end of something momentous. The hotel seemed emptier than ever. Some of the other guests and staff started to spill out through the front doors, asking if it was over.

'Go home, everyone!' American Dave shouted gleefully. No one quite trusted him, and they looked towards me and Fiona for confirmation. We nodded; it was indeed time for everyone to go home.

The sound of a car boot slamming drew our attention. It was Mr Potts; God knows where he had crawled out from. He turned back to look at us for a moment and then got in his car. That was the last time I saw him. Later, when I was putting my own retirement notice in, I found his resignation scrawled on a bit of scrap paper on his desk. It was not quite the ending I had hoped for at Cavengreen, but it was definitely time to draw a line under my time at the hotel. Not that I knew it then, but Helen would soon convince me to write this book, and that would take up most of my days.

Sue has been in prison for a couple of months now, ever since that fateful day. As it happens, she has pleaded 'not guilty' to murder. I am sure she has a good lawyer on her side who will put a case forward for lack of evidence. I don't know how they will wriggle their way out of the fact that she confessed, but I am certain they will come up with something; they always do, these lawyer types.

I am not surprised that I have been called as a witness for the prosecution. A lot of the evidence against Sue relies on things I heard and saw. Fiona has been warned that she may be called too, although nothing has been set in stone and she hasn't been prepped to quite the same level as me. A couple of the others from the hotel have also been notified. It's nerve-racking, to say the least. It's just as well I've got this little book project as a distraction, otherwise I'd be in bits thinking about the whole ordeal. Helen is coming over soon to run through some of the last chapters. I will ask her if it is okay to record this editing session and insert it here, so you can get an idea of what we are up to.

Helen: Good afternoon, Hector. Now, I know you don't always fancy a chocolate cake, so I got you a vanilla slice and then I got myself some chocolate mud cake. A bit cheeky, I know, but who am I hurting?

Hector: You're too good to me, Helen. Just quickly, before we get settled . . . Actually, first things first, do you want a brew? Kettle is already boiled.

Helen: Yes, please. Thank you.

[Pause.]

Hector: I was thinking we could record today's editing session and insert it into the book as a little behind-the-scenes for the readers. What do you think?

Helen: I see no harm in that. However, I'm not sure how interesting it will be.

Hector: It is just a bit of extra content.

Helen: Where did you get to with this morning's recording session?

Hector: I finally revealed the murderer.

Helen: Oh, wonderful! I'm sure the readers will be shocked.

Hector: I hope so. I tried to lead them astray, like you told me to.

Helen: That reminds me, I can't make it to the trial with you. I'll be in London that whole week doing the final edits on your book with my old colleagues. We've got to get this on the shelves sharpish.

Hector: That's okay. I'll be sure to take my dictaphone to
the courthouse, and in the breaks I'll record as much as
I can remember about my time on the witness stand. What
happens then? Should we just add those bits into the book at
the last minute?

Helen: Yes, if we have everything else ready to go, then we'll
add the details of the trial in as more of an epilogue.

Hector: What does that mean?

Helen: A section at the end of the book that concludes the story.
It'll be nice to finish by saying something like, 'And Sue
Bainbridge was found guilty and sentenced to x number
of years in prison.' Something like that, just to tie it all
together.

Hector: I see. Yes, that sounds good.

Helen: Okay, let's get started on today's edit. I'm looking at
chapter nineteen, the part where you talk about American
Dave and his mistress going into the maze for a bit of
you-know-what. It is a shame there was no CCTV out there!
. . . Sorry, I shouldn't laugh. I have some questions.

Hector: Ask away.

Helen: Do you think you should add some more colour in
about the gardens? I like your little side story about the
Spanish gardener in chapter twenty. Every book needs a
touch of romance. I can't believe you told the readers that
I was blushing while you were telling that story. I must have
missed you saying that.

Hector: Just trying to give the readers a little insight into you, Helen.

Helen: Well, they'll just think I'm some sad, single old bat.

Hector: Never. Are you blushing again?

Helen: Oh, give over. Let's get back to this. I loved the background about the maze. Did the Spanish lady plant the rose garden too?

Hector: She did. I helped dig the grass up for the beds.

Helen: Let's paint more of a picture here then. The roses were trimmed back to their stems when the murder happened. Let's add that in so people don't have a picture in their mind of some long, beautiful roses. Because that wasn't the case.

Hector: Ah yes, *Botrytis cinerea*. I think that's what the fungus was called.

Helen: I'll make a note to add that in. And then remind me again why there was an iPad with the murder weapon.

Hector: Presumably it was the one Sue used to message me to come to suite seven, so I'd find the body.

Helen: Yep, got it. And then, this part here: I've typed some of this newspaper article out, but I just need to clarify if I should leave the whole part out about the court case or if I should just omit Sue's name.

Hector: Just take out the name, I reckon.

Helen: Okay, done. Now, there's a bit on the tape that I need you to translate for me. When you've been talking for a while, you tend to turn your head away from the dictaphone and your voice drifts. It makes some bits hard to hear. Try to keep the recorder just below your mouth at all times.

Hector: Sorry, Helen. I don't even realise I'm doing it until it's done. And then I can't remember what I've said to repeat it. Can you hear most of it?

Helen: I can hear it; it is just a little faint. Listen.

Hector: First let me turn this off. It probably won't make sense to the readers if we have a transcript of us recording a recording. I'm sure they get the gist by now anyway.

CHAPTER

It is day one of the trial. I am recording this from inside the men's lavatories at the courtroom.

Apologies Helen for the slight echo. Echo. Echo.

The floor and walls are covered in yellow tiles and my voice seems to bounce off them. All the wooden stalls are empty, so there is no one listening. If anyone walks in, I will pause the tape.

I have arrived at the courthouse a bit early—nerves, mostly. I was told to come down here just in case the prosecution needs me as a witness, but it is unlikely they will. Twiddling my darned thumbs is what I'll most probably be doing all day. It would be far more productive for the book if I was allowed into the public gallery. But that's against the rules. Apparently, it is detrimental for me to observe the trial before being questioned as a witness, as I may be influenced by the arguments presented. There are pros and cons to standing as a witness. The only pro I can think of is that it will be useful for the book, these behind-the-scenes insights. Oh, and I suppose if I can help get a murderer locked up then that is a good deed. But the con is that it's far too much pressure. What if I start to stammer? I've got my notes here from my preparation session with the lawyers. Helen kindly typed them up and printed them out for me. I reread them over and over again on the train. The facts are as clear as day in my head but I'm still nervous. I won't be allowed to read off this piece of paper when I'm on the stand, and my brain gets so frazzled when I try and communicate under stress. You and I both know that by now.

None of Sue's family are here yet, as far as I can tell, although I am expecting to see them around the hallways. I have been told that there might be a bit of a delay getting things started while they select the jurors. I have always wanted to do jury duty, but I have never been called for it. Josie was called twice but got out of it once because of the cancer. The first time she sent a man to prison for ten years for smuggling drugs in from Thailand. In noodle packets, I believe it was. To me, jury duty would be something interesting to do. Especially now I am retired, I wouldn't mind doing my public service. I would like to see how it all works. There is no use watching those American courtroom dramas to get an idea. I have heard it's not quite like that.

That reminds me, I am sure American Dave will show up at some point. I'll do my best to avoid him. At least he's not going to be allowed to bring his camera crew in here with him. There have been a couple of complaints to the local council about him turning up in various locations with his camera and filming without permission. There is no need for that. I am sure the council would give him permission to go wherever he likes if he just bothered to ask. Making the village a tourist attraction would be good for the locals, however annoying those of us who don't run businesses would find it. The Cavengreen murder has put the village on the map, so we may as well take advantage of that and get some money flowing through.

I am not in the village today, of course. I took the 6 am train to Leeds, where the trial is being held. This is where the big courts are. I have been here many a time—to the city, that is, not the courts. Normally when I need some new casual clothes. About once a year I take myself to Marks & Spencer to stock up on polo tops and shirts. I usually get the same top in every colour and rotate between them until they get holes under the armpits or a stain that won't budge.

I am in a suit today. It is the same one I wore to my dear Josie's funeral; the only suit I own. Outside of Cavengreen and the odd funeral here and there, I have no use for suits. But it seems appropriate attire for such an occasion. I am going to head back to the courtroom now and see if they are letting people in.

By 'eck, that was a long day. They made me wait around in a poky, windowless witness room until 3 pm, which is when the judge sent the jury home for the day. As expected, they didn't need me. It is now 3.45 pm and I am on the train, heading home. I have the carriage to myself, so I will get all my thoughts out while they are still fresh.

Okay. When I left you, I was in the men's lavatories. I went to see if they were letting people into the courtroom, and they were. At first, I didn't see anyone I recognised, until I spotted Martin, Sue's husband. His wife being locked away and the revelation of her affair had left him gaunt and weary. He looked like he was trying to blend in, opting to wear a very casual grey jumper and jeans, but everyone knew who he was. There were whispers in the hallways identifying him as the husband of the murderer.

Olive was nowhere to be seen. Perhaps she has been told to stay away. Perhaps she is too angry at her mother to attend. I am not sure how I would feel if my mother was on trial for murder.

Disappointed, I suppose. Unless she murdered my father; then perhaps I would be in the front row, cheering and clapping.

Tap one. Tap two. Tap three.

Once everyone had entered the courtroom, I had a quick peek in through the small glass panel on the door. From that glance I got a bit of a sense of what the room was like. All this helps in my mental preparation for having to stand as a witness. Now I can visualise the room, so I can visualise myself in the room. It's just one less thing I have to wonder about.

The courtroom wasn't how I expected it to be. For some reason, I thought it would be huge, with wooden benches and portraits of old judges. But it was modern. The judge sat in the middle, elevated on a platform against the back wall. To the left was the jury box, with big grey seats that had armrests. Less comfy-looking brown seats made up the public gallery, which appeared to be just on the one level, instead of the two that I had envisaged. The lights were bright, unflattering and clinical. The sort of lights that make your eyelids droopy after a while.

There was a witness box off to the right. It was empty, of course, given that I was outside in the corridor and not giving evidence at that moment. There was no sign of Sue, but I imagine she was tucked away out of view.

And that was day one in a nutshell for you. I spent the rest of the day sitting on a vomit-green settee, alone in the witness room, waiting to be called but knowing I wouldn't be. On my way out of the court, I overheard someone on their telephone complaining that it was a boring day that consisted of opening arguments and little else. I can see how this might drag on for a while.

I heard all sorts of accents chatting away as we filed out onto the street. The trial is big news, not just in Yorkshire but all across the UK. You may have heard about it; perhaps that is why you purchased my book. There were locals in the crowd, but I also picked up lots of accents from down south—presumably press wanting to cover the story. Sue is from a wealthy family and the murder happened at one of the country's best hotels, so it is no surprise the story is of interest.

Hopefully I'll have a more exciting day to tell you about tomorrow.

Bleedin' hell, I forgot to take the lamb hotpot out the freezer this morning to defrost for my dinner. Fingers crossed there's some emergency eggs in the fridge when I get home. Goodnight then.

I was going to leave this chapter here, mostly because I have regurgitated everything that I can remember from the trial. Just quickly, though, I have had an update on the book. I am back home now, by the way. Helen telephoned me just after dinner—emergency soft-boiled eggs with dippy soldiers—to run me through a few of the discussions she has been having with the publisher. As it turns out, they quite like what she has presented them with so far. 'Unique, raw, and joyfully imperfect,' they said. Helen wants to send me some of the sample chapters she has written up, but I trust her to transcribe everything as she sees fit. I don't need to relive it again. This entire process has been therapeutic for me, and once all the words are out and the story is complete, I fully intend on parking the memories in that dusty corner of my brain where I keep my father.

Tap one. Tap two. Tap three.

Helen was as patient with me tonight as the desert waiting for rain. She had to talk me through how to get on to my computer and access the email address that I forgot I had. The publisher has created three mock-ups of the cover art for the book and Helen wanted to know my thoughts. Ultimately, the decision will be down to the publisher's marketing team, she said, but my opinion will carry some weight.

The first one was terrible. It was one of those 'Do Not Disturb' signs. Except this one had a bloody hand hovering next to it, with red blobs dripping off a doorknob. The shade of red for the blood was a bit too red-red, if that makes sense.

Helen told me that the second cover was everyone's favourite, and I agree. It is striking and colourful, yet subtle. It would stand out in the window of a bookshop.

And then there was the third one, which I also liked but Helen said was too clichéd. It is a photo from the back of a man wearing a butler's uniform, holding a silver tray with a bloody knife on it out to the side. Although that makes it look like I am the murderer. If you are reading this, then you will know exactly which one was chosen. Hopefully you agree it is the right choice.

Then we ran through title suggestions. The creative team sent through a whole list of options. I will read a couple of them out for you: *The Cavengreen*; *A Deathly Wedding*; *Check In But Don't Check Out*; *Travel Bags to Body Bags* . . . the list goes on. Since the start of this process there has only ever been one title I have wanted for the book. It was Fiona's idea, actually. She said it is my story, and I agree.

I told Helen, 'I don't care what artwork you put on the cover, or what percentage of the sales I get, but this book has to be called *The Concierge*.'

She agreed.

CHAPTER

28

Day two in court. This morning I remembered to take the lamb
hotpot out the freezer, so based on that I reckon it's going to be an
okay kind of day. At least, that's what I'm trying to convince myself.
I suspect I may be called as a witness at some point this morning.

I am starting my day recording a quick introduction in the men's
lavatories, like yesterday. Maybe this will become part of my routine.
I always like a routine. I am wearing yesterday's suit but with a fresh
shirt underneath. And I've swapped to a green tie. One that Fiona says
makes my eyes 'pop', whatever that means. Not out my head, I hope.
I don't need nonsense like that today. If I'm allowed back tomorrow
after giving evidence, I'll opt for more casual attire, like everyone
else. But only a suit will do for an occasion when all eyes are going to
be on me. Gulp. I said 'gulp' for your benefit. That's not something
I normally do to accompany a hard, nervous swallow.

There was already quite the crowd gathered outside the courtroom
when I arrived at eight, though the doors don't open until nine.

Some buzz must have spread since yesterday, and more people have shown up either to have a nosy or to write about the day's events for whatever media outlet employs them. Sue's husband, Martin, was the only person I recognised in the crowd. He spotted me and I caught him looking, but he quickly glanced away. That's okay. We are hardly friends, merely two strangers who will forever be linked by this awfulness. He might feel awkward around me because I know he is standing by his wife through not only a murder trial but an affair too. I am not judging him. Marriages survive worse blips than that. My father used to beat my mother to a pulp, but she would still defend him if she needed to. Loyalty knows no bounds sometimes.

It is time for me to head to the witness room to reread my preparation notes and wait to see if I am called or not.

It is lunchtime, and plenty has happened since I last spoke to you. I have found a cosy cafe serving toasted sandwiches. Ham, cheese and tomato with a bit of mustard, that is what I have gone for. I barely have an appetite but the courthouse covers expenses for food so I thought I may as well order a little something. They also pay for travel expenses and any loss of income incurred by being here. Not that I am currently employed. Train tickets and the odd sarnie aside, I'll be a cheap witness in the court's eyes.

The witness care officer— that's the person who tells you the who, what, where and when of what's going on while you're waiting at the courthouse—let me know that I'll likely be called up after lunch. I'm trying to play it down for you lot, but by gum, I'm nervous. You'll never guess—although maybe you will, the options are few and far between—who waltzed into the witness room this morning while I was making a brew and browsing the rather bleak selection of biscuits.

None other than Mr Potts. The room is only about four-by-four metres in size, so to say it suddenly felt crowded with the two of us in there would not be an exaggeration.

Mr Potts sheepishly walked around me and took a seat in an armchair in the corner. As far away from me as possible, which wasn't very far. He quickly opened the book he arrived holding and didn't move his gaze from the pages for two hours. The pensive gentleman on the cover led me to assume it was a self-help guide. Lots of the pages were dog-eared.

Not a word was spoken between us. I'd rather not make such a cliché remark as, 'you could cut the tension with a knife,' so instead I'll go with, 'you could hack the intensity with a chainsaw.' That sounds more colourful for the book. Needless to say, we both leapt to our feet to escape our cage of unsaid words when the witness care officer popped his head in to let us know it was time to grab some lunch. I'm not sure what would be worse, spending the afternoon trapped in a room with Mr Potts, or taking the stand in a murder trial.

Taking the stand in a murder trial was far worse than sitting in tense silence with my former colleague. I can tell you that for free.

Tap one. Tap two. Tap three.

The whole thing was a blur. I feel like I blacked out. I thought it best to return to the men's lavatories and record this sharpish before the stress erases it forever. I will have to rack my brain and do my best to recap the information for you. My preparation notes will help jog my memory.

As soon as I sat back down in the witness room after lunch, the witness care officer came in and told me the prosecution team was ready for me to take the stand. Mr Potts glanced up from his book but said nothing.

When I got to the courtroom, there was no one to greet me except an usher. My heart thumped so loudly that it muffled my hearing. I stared at the court usher's lips as he gave me instructions on what to do once inside the room. I was to head to the right-hand side and into the witness box. He told me to leave all belongings in a plastic tray. He was a young fella and laughed when he saw my old mobile telephone and dictaphone. In fact, he had no idea what a dictaphone was.

Heat rushed to the tips of my body, including my ears, toes, fingers, and the end of my nose. And then my father's voice popped into my head. The timing couldn't have been worse. He told me I was useless and deserved another beating.

Tap one. Tap two. Tap three.

Even though he wasn't there to hurt me, I felt my hands start to shake as if he was waiting inside the courtroom with a belt. I tapped my head three times, but my mind was flooded with his voice. I tapped my head three more times, but he was still there.

Call it paranoia, but I felt like the usher was looking at me funny. I moved away and stared out a window at the traffic below. With my full palm I hit my head lightly three times. I closed my eyes, took a deep breath, and pushed my father out of my mind. He dragged his heels and cracked his belt on the floor as he went, but he *did* go. Then the usher called my name. It was time to go in.

It felt like all eyes were on me when I entered the courtroom— not that I looked anywhere except where I had to go. I followed the usher's instructions and walked along the right-hand side of the room to the witness box. I stared straight ahead. I didn't meet anyone's eyes. In my peripheral vision I could see American Dave smirking and chewing gum. I can only assume he was trying to put me off when he started whispering in Paula McDavidson's ear. She giggled and nodded in response. Whatever they were saying, I am sure it was something cruel about the way I walked, looked, or simply existed. Paula has always been an annoying busybody, but American Dave's nastiness was starting to rub off on her. Her personality can't afford to get any worse, but it looks like it has.

The first thing I was asked to do was to confirm my name and repeat a promise to tell the truth. 'I, Hector Harrow, do solemnly, sincerely and truly declare and affirm the evidence I shall give shall be the truth, the whole truth, and nothing but the truth.' That would have made a grand opening line to this book.

Helen, let's discuss later. Although I remember you saying how much you liked the current introduction so I might be fighting a losing battle here.

There was no 'so help me God' tagged on at the end of all that. Maybe because I am an old man, they assumed that I would want to swear an oath on the Bible. I told them that's not for me.

Then the prosecution started their questioning. The prosecution lawyer is a lady called Marie Habib. I met her at my preparation session and boy, is she a real tough nut. Today her black hair was scraped back into a long ponytail that swung around hypnotically as she spoke with conviction. Every word she said was perfectly articulated, and each moment of particular emphasis was accompanied by some very animated black eyebrow raises, almost like a cartoon.

'She confessed. She confessed. She confessed. She *con-fessed*,' Habib repeated over and over. I remember she said it four times, because I wanted her to stop at three. She locked eyes with each juror as she said it. Some of them bobbed their heads in agreement, probably subconsciously; others looked down shyly.

'You heard the confession, didn't you, Mr Harrow?' She looked me straight in the eye.

I nodded.

'If you could answer yes or no, Mr Harrow.'

'Yes,' I said hastily.

'Can you tell the jury what exactly you heard Sue Bainbridge say?'

I looked at the jury and told them exactly what I had rehearsed, that Sue said, 'It was me. I killed him.' Some of the jurors scribbled down notes.

'Thank you. And going back, what day did Sue Bainbridge check in to Cavengreen and who was she accompanied by?'

A quick glance at some of my early chapters and you will know exactly what I said. I stuck to the facts. Everything was going as planned, that is until my mind got the better of me and I began to go off script, much to the prosecution team's horror.

'How would you describe Sue Bainbridge's temperament during her time at Cavengreen?' Habib asked me.

You know, because I told you, that I had read and reread my preparation notes umpteen times. I knew what to say. I was supposed to tell the courtroom about that one single incident in Lavender Plates in which Sue Bainbridge shouted at me and told me I should just confess so everyone could go home. Well, I started by saying that. Habib nodded along, acknowledging I was following our choreography; setting the scene that Sue was desperate to pin her actions on someone, on me. But the nods of approval soon stopped.

'I'm not convinced she was acting like a murderer would act though. She was just stressed, like everybody was. Even I had my moments.'

The defence team scribbled something down.

'It's the conversation in the garden that we should be focusing on here.' I continued, off script, stupidly. I can't explain what came over me.

'Yes, thank you, Mr Harrow, I was just getting to that.' Habib skipped ahead a few pages in her yellow notepad. I had unintentionally thrown her off. She ran her finger down the page as she tried to catch up to my train of thought. 'Mr Harrow, if you could tell the court about the conversation you overheard in Cavengreen's gardens. Who was it between?'

'Mrs Bainbridge and her daughter, Olive. They were . . .'

'Thank you,' she interrupted me. 'And what time of day did you see Mrs Bainbridge and her daughter having this conversation?'

'Three am.'

'And what did you hear Mrs Bainbridge say to her daughter?'

I returned to our rehearsed script, telling the courtroom how Sue was asking her daughter to tell her the truth, repeating that she could help her.

Habib flicked back a few pages in her notepad, to fill in the gaps that I had forced her to skip.

'Just returning to the alleged day of the murder, you were the one who discovered Mr Tatterson deceased in suite seven, is that correct?'

'Yes.'

'And what time was that?'

'About three pm.'

'And to your knowledge, where was Mrs Bainbridge at that time?'

'I had made a booking for her in Lavender Plates, and she was there with her family.'

'And do you know the whereabouts of Mrs Bainbridge before her Lavender Plates booking?'

'I saw her and her husband head out for a walk around eight am.'

'And how did she seem?'

'Fine.'

'And then after that, did you see her again?'

'Only when she returned from her walk around eight forty-five, and then in Lavender Plates, after I'd found the body.'

'That was around three thirty pm, is that correct?'

'I'd say so.'

'So, you didn't see Sue Bainbridge between eight forty-five am and three thirty pm on the day you discovered Mr Tatterson's body?'

'That's right.'

'No further questions, your honour.'

Habib huffed and sighed when she sat down. The defence team were invited to cross-examine me, a moment I had been dreading.

There was a bit of admin to get through at the start as I reconfirmed who I was and the position I held in the hotel. We ticked off a couple of points as I clarified what I had just said to Habib, and then they got into it.

'Would you say you have a good memory, Mr Harrow?' Why I never. The cheek.

'Um . . . most of the time, yes.' Was what I really said.

'But not all the time?'

'Not all the time, no.'

'How old are you, Mr Harrow?'

'Seventy-four.'

'And this event happened several months ago?'

'Yes.'

'Do you often remember conversations that have happened several months ago word for word?'

'Not normally.'

'But you remember Mrs Bainbridge's conversation in the garden with her daughter?'

'I remember the gist.'

'Ah okay . . . the gist.' With raised eyebrows the defence lawyer turned and smirked at the jury. 'No further questions, your honour.'

I feel deflated. Like I have just played the part of the unreliable, old witness. Like I have been made to look a fool. This whole book, all of your reading it, you're doing so because you have faith in my retelling of this story. Don't listen to that silly defence lawyer. The sort of things that happened at Cavengreen are the sort of things one doesn't forget. Old or not old.

On my way out of the courtroom, I asked the witness care officer if I was allowed to sit in the public gallery this afternoon and for the rest of the trial. He said yes. At least Helen will be pleased.

The court took a twenty-minute break, enough time for me to record that last part in the lavatory. When we resumed, I loosened my tie and took a seat in the gallery. I could see things a lot clearer without all the stress blurring my vision. American Dave was there still. I could hear him before I could see him. I found a seat in the third row, and as people were filing back in I heard a familiar voice arguing with the usher. I turned to look. American Dave was being told to remove his cowboy hat or he would not be permitted in the courtroom. He was not best pleased, having been allowed to wear it that morning. He huffed and puffed and eventually snapped, 'You better not lose it.' He ruffled his hair as if he was self-conscious about it. He took a seat directly behind me and leant forward to whisper, 'Howdy,' over my right shoulder.

'No film crew following you today?' I asked him.

'Not allowed in the courtroom,' he replied. I could tell he was still chewing gum without even looking at him, just by the sound of something sticky chomping between his teeth.

Every seat in the gallery was filled, with another row of spectators huddled in some standing room at the back. Sue entered in handcuffs. She scanned the room, presumably looking for familiar faces, and she smiled faintly at her husband. I leant forward to see his reaction; he smiled softly back at her.

It was the first time I could get a clear look at her. She was a shadow of the glamorous woman who had first entered Cavengreen. Instead of high heels and a designer dress, she was wearing an ill-fitting grey trouser suit. Her brown hair was sprinkled with wiry grey. Without make-up, her skin looked dull. She appeared frail and exhausted. I imagine she hasn't been able to eat much because of stress. Saying that, I lost half a stone over those four days at Cavengreen.

Patrick, the groom, was sitting next to Sue's husband. There was no Olive. Behind them sat the twins, both dressed like they were going to a celebrity's funeral, with black suits and ridiculous dangly gold earrings. I locked eyes with one of them—Oksana, if I remember correctly. She poked her tongue out at me before turning away and whispering something in her sister's ear. They both turned and glared at me, but I looked away. I am not here to be part of their foolish gossiping. I am here for the trial, so I can finish my book.

It was impossible to tell who in the room might have been a friend or family member of Bruno. You'd think there would be a few people there from his side. Perhaps as the trial goes on, I will be able to identify those people for you.

When they brought the jury out, I studied them to try to imagine which way they would sway. There were eight men and four women, all of them stony-faced. One of the men—the oldest-looking, in my opinion—identified himself as the foreman. It is his job to ask any questions the jury might have and, ultimately, he will announce the verdict. Like I said, I would be quite interested in doing jury duty, but I don't think I would raise my hand to be the foreman. Reading out the verdict, changing someone's life forever like that, that doesn't sound like it would be for me.

I thought they might have brought Mr Potts out to stand as a witness, but they didn't. The confession continued to be the main theme of the prosecution's argument the rest of the day, but Marie Habib also added a few other bits and pieces in there. There was no evidence of an alleged affair with Bruno. Only a single text message from Sue to Bruno on the morning of the wedding, saying, *Don't you dare ruin today*, connected them.

'A clear threat,' was how Habib described it.

The message was shown on a TV screen, with paper copies handed out to the jurors. Habib then put forward a theory that Sue had to kill Bruno to prevent him from telling her husband of their affair. The defence yelled, 'Objection,' at that point, citing speculation. The judge asked for that moment to be removed from the transcript and dismissed by the jury. Surely the seed had already been planted in their heads. The judge seems like a smart man. I mean, I am sure you have to be very smart to be a judge.

The prosecution brought up a photograph of the items found in the maze; it was the first time I had seen the murder weapon. Journalists frantically scribbled in their notepads. The photograph showed the bloody knife, the iPad and a pair of boots on the muddy ground.

The argument was that the boots *could* have fit Sue, despite being one size too big. They argued that using boots that were too big would be a great way to throw the police off her scent.

Sue kept her head down the whole time, not showing any emotion or giving anything away. Everything hangs on that confession. I am presuming that the defence will try to explain that away tomorrow.

Yesterday was a complete disaster. I missed a full day in court and a full day of recording. You will never believe it: I got to the train station at 6 am and American Dave was there waiting for me with his camera crew. There was no reason for them to be there at that time. Leeds is two hours on the train and court doesn't start until ten. I like to go early and have breakfast and a coffee at my regular spot before heading to the courthouse. He had left his cowboy hat at home, but that didn't stop him from turning up in denim jeans tightened by a chunky belt buckle with a picture of a horse pulling a cart engraved on it. He had a black shirt with tassels on the back. Round here, he looks like he is in fancy dress. This is Yorkshire, not the Wild West.

American Dave was with Paula McDavidson, who immediately started boasting about the cowboy hat that American Dave had ordered her from the States. Apparently she has quite the collection now, she bragged. She told me she intends to wear them in her to-camera interviews for the documentary. I told her I didn't care.

The platform in our village is not big, so it was hard to avoid them. There is a small ticket booth, one bench, and that's it. If it rains, you get wet. Those big trains that pass through on their way to Leeds make the whole platform vibrate, it's that old. Those that do stop only open the doors to one carriage, since that is all that fits on our platform. There was no escaping American Dave and his gang. Every time I edged away, they moved closer.

'Behind the yellow line!' Paula McDavidson shouted at me when part of my foot touched it. She howled with laughter like a school bully, the camera capturing every moment of it. I am sure she is very proud of her behaviour.

I ignored and ignored and ignored them, biting my tongue and breathing deeply at their provoking remarks. American Dave was quizzing me about why I needed to be in the courtroom every day, whether it was because I was writing a book, like Fiona had mentioned. He told me that he was going to tell the story of Cavengreen and I had better watch out, because he wasn't going to let my book come out before his documentary. I didn't react. You lot should know by now to take whatever is in his documentary with a pinch of salt. Yes, I want my book to be released first, but what will be will be. My story is the truth, and his is a load of cow dung.

But then he went a step too far. 'How 'bout this, Hector? If you attend court today, I'll fire Fiona,' American Dave said, a smirk plastered on his face and chewing gum rolling around his mouth. This man has sunk to a new low. He said I could come to court the next day, but that day I had to stay home. He knew that missing the defence argument would be detrimental to my storytelling. That was his plan.

My face burnt as I tried to hold back my anger. Paula McDavidson sucked in her cheeks and bounced on her heels as she giddily waited for me to respond.

'He's serious, you know, Hector,' Paula felt the need to add.

'As serious as a murderer, that's me.' American Dave winked. 'Come to court, your friend gets fired. Stay home today, and she keeps her job. I reckon she needs the money, don't you?'

There was no use bargaining with him. To bargain with a fool would make me an even bigger fool. I gathered my things from the bench and left the station, the sound of their howling laughter following me.

I can't tell you how defeated I felt when I got home yesterday. That is why I couldn't record anything for you.

Fiona telephoned around lunchtime to leave a message about catching up for a coffee on the weekend. She was shocked when I picked up the telephone, and instantly knew something was wrong. But I chose not to tell her what had happened. As far as she knows, I have got a migraine. There was no use worrying her; she has been through enough and no book is more important than our friendship.

So, that was yesterday. That is in the past and now that I have told you about it, I fully intend to move on. Today is a new day and I am back in the men's lavatories recording my introduction. I will chat to some of the court watchers today and see if they can fill me in on yesterday's proceedings.

Hang on a tick.

Sorry about that, Helen. A gentleman needed to use the facilities. That flush must have made a right racket on the tape.

Where was I? Oh yes. Court watchers are people who sit in the public gallery at trials as a hobby. There are only two types of people who I can imagine doing something like that as a hobby: nosy buggers like Paula McDavidson and people who get their energy from other people's misfortunes, like American Dave.

From listening in on conversations, I have identified a few court watchers in the crowd. There is a woman—mid-fifties, I would say—who looks tough, judgemental and unforgiving. I don't think I'll talk to her. There is a young woman in a headscarf who doesn't look a day older than nineteen. Imagine being interested in murder trials before you hit your twenties. Perhaps she is studying law at university. Then there are two other women, both of them around thirty or forty. There are a few men, too. One of them stood out to me: he has dark skin and orange glasses. He looks eccentric and wears a jumper with a picture of a dancing pig stitched onto it. This is not to say he will be a big part of my story; I just want to set the scene, and this man certainly looks like quite the character.

This is a place where bad people come to get punished and innocent people come hoping for the best but expecting the worst. If these walls could talk, I am sure they would cry. I am not sure what to expect today but, as usual, I shall fill you in later.

The days must feel so quick to you, with me leaving you in the morning and then returning hours later. But I tell you what, they drag for me. On the positive side, I was completely wrong about yesterday's court agenda. It wasn't the defence argument at all. That shows how much I know. Yesterday was a continuation of the prosecution's argument, where they addressed some bits of evidence. That is what one of the court watchers told me, the young girl who, despite my assessment, is not studying law. She just likes having a nosy at particularly high-profile trials. She said the court only sat for two hours yesterday before the judge sent the jury home for the day. I can't tell you how happy I was when the watcher told me all that. American Dave must have been seething when he realised I didn't miss too much. Nevertheless, a day not in court is a day missing from this story.

Today was jam-packed and did not end quite as I had expected. In fact, it couldn't have gone any worse. I'll get to that.

I was surprised that it was *still* the prosecution's turn to present their argument. There were no new faces in the gallery; it was filled with the same journalists, court watchers, and friends and family as before. The twins seemed to think it was a fashion show and were wearing matching bright pink trouser suits. Hardly appropriate for the occasion. I know full well they are dressing up because photographers spend the day camped outside the courthouse. Me, I always sneak out through a side exit, but the twins strut out through the front as if they are stepping onto a runway. They pretend to shield their faces from the camera lenses, but I can tell they are loving every second. American Dave also gives the cameras a good show. One time I saw him pretend to throw an invisible lasso over Paula McDavidson and she played along as if she were being dragged towards him.

It is just me and Martin Bainbridge who use the side door. Not at the same time, of course. He holds back so as not to bump into me. It is a well-rehearsed routine now. I am sure he was somewhat thrown off when I didn't make an appearance yesterday. People like consistency, especially in moments of chaos like this. It is obvious he doesn't want to speak to me. Not that I would hassle him; I would probably just tell him I hope he is okay. His wife might be an adulterous murderer—although still innocent until proven guilty—but that doesn't mean the poor bloke should be dragged through all this.

That is another tangent I have let myself go off on. Back to the courtroom. I am yet to identify any of Bruno's family members, which is bothering me. Surely someone cares that he is gone. A couple of the jury yawned as the prosecution began their argument for the day. They looked bored to tears. The judge even made a joke about it at one point. He asked if they would like him to sing them a lullaby. There were no more yawns after that. It is funny how you would think a murder case would be fast-paced and exciting, but as it happens, it is a lot of admin and going through the same details over and over.

The prosecution spent the morning reminding the jurors once again that, well, Sue confessed. I'm sure the defence will blame stress and exhaustion for a moment of madness designed to save her daughter. A few of the jurors nodded along as the prosecution joked about how the defence would have a hard time arguing that the confession was false. One of the female jurors smirked, scoffed, and folded her arms.

In the afternoon, the prosecution announced that they were going to call another witness. That's right: second up in the stand was none other than my old pal, Mr Potts. I was wondering when he would show up again. He entered the courtroom looking just as exhausted as he did on that final day at Cavengreen. He had spruced himself up with a tailored suit and tie, but that didn't disguise the fact that he looked like he might have had a tipple or two that morning. Only I would have noticed, though. I am more familiar than everyone else with how Mr Potts's face changes when he has had a drink.

A woman who could have been his wife sneaked in and stood at the back of the public gallery, stress plastered all over her face.

The prosecution started their questioning. That's when I made the down-right stupid mistake that would cost me, and you for that matter, the next part of the book. The classic fool that I am. At the time, I thought I could get away with it. I should have known better than to try and be sneaky. I just wanted to be able to deliver you the most accurate information.

My dictaphone was tucked in the inside pocket of my jacket. Slowly, subtly, I reached inside and fiddled for the record button.

Doubting whether I had my finger in the right spot, I peered inside and lifted the dictaphone ever so slightly up and out of my pocket.

'He's recording! Stop everything, y'all!' An outstretched finger attached to the hand, arm and body of that meddling American Dave pointed in my direction.

'What is going on over there?' The judge snapped, rising to his feet. Everyone looked at American Dave and then followed his finger to me.

'This man, Hector Harrow, has a recording device in his pocket. I just saw him y'all. That is prohibited. There's a sign out in the hallway saying so.' American Dave proudly looked over at the judge awaiting his congratulations.

'Is this true, Mr Harrow? Are you recording inside my courtroom?'

My mouth hung open, wanting to say something, but not able to find any words.

'Both of you, step outside.'

'Why me? What did I do?' American Dave barked.

'Leave my courtroom!'

Outside in the hallway, the usher asked me to turn out my pockets. He saw the dictaphone. American Dave triumphantly shouted that he was right. He wasn't allowed back in the courtroom, though. The usher was joined by someone else from the courthouse. A suited man with an angry face. He asked me to play what was recorded on the dictaphone. I begged him not to make me, but he insisted. American Dave leered over, practically resting his chin on my shoulder as I was forced to rewind and press play. The tape started with me, in the men's lavatories, demonstrating how echoey the tiles are. My face went red with humiliation. American Dave sniggered behind me, his warm breath hitting the back of my neck, making me squirm. After the longest fifty seconds or so of my life – apart from when I discovered Bruno's dead body . . .

Tap one. Tap two. Tap three.

. . . I was permitted to turn the recording off. American Dave let out an over-exaggerated laugh as he punched me in the arm.

'Let's just say I'm not worried about what will be better, my documentary or your book.'

That man is a hero in his own mind, and his mind only. 'Who on earth would want to read a book filled with your jibber-jabber?'

Embarrassment consumed me. It was like someone had just read my diary. I felt completely exposed, vulnerable.

'Ah, see you later buddy.' American Dave slapped me on the back and then walked off down the corridor, still laughing. After a few strides he jumped up and clapped his feet together in a leprechaun kick. I'm surprised he didn't accompany the move with a 'yeehaw'.

The court officials instructed me not to return to the courtroom. They banned me. Getting banned from places is becoming quite a habit of mine all of a sudden. After seventy-four years of not causing a fuss, it's a little overwhelming to suddenly be considered a disruptive old man.

So, please forgive this bump in the road. It was my intention to bring you all the insights from inside the courtroom, but it seems that won't be the case. I hope you aren't disappointed.

CHAPTER

30

I am at home in my dressing-gown. My mood is low, I must admit. It seems I have become a nuisance. And I am worried about the book. Perhaps I have bitten off more than I can chew. I want to give you the ending you deserve, but I am not sure finishing the book with a vision of me sipping tea in my dressing-gown will suffice. It is chamomile, in case you are wondering. Helps calm my nerves.

Helen is coming over this morning, to join my 'pity party' as she described it with a little giggle. Hopefully she turns up with cakes and distractions. She wasn't planning on paying me a visit, but when I got off the telephone with her this morning, she called me right back and said she would be over at ten to cheer me up. Best get some proper clothes on then, for Helen's sake.

Helen is here. She says she's worried about me, because apparently I seem sad and look like I have lost weight. I keep telling her I'm not sad, I'm just flat. And a bit of weight loss isn't going to harm me, what with all these cakes she's been bringing round.

As soon as she walked through the front door she started faffing about, tidying things that didn't need tidying and fluffing already-fluffed cushions. Not to sound ungrateful, but she need not fuss around me like that. These Danish pastries with flaky almonds are quite enough. Thankfully she brought over a whole cake box full, and we have a pot of English breakfast to enjoy them with.

The sun is shining, so we are sat at the garden table—in a shady spot, of course. Two minutes in sun like this and I would be lobster red. It is one thing getting kicked out of the courtroom at a murder trial; it is quite another having to bear the points and stares that come along with causing such a scene looking like I've been turned inside out. A recapping of my antics was broadcast on the six o'clock news.

Helen has brought over pretend books bound in the cover the team has chosen. I am pleased to see that they went with option number two. It looks good. To be honest, it is probably not the best day to show me this. On any other day I would be chuffed to bits to see this project of mine come to life, but today I feel like a right grump. Poor Helen has to endure my company, although she is too nice to say anything other than that she's happy to be here. You can't see her, but she just mouthed, 'I *am* happy.' That is the sign of a good friend, eh? When they still want to be around you even when you are being a miserable git. She thinks the stress of the trial and the book have finally got to me. I am too stubborn to agree, but Helen is smiling behind her teacup because she knows she is right.

We should have asked a court watcher to take notes for us inside the trial today. That was Helen's idea just now. Bloody brilliant, isn't she? I will get on to that tomorrow. At least that way we will have some sort of connection inside the room. That is what you lot want to hear about, not me blabbering on about the weather. I will offer someone fifty pounds . . . Oh, wait, Helen is shaking her head and gesturing upwards.

Are you bloomin' joking? Okay, fine, one hundred pounds per day to take notes for us. It better be good stuff at that price. How many copies of the book will I have to sell just to get back—

Who the devil? Someone is at the front door. Who the heck could that be? Everyone I can tolerate right now is sitting in this garden. I am not answering it.

Helen has gone to get the door. She probably just wanted a break from me. She can be a bit hippy dippy sometimes, and she says I am putting too much negative energy out into the universe. That is a very London thing to say, I reckon. No one in these parts talks about energy or juju. My juju is bad today, in case you hadn't guessed. This is very unlike me. I am not the type to be full of beans, bouncing off the walls, like some people are, but I am normally happy, or at least content. Today I am grouchy. That is a good word for it. And I tell you what, that level of grouch is about to get a whole lot worse now that Mr Potts is standing in my garden.

Mr Potts said he didn't want to be recorded. That is a bit bloody rich coming from him. Although, I'm not really one to comment either now, I suppose. He popped round armed with a few things he wanted to say. The first was an apology, which I accepted. It is my belief that whenever anyone comes to you, hat in hand, and makes the effort to apologise, as long you believe it to be genuine, you should accept it and move on. Now, that doesn't mean you have to be all buddy-buddy with that person, but it does mean that you can put them out of your mind.

He seemed genuine enough to me. He told me he had reached out to a counsellor and was working on his relationship with alcohol. He's reading self-help books too. Told you so. He doesn't want to make excuses, but he believes that is part of the reason why he did what he did with the camera inside Cavengreen—he was not in his right mind. That and the money, a wad of which he had stuffed in an envelope and tried to hand to me. I didn't want it. I told him to take it with him when he left, but I have just found it wedged behind the clock on the mantelpiece. I will donate it to the local dog shelter—or to Bruno's family, if I ever identify them.

Mr Potts said today was day one of no alcohol. Even this morning he looked better than during those four days at Cavengreen. His face looked freshly scrubbed and he was wearing a nice casual shirt and chinos. He almost resembled the man he used to be. He told me that his relationship with alcohol was already dicey before the murder; he just hid it better. That is none of my business, and I certainly don't want to embarrass him any further. He is on the up, that is all that matters. He sold his house and is renting a flat in Leeds with his wife and son until he can find a new place to work. He said he was on his way to a job interview at a hotel in Manchester. The move will do him good, I think. They always say the best time to break a bad habit is during a big life change. It gives you an opportunity to reset your routine, something like that.

The main thing Mr Potts came here to discuss was Olive, the bride. He told me he has been replaying everything that happened at the hotel in his head, and he firmly believes Olive was somehow involved in Bruno's murder. I must admit, I agree. I keep revisiting the conversations I overheard, and something doesn't quite add up.

Mr Potts said he saw Olive lurking around the back of the courthouse with her husband yesterday. They were arguing. Mr Potts claims he heard Patrick say, 'You hid the murder weapon. I am not going in there with you and pretending we're not involved.'

Helen interrupted at that point. She thinks it is very likely that Olive killed Bruno because *she* was the one having the affair, and then her mother felt the need to confess to protect her daughter from a lifetime in prison. It makes sense. Why would Bruno be at Cavengreen on Olive's wedding day when he was having an affair with her mother? He must have been there to stop the wedding.

The three of us speculated like old friends. Every so often I would remember that Mr Potts is no friend of mine and scowl a little at his presence, but he had brought up some useful information. That is, if it is true. Mr Potts can hardly be trusted; he has proven that in the past. But what business would he have giving me false information?

We explored the idea that Olive murdered Bruno to stop him ruining her wedding. Or perhaps Patrick is the real murderer, fuelled by jealousy after finding out about his wife's betrayal. The jury has all the evidence it needs to send Sue to prison, but what if we have it all wrong?

CHAPTER

31

Shh. I am trying to be incognito. That is why I am whispering. Not that you can hear, and not that it's necessary. There is no one around. I made it into the courthouse, and I am back in the men's lavatories, recording an introduction to my day. My outfit consists of a very un-Hector-like combination of a black jumper, black pants, black shoes. Like a cat burglar, but a less agile one with a dodgy hip. Technically, I'm not breaking any rules. The court officials said I wasn't to return to the courtroom. They didn't say anything about me being in the building. I breezed through security. Admittedly I was nervous. I imagine it's how drug smugglers feel at airport security. But the show, or the book, must go on.

Helen encouraged me to head down here to engage a court watcher. I told Helen it would be easier if she came down here and took the notes herself, but she doesn't want to muddy the lines between creator and editor. It would have been good to have someone I trusted on the task, but I get where Helen is coming from. She doesn't want to meddle too much in *my* story.

Nerves. I have lots of them. My plan is to observe the crowd gathered outside the courtroom from afar, lock in my target, and then quickly approach them with my offer before word of my appearance spreads. I have a notepad and pen in my bag to give the court watcher, plus one hundred pounds in cash. If they don't agree to help me, I will ask a couple more and then leave it. I don't want to draw too much attention to myself, and I am not entirely sure what I am doing is legal. At the very least, I am confident it would be frowned upon. However, the way I see it, it's no different to the journalists coming in and scribbling notes.

Right, I will be back shortly to let you know how I go. Wish me luck.

'Weren't you banned?' the court watcher said when I approached her with my offer. I politely told her to keep her voice down, but a few heads had already begun to turn. She abruptly dismissed my proposal, emphasising that this was her hobby; things like taking notes for other people turned it into a job and that was not what she wanted.

Acting fast, I quickly beelined for that eccentric court watcher I told you about, the one with the dancing pig jumper. He described my offer as 'scandalous' and was happy to accept my money in exchange for notes on the day's proceedings. Hopefully this system works well. I'm interested to hear what is said in that room today. After my chat with Mr Potts, I am not wholly convinced that Olive wasn't involved as well as—or even instead of—her mother. But that decision is the jury's job at the end of the day. Beyond reasonable doubt and all that.

I am recording this in the back alley behind the courthouse. This is the place where I have agreed to meet the court watcher to exchange the goods and money in a few hours. Now that the wheels are in motion, it all makes me a bit giddy. I've a few hours to kill between now and our rendezvous. Might pop to Marks & Spencer for a polo . . . why I never . . . what is she doing here?

Back home, in my dressing-gown, cup of tea in hand. I have got to record this tonight. You need to know what happened earlier.

At the back of the building, there were cars parked half across the pavement and plenty of traffic noises from the surrounding streets, but there were only two people: me and Olive.

She wore a long green dress and, when I first saw her, she was kicking stones with the side of her sandals. Her blonde hair was pulled back in a ponytail. Her eyes were red and puffy. When she saw me, she frowned and looked away. That didn't stop me walking over to say hello. In my eyes, today was the last chance I would be able to get some first-hand content for the book.

As I approached, she turned and walked in the opposite direction. 'Olive, wait!' I called after her.

'Just leave me alone,' she shouted back, picking up her pace until she was moving quite fast. If it weren't for the uneven pavement, I never would have caught up, but her sandal was snagged by a dip in the concrete, and she landed on the ground, her handbag skidding ahead of her, spilling its contents everywhere.

When I got closer, I noticed a bloody graze on her knee and a few cuts to her palms. She ignored me when I asked if she was okay and again when I offered a hand to help her up. Instead, I bent down to collect the belongings that were scattered on the road. I managed one lipstick and was going to pick up a pen when my hip locked in place and I rolled to the side, landing with a thump between two parked cars.

Olive sprang to her feet and helped manoeuvre me onto the pavement, where we sat side by side on the kerb, nursing our injuries.

'My mother is innocent, you know,' Olive said, her voice defeated.

'But she confessed, Olive,' I reminded her.

We both stared at the road ahead instead of looking at each other.

'She confessed to protect me.'

'So, you killed Bruno?' I asked her. It felt brash in the moment, but I knew I would never have another opportunity to speak to her.

'No,' replied Olive, 'but neither did she. Someone else did and they are getting away with it.' A slightly angry tone had crept into her voice.

'Who was having the affair?' I asked.

'I was,' she replied. 'But it ended when Bruno's wife Deborah found out. Listen, you can't help us, Hector. Not unless it was you and you want to confess.' Olive turned to face me as I shook my head from side to side.

'You must know how it looks, Olive.' That is what I told her.

'If I had killed Bruno,' she said, 'I would never let my mother take the fall for it. Someone else in that hotel killed him, and I am going to find out who.' She shoved the rest of her spilt belongings into her handbag, stood up, and stormed off down the street.

I sat on the kerb a while longer.

'There he is!' It was the twins, suddenly appearing around the corner with a swarm of photographers following them. They marched towards me.

There was no use trying to escape. My hip had buckled and I couldn't get up without assistance. I sat on the pavement, helpless, waiting for the cameras to be shoved in my face.

Then I spotted one of Olive's lipsticks wedged under a car wheel. The top of it had rolled off and was nowhere to be seen. The sound of cameras clicking and people shouting in my face got louder and louder.

'What are you doing here, Mr Harrow? Didn't they kick you out?' One of the photographers yelled as he clicked his camera.

The twins hovered behind me, making sure to be in every shot. But my eyes were focused on something else. Leaning forward slightly, I pulled Olive's lipstick out from under the wheel. And then a revelation hit me like a tonne of bricks.

I need to speak to Fiona tonight.

CHAPTER

Fiona just breached hotel protocol. I told her I needed Olive's telephone number from the reservations system, and she wrote it down and dropped it off for me. It is absolutely against hotel policy to share guest information, but when I told Fiona what I thought I knew, she gave it to me straight away. And she wished me luck. By gum, do I need it.

The telephone number has sat on my bedside table for the last two days while I have mulled over what to do. If I play this right, an innocent woman will avoid prison. To be honest, I haven't been keeping up with the court case. In my eyes, none of that matters anymore. They are clutching at straws, and I am grabbing at solid rocks. I have seen bits and pieces on the news about the defence's argument. They are relying on the lack of physical evidence—fingerprints and the like. Surely that will cast enough reasonable doubt in the minds of the jury. But the clock is ticking. Depending on my next move, I could get the whole case thrown out before the jury even starts deliberating.

That will save Sue the stress of the verdict. She is innocent, I know that for sure now. But who would believe the wild ideas of an old man who gets kicked out of courtrooms? Nobody, especially not when the woman on the stand has made a verbal confession in front of witnesses. I need concrete evidence to take to the police.

I just got off the telephone with Olive. As you can imagine, I was nervously pacing up and down the garden in my dressing-gown, cup of peppermint tea in one hand, telephone in the other. It rang three times before she answered. Lucky. My words came out in a splutter; in fact, I am not quite sure what I said was proper English. I took a moment to compose myself then, after a deep breath, I said, 'It's Hector, from Cavengreen, I need to speak to you.'

Olive was angry at first. She told me to leave her alone. But she didn't hang up. Surely if she really wanted me to leave her alone, she would have hung up. I persisted. I told her that I wanted to help get her mother out of prison. Of course, she was interested in my proposition. But we couldn't talk about it over the telephone. I told her to come over. This was a conversation we needed to have in person.

Like I said, I need concrete evidence. So, I am going to record my conversation with Olive. That poses one problem, though: I need Olive to agree to being recorded. Fiona was adamant about this. She told me it is illegal to record someone without their permission, and for that reason the recording could never be used as evidence. Even if I did record Olive confessing to the murder on tape, the police could never use it.

Fat chance she would confess to anything if she knew I was recording. It is going to be tricky, but Fiona had a good idea: She told me to say the words, 'I'm recording you, is that okay?' but to make it sound like a silly joke relating to my recent courtroom antics. That should throw her off thinking I might actually have a recording device hidden under my puzzle books or in my teapot. She is coming over at eleven. That gives me just enough time to take a shower. All going well, this could be the last chapter in my book.

Olive should be here any minute. It is rather exciting, don't you think? And nerve-racking at the same time. All my eggs are in this basket, and if it doesn't play out right, then I am in more than a pickle. In fact, if this goes arse up, there will be no book. I am not publishing something that ends with the wrong woman behind bars. You lot can watch American Dave's documentary for that. Mine will be the full, complete story. Helen will transcribe my conversation with Olive for you.

Hector: Eh up. Hello, I mean.

Olive: The taxi had no idea where he was going on these small lanes.

Hector: Happens all the time. Come in. Come in.

Olive: I'm a bit overdressed; I'm meeting Patrick and the twins for lunch back in Leeds later.

Hector: Well, it's a lovely yellow dress. Take a seat. Can I get you a brew?

Olive: Brew?

Hector: Cup of tea.

Olive: Sure. Thank you. Your home is so . . . cosy. And quaint.

Hector: I'm sure it's tiny compared to where you live down in London. Do you have one of those rooms just for wine, like Cavengreen had? Me, I've had the same bottle of red tucked behind my breadbin since last year. Not to mention, you get much better weather down south.

Olive: I was surprised how much chillier it is up here, even during summer. There have been some lovely days, though. Like today.

Hector: I bet you can't wait to get home.

[Pause.]

Hector: Biscuit? Those ones are Hobnobs and those ones are chocky digestives.

Olive: No, thank you.

Hector: I just want to let you know I'm recording this conversation, is that okay? . . . Oops, I've got crumbs all over my trousers.

Olive: Uh . . . sure. Oh, I get it. After what happened in the courtroom.

Hector: Not my finest moment.

[Pause.]

Olive: Why am I here Hector?

Hector: I need to tell you some information that I think, actually, I know, will free your mother.

Olive: Go on . . .

Hector: That you killed Bruno.

Olive: Not this again. I thought you had something concrete to
help prove my mother's innocent.

Hector: I do.

Olive: Well, what evidence do you have then?

Hector: Your guilt is my evidence. Come on, Olive. Why did
you kill Bruno?

Olive: I . . .

Hector: It's time to tell the truth, Olive.

Olive *[sniffling]*: You won't understand.

Hector: I don't need to understand. But if we work together, we
can free your mother. You can't let her take the fall for your
wrongdoing. It's not right.

Olive: I know.

Hector: Why don't you tell me what happened?

Olive: Well, okay—but try not to judge me. It all started five
years ago. Bruno was one of my professors at university.
Despite the age gap, we struck up a friendship over our
mutual passion for classical poetry. That friendly bond over
poetry quickly evolved into a friendly bond over poetry and
fine wine. We would meet on Thursday evenings at a small

wine bar with just ten seats and dim lights. We would share a bowl of truffle fries and a bottle of whatever we fancied. My favourite was chardonnay, his was pinot. I always let him choose the wine.

After wine, we would go to a jazz bar, where we would get lost in the sultry sound of the saxophone and each other's eyes. The connection between us was electric. Not to mention, I found him so handsome. We used to talk and kiss in the corner of the jazz bar. I would try to tempt Bruno back to my flat, but he always said no. He made sure he was home by ten at the latest. Instead, we would have quick encounters between lectures in his office.

I was well aware that Bruno was seeing someone at the time, a woman named Deborah. He said it wasn't serious and that he had no intention of proposing. He and Deborah shared a flat in Camden, but they lived mostly separate lives during the week and then were busy socialising with friends on the weekends. It was rare they spent time alone, just the two of them.

At the time, I was single and, I must admit, I put pressure on Bruno to leave Deborah for me. But he questioned our age gap. Being some forty years older than me, Bruno told me he would never give me children, and he feared one day I would tire of him and meet someone else . . . And I did.

I met Patrick when we were university graduates working for *[name of bank redacted for legal reasons]*. He was handsome and charismatic, and I was instantly attracted to him. I didn't rush into anything, though. Bruno still made me happy, even if he couldn't give me his whole self. Instead, I teased Patrick, rejecting his advances but flirting outrageously. He followed me around like a puppy dog. Until one day, a year or so after we'd first met, Patrick told me he had met someone. Before that, I had never considered how I felt about him. He was always just there when I wanted him to be. That day, I dragged him into the filing room and kissed him. We moved in together six months later, and he proposed one year after that.

I'm sure this all sounds very romantic, but just to remind you, I was with Bruno that whole time. In fact, it wasn't until the day Patrick proposed that I ended our affair. Bruno was wildly jealous and tried to win me back. He told Deborah everything, and left her. It was too late, though, and I told him repeatedly that it was over. But then we started meeting up in secret, trying to find closure, and those moments always led to a shared kiss.

Every time it happened, I felt so guilty. I honestly wanted to spend the rest of my life with Patrick. I still do. He makes me happy. He's from a good family, he wants to be a father and he has a promising career. But it was so hard because, despite all the great things about Patrick, he still wasn't Bruno.

As the wedding day approached, I became increasingly anxious about my relationship with Bruno. I stopped answering his calls and didn't respond to his texts. He threatened to turn up at the wedding and tell Patrick everything. I hid my anxiety from everyone—except my mother; I confided in her. Only my mother knew of the mess I had got myself into.

We were both on high alert when we arrived at
Cavengreen, fearful that Bruno would appear at any
moment. I tried to push the thought to the back of my mind,
dismissing his threats as nothing but that. I hadn't heard
from him in a week and hoped he'd come to his senses and
calmed down. But the morning of the wedding, I was beside
myself with stress. I had no idea he was even at the hotel
until that evening.

Right before my first dance with Patrick, I received a
message from Bruno, telling me he was at Cavengreen, in
suite seven. He said he wanted to see me. I replied, asking
him to wait. But he threatened that if I didn't go to him, he
would crash the wedding. So, I told him I would sneak out
later to see him. He was to leave his terrace door unlocked
for me.

After . . . you know . . . consummating my marriage,
I put on a dressing-gown and slipped out while Patrick was
asleep. I went down to the terrace and opened the door
to suite seven. Bruno was waiting inside with a glass of
champagne in his hand. He said a sarcastic congratulations
before drinking the whole glass in one go. I remember him
wincing from the bubbles.

We sat on the end of the bed and Bruno tried his best to
win me back. He looked at me with those eyes of his and,
foolishly, I let him kiss me. But I stopped him before we got
carried away.

To me, Bruno felt safe and masculine, while my husband
was young and inexperienced. Bruno begged me to run
away with him. He grabbed my hand and pulled me
towards the door. I snatched my hand back and fled for

the terrace. He tripped me up from behind and I fell to the floor. He flipped me over and pinned me down. I struggled, but he was too strong, so . . . I gave in.

In that moment, I knew I had to play a different game. I told him I would leave with him, but only if we made a proper go of things. No Patrick, no Deborah. Bruno agreed: he had finally got what he wanted.

He kissed me on the lips. That final kiss made me feel sick, but I tried not to let my true feelings show. There was a knife resting on Bruno's minibar; I had noticed it when I first entered the room. It was a steak knife that Bruno had obviously used for his dinner. I edged closer to it, smiling sweetly at Bruno as he gathered up his things. I grabbed the knife and held it behind my back. Bruno opened his arms out wide for a hug. He was so happy.

My hands were shaking as I walked towards him. I knew I had one chance. I waited until I was the perfect distance away and then swung my arm around and plunged the knife into Bruno's heart. His eyes widened and he gripped his chest as blood spilt everywhere. I leapt backwards to avoid the splatter. My heart broke as my first love dropped to the ground.

There was no time to lose. I grabbed Bruno by the arms and dragged him backwards into the bathroom. I can't explain what was going through my mind; perhaps I thought if anyone entered the suite to look for him they'd just think he'd gone out. Then I took the iPad and knife and slid out the doors.

Back in my suite, I panicked. I ran into the downstairs bathroom and wrapped the iPad and knife in a towel, placing them in the bath. Then I slid back into bed.

That's when Patrick woke up, wanting to consummate our marriage again.

Hector: And that was it? You thought you'd get away with murdering a man?

Olive: I hoped. Patrick snored away next to me, but I didn't sleep at all that night. I kept thinking about going to prison. I wouldn't cope very well. Not with the way I speak and look. I was determined not to end up there, so I started to think of a plan to dispose of the murder weapon.

Hector: But first, afternoon tea?

Olive: But first, afternoon tea. I felt completely numb as I slipped into a flowing white dress, straightened my hair, and applied some pink lipstick. Each moment felt undeserved now that I had killed someone. Patrick was hungover, searching for painkillers. I knew they were in the downstairs bathroom, so I went down to fetch them for him, telling Patrick that I wanted to spend the rest of my life looking after him.

It's while I was down there that I used the iPad to message you at the concierge desk, asking for ice for suite seven. Guilt had overwhelmed me. I wanted Bruno to be found by someone, so at least he wasn't alone anymore.

Hector: And tell me, what went through your head when you saw me burst into Lavender Plates in such a terrible state?

Olive: You were so frantic; you could barely breathe. I was the only other person in that room who knew why. I was concerned for you, but most of all I was relieved that Bruno was no longer a hidden corpse but a poor murdered soul. It comforted me when a whole team of police showed up to seek justice for my old lover. But I had to make sure they didn't find out it was me.

When afternoon tea was over, I confided in my mother. Like most mothers would, she vowed to protect me—no matter what. Together, we came up with stories of self-defence, but I knew there had been no struggle. I told my mother that I killed Bruno in a moment of madness.

[Helen stops the recording and asks Hector about the moment when he overheard Olive telling her mother that she didn't do it. Hector replies that he doesn't know what Olive meant by that. He suggests they might have been rehearsing the lies they were going to tell.]

Olive: Things got complicated when Mum and I returned to the bridal suite. Patrick had discovered the murder weapon in the bathtub, and I had to think fast. So, I told Patrick that my mother had killed Bruno in self-defence, because he was threatening to expose their affair. Mum looked alarmed when I said that, but she went along with it. So all this time, Patrick has believed that my mother was the one having the affair with Bruno. And as my new husband, he promised to help protect us both.

Hector: And how do you feel now, knowing that coming forward to save your mother from prison will mean that Patrick is going to find out about your affair?

Olive: Devastated. I loved both men, and now I've lost them both.

Hector: Any regrets?

Olive: Many. I wish I had ended my relationship with Bruno
before it had really begun. I wish I had been wiser, and
realised he would never leave his partner for me. I wish
I had cut him out of my life when I met Patrick. But most
of all, I wish I hadn't killed him. At the time, it seemed like
the only way I could escape him. He didn't want to let me
go and I thought killing him would get him out of my life
without Patrick having to find out about the affair. But now
he is going to find out anyway.

Patrick wanted to call his lawyers to help us out of the
mess we had found ourselves in, but I managed to convince
him that we couldn't tell anyone. My mother went along
with everything, but I am sure she regrets that now.

The plan was to act normal for as long as possible. Tell
the police nothing. But we still had the murder weapon. On
day three, the police were getting closer to searching our
suite. We needed to make our move. Patrick made sure the
coast was clear so Mum and I could hide the knife. I am
sure he will feel foolish now for helping me. I just hope the
police don't come down hard on him.

In the early morning, Patrick went out into the garden,
dressed in his bathrobe to check that no one was about,
and when he gave us the signal we took the knife, iPad and
boots, all of which we'd wrapped in a towel, and made our
way to the centre of the maze, fearing that we would bump
into another guest at every dead end or blind turn.

When we reached the centre, I put the bundle down, grabbed my mother's hand and, flooded with adrenaline, together we ran out. I was relieved to have got rid of the evidence and my mother seemed to be too. Looking back, I know now my mother was scared of what she had got herself into. I feel so selfish. But I didn't think it would come to this.

Well, now you know the whole story. What happens now?

Hector: Let's get this book published and on the shelves, and then we can put the right woman behind bars, where she belongs.

The End.

CHAPTER

33

Believe me, I can imagine how surprised you are to be here. But you see, I had to make it look convincing—the end of the book, that is. Helen sent the final draft off to the publishers last week. But I am afraid the book is not finished. Helen is on her way over now to chat about things and help me piece together the real ending to this story. Helen has done a wonderful job this last month. We were joking the other day about how funny it is that some of you will be reading this next to a swimming pool while on holiday, or on the train to work, when for me it was such an intense time in my life. For you, it is just another book that you will forget about soon enough.

Let me tell you where we are up to while I wait for Helen to arrive. Not that much time has gone by since I last spoke to you. In fact, Sue's trial is still ongoing. From what I have seen on the news, the closing statements are due to happen later this week. But that is neither here nor there. It is only important because I want *The Concierge* to be on the shelves sharpish after the case is wrapped up, if not before. I haven't heard anything more from Olive, not that I expected to. For all I know, she has done a runner to Spain, but that will not stop the truth from coming out in this book.

Everything you have read so far has already been typed up by the lovely Helen and has gone through a hefty edit. The team at the publishing house have been working day and night to get it done, bless them. They liked the ending. They thought it was quite the twist, exposing Olive as the real killer, and the fact that my book has that exclusive should make it pretty popular. Even if I sell one copy, as long as it is to Detective Raj or someone else at the Yorkshire Police, then I will be right chuffed.

Helen told me she really enjoyed working on a book again. Now that she is retired, she misses her old life. I understand. Helen has been the one spearheading this whole process. I think she thinks I need the money, pronto. So, best to get it onto the shelves as soon as possible. I always thought a Christmas release would be nice. I like the idea of being a stocking filler. But this will be out way before then.

Helen is here; I can hear the gate. I will tell you what I will do: I will pop the dictaphone on the table, so you get to read exactly what is said between us. It is easier than me explaining it all later and forgetting bits.

Hector: For the purpose of the dictaphone, I would like to announce that Helen has arrived. That made Helen giggle a little. Are you happy for me to record this?

Helen: That's fine, Hector. And good morning.

Hector: To set the scene, Helen is wearing a lilac blouse and a pair of light blue jeans. I am pleased to see she is holding a box from Maude's Bakery.

Helen: Very good Hector. Setting the scene. You're quite the pro now, aren't you? I've brought along my laptop, but I really can't imagine what kind of alternative ending you're considering. The publishing house love it as is. Everything is ready to go, so what's this all about?

Hector: I know, I know, I'm sorry to be such a nuisance. But I've remembered a few more details that are crucial to the story. I need your help piecing everything together, as it is all a bit muddled in my brain.

Helen: Well, spit it out then, Hector. Come on. Time is of the essence. Can you get me a knife for these cakes? I thought we'd share a passionfruit tart and slice of lemon meringue pie today.

[Pause.]

Hector: Here you go. Thank you, Helen. Thank you for all your help telling my story. You and I both know I couldn't have done it without you.

Helen: You are very welcome, Hector. It has been an absolute pleasure.

Hector: Let's sit over here on the settee. Tea?

Helen: Yes, please. That'll be lovely with a little sliver of lemon meringue. You know it's one of my favourites.

Hector: I know.

Helen: So, what have you suddenly realised that you've left out of the book?

Hector: This is a tough one, Helen. We've been friends for a
long time. But over the past week or so I've realised, I wasn't
writing *my* story after all.

Helen: What on earth do you mean, Hector?

Hector: I realised that I was writing *your* alibi.

[Pause.]

Hector: For the purpose of the dictaphone, Helen has stopped
cutting the cake and is frown—

Helen: Oh, shut up with the dictaphone, Hector! I haven't the
foggiest idea what you're talking about. *My* alibi?

Hector: Yes, *your* alibi. There's a reason why you were so insistent
that I write my book, that you would be the one to help me,
and that once it was finished, you'd do everything in your
power to get it published, to expose Olive as a murderer.

Helen: Yes, because we're friends, Hector. I'd do anything
to help you and I thought you would be excited by the
opportunity. You know how much I love books; this seemed
like it would be a wonderful story.

Hector: That may be so, Helen. But to spend so much time
with an old grump like me for no benefit to yourself . . .

Helen: I enjoy your company, Hector. And I enjoy helping new
authors find their feet.

Hector: And I've really enjoyed this process too. But I have said
it all along: this was to be a *true* story. And right now, it's not
that. The book is unfinished.

Helen: I'm sorry, Hector, but you've completely lost me. The book *is* finished. Sue is on trial. She confessed to the murder to protect her daughter, the real killer, who has been exposed in the final chapter of your book. It couldn't be a more perfect ending.

Hector: Except that Olive didn't kill Bruno.

Helen: She . . . she didn't?

Hector: No. You did.

Helen: What are you talking about, Hector? You've completely lost your marbles.

Hector: I was beginning to think that too. But it was after something you said during one of our last editing sessions that everything started to make a little more sense. The conversation I witnessed between Olive and Sue, when the bride was insisting she had nothing to do with this murder: she was telling the truth, but her mother didn't believe her.

Helen: And what exactly did I say that makes you think you can point the finger at me? I wasn't even there.

Hector: Except you *were* there, Helen. Two Tuesdays ago, we were sitting here discussing some details about the book. I had a vanilla slice and you a chocolate mud cake. We were talking about the hotel's gardens, setting the scene, and you suggested we include a detail that I know for a fact I hadn't spoken about. You said we should mention that the roses had been clipped back to their stems.

Helen: And suddenly I'm the murderer? Because I told you
about the roses?

Hector: There is no possible way you could have known that
the roses had to be clipped back the previous morning
because of a type of fungus called *Botrytis cinerea*. The fungus
is believed to have been the result of particularly humid
temperatures in the weeks leading up to the wedding. It isn't
possible that you could have known that. Only myself and
the gardeners knew. But somehow, you *did* know.

Helen: This is ridiculous, Hector. I'm leaving. Let me know if
you'd like to proceed with the book or not.

Hector: I thought nothing of it at first, but after Olive
mentioned Bruno had been in a relationship for ten years
but never proposed, I remembered that was exactly the case
with your ex-partner. You always complained to Josie about
how he had never proposed—she told me all about it. That
sparked another memory. A memory of you and him staying
at the hotel.

Helen: Nonsense. I've never been to Cavengreen.

Hector: You have. Fiona confirmed it for me on the system.
The records say that you stayed at the hotel for two nights
about eight years ago. You were celebrating your two-year
anniversary with your partner.

Helen: Oh, of course. I remember now. Hector, it's not a big
deal; I'd just forgotten, that's all.

Hector: Nobody forgets Cavengreen. That's when it occurred to me: I never forget a face, but I do forget where I know people from.

Helen: What are you talking about?

Hector: The victim, Bruno. You were in a relationship with him.

Helen: You've got it all wrong, Hector.

Hector: I remember meeting Bruno back then. This whole time I thought he might have been a celebrity or someone off the telly. When I realised who he was, I knew I had to speak to Olive again.

Helen: But what about the conversation you had? She confessed to being the real murderer.

Hector: That was staged. Fake.

When I first thought about inviting Olive here, it was with every intention of exposing her as the real killer and getting our ending. But after Fiona confirmed your stay at Cavengreen, and the memories came flooding back to me, I devised a new plan.

When Olive arrived, I told her what I knew and showed her a photograph of you. She confirmed that you were Bruno's partner and had been to see her, threatening to expose her, the week before the wedding. You knew that their affair had started up again last year, and when Bruno left you for her you were angry. You knew he was going to try to stop Olive's wedding, so you sneaked into his room that morning at Cavengreen and killed him.

You knew there was no CCTV of the terrace doors. You encouraged me to write my story to solidify your lies in the pages of this book. This was your alibi. That is why you asked me to change your name so you could be a ghostwriter, isn't it, Deborah?

[Note from Hector: I should probably add that this last chapter has been written up by Fiona. A big thank you to Fiona. She very kindly offered to help me finish my book. And I would also like to add that I asked Fiona on a date last week, and she said yes. That part is not really relevant to the story, but I thought I should let you readers know that my life after the murder is looking up. There is no need to worry about me. I am fine.]

Helen (Deborah): But Olive confessed! It's on the tape that we're going to hand to the police.

Hector: Like I told you, none of that was real. It was staged. Olive agreed to help me if it meant we could expose you as the real murderer. She told enough of her own story to make it believable; the truth about her relationship with Bruno, how she sneaked into his suite to see him the night of his murder, and how she had to dispose of the murder weapon that you planted in her room, fabricating a story to her husband of her mother's affair with the victim so he would help her. But I ran another dictaphone at the same time, and that one has the full conversation on it, including the part where we discussed faking our conversation for you. She recorded it on her telephone too. You had to believe that the book was finished, that nobody was on to you. Olive helped me with that.

Helen (Deborah): I can't believe you would do this to me.

Hector: Surely you must have been wondering why Olive
confessed to a crime that *you* committed. I can't believe you
didn't raise all the inconsistencies and holes in her story. As
the editor, you should have asked. But you didn't. You were
too desperate to type 'the end' and have Olive's confession
committed to these pages forever. You didn't even ask
why she couldn't explain what she was thinking when she
dragged the body to the bathroom, not to mention why she
didn't make sense of the boots or the iPad. Perhaps you can
fill in those blanks for the readers.

Helen (Deborah): You deceived me, Hector!

Hector: I'm sorry, Deb. But it is time to tell the truth. The
police are on their way, so how about you start now? Come
on. Give *The Concierge* the ending it deserves.

Helen (Deborah): He left me, Hector. The love of my life left me
for a woman forty years his junior. I was heartbroken and
humiliated—and *furious*.
     When he said he was going to Cavengreen to stop the
wedding, I knew it was my opportunity. I went there with
the intention of killing him. I remembered you telling me
once about the lack of CCTV on the terrace, so I hid in the
maze garden from five in the morning, knowing that Bruno
always, without fail, has a cigarette at six before showering.
For one long hour I stared at those clipped roses. And then
Bruno stepped outside and smoked his cigarette, at the same
time revealing which suite was his. I waited a while longer,

then made a dash for his room. When Bruno got out of the shower, I was waiting there with the knife. He didn't even have a chance to say anything before I plunged it into his chest, aiming for his heart. He tried to grab my wrists and fight me off, but it was too late; he was already growing weak.

As he fell to his knees, he looked at me despairingly. I stared into his eyes for the last time, feeling nothing as I watched the life drain from him. I took great comfort in knowing that he was gone. But then I had to make sure I wasn't caught.

Hector: So, you framed the bride?

Helen (Deborah): I wanted her to suffer like I had done. I knew it wouldn't be hard to make it look like she had done it. She had a motive. However, I didn't anticipate that her mother would take the fall for her. That's not what I wanted.

Hector: Tell me how you did it, Deborah.

Helen (Deborah): Hector, I'm not sure I'm ready . . .

Hector: You've been holding on to this secret for long enough. Don't you want to get it off your chest?

Helen (Deborah): Well, I have no choice now that you've caught me red-handed. Sorry, I suppose it's not funny.

Hector: We're at the pointy end of the story, Deb. Why don't you fill in the blanks?

Helen (Deborah): I put the *Do not disturb* sign on the door and planned to wait in the room until 3 pm, when I knew the hotel hosted afternoon tea in Lavender Plates. I'd attended myself when I stayed all those years ago. And I knew I needed to wait longer than eight hours, to make it harder for the forensics team to determine an exact time of death. That was necessary to help me frame Olive.

I sat on the end of the bed, staring at the body, for over two hours. I dragged it to the bathroom after rigor mortis started to appear in his face. I just couldn't bear to look at him like that. And you're lucky I did. If I hadn't dragged his body, you might be in prison now, Hector.

Hector: Lucky? Hmph.

Helen (Deborah): Do you know what it's like sitting in a room with a dead body all day? No, I don't suppose you do. Well, it's horrible. It feels like you're being haunted.

Hector: You had just murdered someone, Deb. I wouldn't be surprised if Bruno *was* haunting you.

Helen (Deborah): Just before three, I heard everyone chattering as they walked past the suite on their way to afternoon tea. Through the peephole I saw her—Olive—passing by with her new husband and what I presume were his groomsmen. Part of me wanted to dash out and kill her too, but I had to control myself. I waited another fifteen minutes, and then I took the *Do not disturb* sign off the door and used the iPad to message the concierge service asking for an ice bucket. I knew you'd be the one to find the body.

[Note from Hector: It was at this point that I paused the dictaphone and left the room. I took it with me, of course, just in case. I needed to take a few breaths in the kitchen. The kettle was still hot, so I made

another brew. Deborah—that's Helen to you—meant and still means a lot to me, but this was when I realised that she was no friend of mine. To put me in a situation where I would find a murdered body, a sight that will haunt me for the rest of my life—she knew what she was doing, and she didn't care. I half-expected Deborah to have done a runner while I was brewing my tea, but when I returned to the lounge room she was still there.]

Helen (Deborah): I'm sorry, Hector, but it had to be you that found the body. I knew that they'd never suspect you, and that with everything you see and hear at the hotel, you'd somehow lead them to Olive.

Hector: But they did suspect me, Deb. They made my life hell for those four days. They called me a murderer. In the hotel that I've dedicated my life to for the last fifty-odd years.

[Hector taps his head three times.]

Helen (Deborah): Stop doing that, Hector. The tapping won't make it go away. And it was never my intention to get you in trouble.

Hector: So how did you go about framing Olive?

Helen (Deborah): The last time I saw Bruno, he asked to borrow my laptop for a business call. Somehow his phone linked to my device and I started getting his emails. It was mostly boring stuff, work updates and bills. But on the evening of Olive's wedding, emails started come through with her name on them. Bruno and Olive were exchanging messages. He told her he was at the hotel and wanted to see her. She begged him to leave but, when he refused, she said she would visit his room after midnight. Around 1.45 am, Bruno got another email from Olive saying it was nice to see him but that he had to move on. She ended the email with: *I will always love you.* It was set up almost too perfectly. I thought the police would find the emails, arrest her and be done with it. I didn't expect Detective Raj to be as incompetent as he was. The way I planned this, it should have been an open-and-shut case. Thank God I planted the murder weapon in her room.

Hector: Oh, Deb.

Helen (Deborah): I know. I knew I'd only have minutes before you would be at the door, so I quickly grabbed the knife and iPad and raced out onto the terrace, then I ran over to the bridal suite and peered through the window to make sure there was still no one around. Fortunately the door was unlocked. I slipped my bloodied boots off and went inside. I placed the boots, iPad and murder weapon in the bathtub and threw a towel over them. The items had to be easy enough to find eventually. It was the perfect place in which to hide the weapon in plain sight. Then I ran shoeless across the gardens. I'm surprised nobody saw me, but I managed to make it out the back gate completely unnoticed. It couldn't have gone better.

Hector: Until now.

Helen (Deborah): Until now.

Hector: Didn't you think your friends at the publishing house would put two and two together when they realised that my book, the book *you* helped me write, was about your partner's murder?

Helen (Deborah): They never met him. No one did. We led very separate lives.

Hector: You could have just let him go. You didn't have to kill him.

Helen (Deborah): I know that. And believe me, I tried to stay away. But I was consumed by this desire to make him pay. Once I got it in my head that I wanted to kill him, I knew I was going to. He'd made me look like such a fool.

Hector: That's not a reason to take someone's life.

Helen (Deborah): Not always. But on this occasion, it was. To me, at least.

Hector: And who would have thought it would be me—just an old concierge—who would figure it out?

Helen (Deborah): You're more brilliant than you think, Hector.

Hector: I believe I just heard a car pull up outside. It looks like our friends have arrived.

Helen (Deborah): The police. Ah, yes. Well, I guess this is it then.

Hector: I guess so. Take care, Deb.

Helen (Deborah): It has been a wonderful adventure, Hector. I think you've got a bestseller on your hands.

Hector: I'd better go let them in. Ready?

Helen (Deborah): As I'll ever be.

Hector: One last thing before you go, Deb. Why are you being so open with the truth now?

Helen (Deborah): You know I'll do anything for a book, Hector. And now this one certainly has the ending it deserves.

The End. Seriously.

NOTES AND ACKNOWLEDGEMENTS

If only I could tap into your imagination and see your version of Cavengreen. I would love to have a nosy at how you set out the tables and chairs in Lavender Plates, and what your lobby looked like. For those of you who are curious, the closest place I could find in the real world to the world in my head is a rather lovely hotel in the Yorkshire Dales called Grantley Hall.

Your version of American Dave would also interest me. For me, he has actor Stephen Dunham's face with Matthew McConaughey's voice. Topped off with a big cowboy hat, of course.

There is a little nod to Manchester in the book. That is where I was born and raised. The people of the north of England have so much personality without even knowing it. Thank you to my parents, Jackie and John, for bringing me up in a place filled with future book characters.

You may also have spotted the nod to Australia. My UK family would agree with Hector when he says it is too far away. I live in Melbourne now with Philip and our daughter, Sienna. And by the time you are reading this, our second daughter, who is kicking my insides as I type, will have arrived.

I want to say a never-ending thank you to Robert Watkins from Ultimo Press for taking a chance on the first unsolicited manuscript of his career. I am grateful he saw something special in it. Which brings me to my beta reader-turned copyeditor (who I found on Airtasker of all places!), Sophie Bellotti, for helping me get my submission ready.

This story is time-stamped in my mind as being created while on maternity leave. This is the book of Sienna. Thank you for being a wonderful napper so I had the time to get this done.

Abby Corson has been a luxury travel and lifestyle writer for over ten years, with her work featuring in magazines and newspapers including *Vogue Australia*, *The Age* and *The Herald Sun*. Born in Manchester, England, Abby now lives in Melbourne. *The Concierge* is her first novel.